When the Dead Rise

Nicholas P Williams

Cover Designer: Andjela Vujic
Editor: Emily Williams Writes

First Edition
ISBN: 978-1-3999-6112-7

lit by the warmth and glow of the candle at his side. The candle elicited no warmth in the pale skin of his face or the icy glaze of his eyes. In his niche hidden away from the prying eyes of the crew, the stranger leafed through an old tome he had found in the spoils of the Savage Dawn's hull. As the candle flickered it traced shadows across the man's face, forming the appearance of a diminishing frown then a grotesque grin. The candle flickered as the ship rocked more violently than before and fell from its perch, but it was saved by the lighting reflexes of the mysterious figure.

In the distance he heard the sound of orders being given to the crew, "Secure the rigging, weight the anchor," and the excited footfalls of the crew bustling like mice ready to desert the ship. As the stranger heard the squeal of the rusted hinges on the hull door cry out as it was opened, he extinguished the flame of the candle, placed the book inside his coat, and melted into the blackness of the shadowy hull.

Gazing out of the elaborate arched window of the great spire of the Order's headquarters, the grand master, Guilherme Gallion, watched with interest as a rusty old ship pulled into the Uvrenmouth harbour. He raised a decrepit hand to his chin and mused to himself as to the contents of the ship and to its fortunes in ventures abroad. As his spindly fingers wrapped around his facial hair like a spider capturing its prey, his solemn brooding was harshly interrupted by the door to the chamber slamming open.

The noise distracted Gallion from his musing and he turned to face the intruder, a scowl etched across his face that needed no words to convey the displeasure he felt at the unannounced interruption.

"Do you not know how to knock, Carstair?" Gallion questioned rhetorically, before rolling his eyes and returning to the great ornate desk he had risen from only moments before.

"Apologies Grand Master," Carstair returned apologetically realising his intrusion had been clumsy, "but the Savage Dawn has returned from her voyage."

"I am aware," Gallion quickly returned, though there was no enthusiasm in his voice, just a calculating finality. "Go to the ship and see that everything is in order." In no mood for delay, he continued, 'Amongst its treasures I am expecting several books, retrieve them for me." The order was delivered with such coldness that Carstair knew he need not respond. As he turned to carry out his chore, Gallion added, "And Carstair, those books are very important to me – to us. Do not let me down." Gallion dismissed Carstair with a subtle swish of his hand and rose to once again peer out of the great window of the chamber.

Carstair left, gently closing the door so as not to cause anymore intrusion on the Grand Master and made his way down the spiral staircase, pondering on Gallion's final words.

In the great chamber of the Grand Master, Gallion once more drew his hand to his mouth, his lithe form rigid as his bony hand smoothed out his beard and a sickening smile slowly traced its way across his features.

Chapter 2

Carstair stepped into his quarters on his way to the ship, still unsure if he had angered the Grand Master Gallion. He heaved the door open with a wide, heavy hand and shouldered his way into the room in an ineloquent manner. Carstair was a large, heavy-set man but tall with it which made him an imposing figure; one of the reasons he had been chosen by the Grand Master to carry out tasks he wanted to be sure were seen to completion. He did not possess the grace in battle that some of the soldiers did, nor was he as book learned as some of the archive attendants, but he was strong in body and character and loyal to a fault.

He slid his ankh around his neck, the symbol of the order that would grant him passage almost anywhere in the city and slung a heavy weatherworn leather jacket around his shoulders, sliding his arms in and shrugging to get it to fall into place. The sliver ankh shone as it peered from beneath his shirt and he found himself reaching for it to check it was there before he set off. The ankh was as much a symbol of hope and determination for the order and those they protected as it was the scourge of the undead whom they hunted.

Before he re-emerged through his chamber door, he

checked his coat for his weapons, a silver dagger concealed in the small of his back and two ornate pistols that had been given to him by the Grand Master himself were harnessed either side of his hips, always at arm's reach. The Grand Master had once told him that they were not as valuable as they seemed, although Carstair doubted that as they were made from a beautiful hard wood and inlaid with gold filigree that wove around the barrel and handle like grasping octopus tentacles. In any case, they held a priceless value in the gesture they represented to Carstair. They had never failed to hit their target and with the ornate silver bullets that the gun fired they had never failed to take down the quarry they hit either. Satisfied that he was suitably dressed for his task he ran a hand through his shaggy brown hair and rearranged a few stray tufts in the mirror on his exit from the room.

Glancing to either side to see if his vanity had been observed, he swiftly made haste out of the order's citadel, taking great strides as only a man of his stature could, his open coat tails billowing in the gusts of wind that his frame created.

As he emerged from the citadel's gates, he was taken back as a warm wave of street air hit him. The difference between the clean, clear air of the citadel and the dusty swell of the street was never more apparent than in the moments passing the great arch of the citadel. He watched monetarily as the crowds of civilians made their way about the city, some entering the bustling open markets and others heading to work. Sometimes he envied the simplicity of their lives; the not knowing or at least not remembering the great struggle that had happened all those centuries ago, the struggle that he and his kind fought to keep from their minds and doors. But it was his lot in life and he took solace in the noble duty he had undertaken.

As he strode into the busy streets, the glistening ankh that still peered from beneath his clothes ensured that almost all who saw it moved to get out of his way and he quickly passed amongst the throng of marketers, peddlers, and those buying their wares. Moving briskly between streets and downs stairs towards the harbour he kept a watchful eye on the crowd around him. Often servants of the order would be watched by those around, some out of fear, some in awe, but some with more sinister motives, so it never hurt to be cautious. Today, however, Carstair felt the burning of another's gaze upon him as though it was carried along on the warm breeze that was washing in from the sea. He could see nothing to worry him though so he pressed on, yet as he did the shadows moved in his periphery and his hand restlessly felt for the shape of one of the pistols hidden beneath the great coat as it continued to billow around him, giving him some comfort.

Reaching the harbour, Carstair silently gave thanks that it seemed only the first of the boxes were being removed from the hull.

"Where is the captain?" Carstair barked impatiently in the general direction of the crew that were unloading the boxes under the growing intensity of the morning sun.

"Who's asking?" one of the crew petulantly shot back, but as soon as they caught sight of Carstair they thought twice about such impudence. His considerable frame was enough to elicit such a response without the order's symbol being shown.

"He's in the hull taking stock," came the more sombre reply of the crewman's partner.

Carstair nodded but gave no more acknowledgement of the crew, grabbing the cold iron railings and hoisting himself onto the ship with a speed and ease few would have thought him capable of.

He quickly surveyed the deck of the ship, watching a few deck hands run back and forth tying ropes or moving cargo. Once he spied the hatch that led into the belly of the ship, he made a beeline for it, not wishing to be held up any longer.

Reaching the hatch, he peered into the gloom and was met by little but the stale smell of old boxes and long forgotten treasures. It was not unpleasant, but not a smell he was used to, and he recoiled instinctively at first before allowing himself to stoop lower, to get a better view into the hull. All Carstair could see were walls of boxes dimly lit in the flicker of candles, however, he could make out a larger glow a little further into the hull, a lantern he thought, and he heard the footfalls of men at work, heaving the cargo of the hull around to some discomfort.

"Captain?" Carstair questioningly bellowed into the gloom. He waited for a response, and just as it seemed none would come...

"Who's asking?" echoed from the darkness back at him.

Carstair stalled at this second remark of disrespect and thought whether or not the crew was composed entirely of disrespectful churls, but composed himself enough to return, "I am Carstair, emissary and attendant of the Grand Master Gallion of the Order of Uvrenmouth. I am here to seek audience with the captain of the Savage Dawn, you have something for my master," he sent back into the dimness with all the authority it deserved.

He heard more movement and a few grunts of anguish, but as he felt the choler rise in his throat and prepared to descend into the darkness to address this surly crew face to face, a figure began to form in shadows which manifested itself in the form of a grizzled face staring up at him. As he continued to stare back, the face caught a glimpse of the ankh and softened as he seemed to accept that Carstair was who he said he was.

The captain of the Savage Dawn ascended the steps that led down into the hull and shielded his eyes as the sunlight pierced them, now accustomed to the darkness below deck. "Captain Rangehorn. I have been expecting a visit from the order," he ventured, offering his hand to Carstair. The Captain was no small figure but in Carstair's hand, even his was dwarfed. They cordially shook hands and Carstair opened his mouth to speak but the captain got there first. "The box you seek is marked with the symbol of your order, master Carstair, you should—"

"Attendant," Carstair interrupted a little embarrassed, "I am no Master."

"Apologies, attendant Carstair," the captain continued almost mockingly, "you should find it is to your expectations, I will have one of the boys fetch it up for you now." The captain trailed off and any sport he had found initially in jesting had long vanished.

He descended back into the abyss of the ship's hull and Carstair heard the muffled orders he gave to the crew. On the deck, under the now unrelenting sun, Carstair began to sweat; his brow glistening and his shirt becoming tacky. It was not unusual for the mid-morning sun to blaze as it did but Carstair couldn't help feel that he was still being watched and the perspiration was as much to do with the sun's rays as the discomfort he felt at the thought of his surveillance.

It was not long before the crew emerged from the ship's hull heaving an archaic yet beautifully decorated wooden chest. The chest was no more than three foot in length and maybe a foot in depth, but the crew were clearly having to put in a lot of effort to get the chest up the stairs to the deck. As they finally got it out of the hold and into the sunlight, they let it drop unceremoniously to the ground and it landed with a dull thud that made Carstair's eye twitch, the only visible sign at his annoyance at their disregard for it.

The crew, unbothered by what would now happen to the chest, retired to a barrel of fresh water to get a drink before they had to return to their laborious work. Alone with the box, Carstair marvelled at the ornate metal work that encapsulated the dilapidated wood that in turn held his quarry. He also thought it was somewhat of shame that the crew had desecrated such an aging and wondrous piece of history by stamping a huge black ankh symbol on the side in ink that had run in places. Nevertheless, he flipped the two metal clasps that sat on either side and opened the box, moving his head away, expecting an explosion of dust or the reek of century's old stale air, but neither came.

Carstair was almost disappointed; opening the crate had no more ceremony than opening a trunk of clothes. It was not what he had expected from something the Grand Master coveted so much. Peering in, he let his eyes fall over the assortment of books that lay in the chest. Most were intricately bound in various colours of leather, their spines displaying titles that he could not pronounce, and some that he thought he ought not to. Those he could read included 'The Book of Arcane Damnation' and 'The Chronology of the Macabre', and he thought to himself about their power.

The contents of the crate were jumbled, no doubt thrown about during its time aboard the Savage Dawn. Carstair rummaged through, moving books from side to side, though this was mostly for show as he did not know the manifest for what should or shouldn't be in there. He decided that all was in order and closed the chest shut, locking the latches as he did so. Just as he was about to depart the ship with his prize, a familiar voice called to him.

'Everything in order master Carstair?' the captain shouted, his head just visible from the hole in the deck.

'It would seem so Captain Rangehorne, the Order thanks you for your service.' With that, Carstair turned his back on the captain and began lugging the crate towards the ships edge, having seemingly less trouble than two of the crew had getting it onto the deck.

'And we thank them for funding this voyage!' the captain offered.

Carstair did not turn to acknowledge this, but if he had he would have been acknowledging no one as the captain had already descended to catalogue his plunder.

Heaving the chest onto a cart he had acquired from a ship hand at the docks, Carstair did a final survey of the area before starting the journey back to the citadel. The crowds continued to pulsate around stalls, workers carrying fresh produce from the harbour into the markets, and Carstair slipped away to deliver to his master what he had collected.

In the shadows of the fishing crates of a nearby trawler, a man emerged dressed in dark trousers and cloaked and hooded. The trousers were well worn but there was no mistaking their pedigree; they had been made from the finest leather, making their way down to an equally impressive pair of boots that rode up the stranger's shins, tight to the flesh. It was not possible to see what resplendence the man was wearing under the large overcoat that was drawn around his body tightly. Though the drab and ageing material of the coat did not compliment the splendour of the bottom half.

The stranger watched Carstair leave the harbour

through an archway, and despite the hood that concealed much of his pale face, a look of concern was etched across it. The stranger turned into the streaming light of the marketplace and withdrew the hood that had been helping him remain concealed. As he did so, shoulder-length hair flooded out of the hood. It was jet black and made a stark contrast to the pallid contours of his handsome face. His eyes had an icy blue hue that looked as though they could hypnotise any that looked upon them, yet they also seemed tired and weary as though they had seen more ages than the youthful face that housed them suggested. His mouth was chiselled, but the lips thin and greyish. All his features were pronounced, making him seem more like an old man inside a younger man's body.

The stranger moved amongst the market crowds with an ease and guile that made it seem as though he were barely making any footfalls at all. Silently, he shifted between stalls and although he was clearly there it seemed he moved more like a ghost among the living. Finally, the stranger stopped, spotting a young boy running messages between the different traders of the market. He made his way over to him and stooped a little to talk.

'Boy,' the stranger spoke in a soft tone that encapsulated the boy immediately. His words descended on the boy like a spell and kept him fixed on what the stranger had to say. 'Can you get a letter out on the next post ship that leaves this place?' his words cascaded slowly and purposefully and enraptured the boy in his daze.

'I can mister,' the boy finally replied as the haze he had felt lifted somewhat.

'Good.' With that, the stranger unbuckled the belt that had kept the shabby coat pulled around him tightly and had kept his form from drawing attention. As the coat released its grip on his body, the shirt beneath became more visible. It was a little tattered and covered in dust and marks that looked almost rusty, as though he had spent some time leaning against rusty metal that had absorbed into the blemished white of the once proud shirt.

The stranger delved into the jackets inner pocket, returning to the light with a letter sealed with ruby red wax. The address was written in an expensive ink and a hand that was beautiful to look at and impossible to replicate. The stranger offered the letter to the boy, a gold coin held above it under his thumb. The boy reached out and grasped the letter and coin and in doing so brushed the long, elegant fingers of the stranger's hands. The boy recoiled somewhat for even in the baking midday sun the hand felt as ice to touch.

'Do not be afraid,' the stranger soothed the boy, 'there is payment enough for posting and a reward for your service, have you ever seen a gold coin such as that?' he continued, his voice easing the boy's reluctance.

'No sir, thank you sir!' the boy managed to blurt out and with that he turned, letter and coin in hand and ran into the crowd towards the post master's building. The boy had told no lie that he had never seen such a coin. It was rare indeed to see gold coins in Uvrenmouth; the traders and population dealt almost entirely in silver.

Chapter 3

Twilight began to descend on Uvrenmouth, the unusual hostility of the sun that day relenting into the coldness of night. The markets were packing up and many were heading to one of the numerous watering holes the city had on offer.

It had been several hours since Carstair had delivered the chest of books to Grand Master Gallion. As he had entered the chamber bearing the full weight of the chest, the delight felt by the Grand Master had been visibly manifested across his features. His eyes had narrowed as his pupils dilated at the treasure being presented to him. He Was clearly relishing the prospect of the chest's contents.

'Thank you Carstair, you have done our Order a service by recovering these books,' the Grand Master spoke, although his mind was clearly elsewhere.

'I just picked them up from the ship,' Carstair protested, feeling the words lauded too much praise on him.

'There are many who would like to get their hands on these books, and that is why they must be kept here under our protection,' the Grand Master returned in the same placid tone, ignoring Carstair's embarrassment.

'There is but one piece of the puzzle left now Carstair, a key, which will allow us to unlock the dark mysteries the books hold, without it they are quite unremarkable,' Gallion lamented. No longer did the Grand Master even seem to be talking to Carstair but rather to himself in a trance he could not shake.

'There was no key in the box Grand Master, the curs on the boat are not holding out on us?' Carstair questioned awkwardly.

'The key is a cypher, do not think so literally Carstair,' the Grand Master scolded absently.

Carstair looked on a little concerned at the power the books seemed to be exerting over the Grand Master, curious and afraid all at once at the contents. As the night drew in the shadows cast by the candlelight began to grow and dance across the walls like carefree children in summer's throws. Those same shadows cast their form across the face of the grand master and almost appeared to be licking at him like great tendrils of some long-forgotten beast. Unnerved by the play the shadows were enacting around the room, Carstair made to take his leave.

Seeing the Grand Master search through the books, much more carefully than he had earlier in the day, Carstair felt a pang of guilt at his heavy handedness. This was quickly extinguished at the great commotion that began in the great hall of the citadel. The sound of men at arms rushing from their posts and the subtle bell that signalled a supernatural occurrence brought a look of horror to Carstair's face. There had been no intelligence to suggest that such an occurrence may happen and their scouts were ever watchful for the signs of the unnatural.

'Go. They will need your leadership,' the Grand Master managed in the most matter of fact tone he could muster, barely put out by the obvious unnerve of the citadel.

'Grand Master.' Carstair offered and half bowed as he was already turning to leave the room and return some civility to proceedings. He shut the door carefully behind him and rushed down the spiral staircase that led form the Grand Masters chambers. His feet pounded at the flagstones as he descended, the shadow he cast in the torch flame maniacal as he rushed to the bottom. Bursting from the stair well he found the hall awash with bodies, unnerved by the suddenness of the alarm and unprepared for such an occurrence.

'What's going on?' Carstair barked at one of the librarians rushing around with a scroll of paper in his hand.

'We received communication from one of our watchers that an unknown entity has entered the city... unchecked,' the librarian stuttered through fear, whether of himself or the entity, Carstair could not tell. 'It is a...' the Librarian stalled again.

'Spit it out brother!' Carstair interrupted, 'there is no time for hesitance.'

'It is believed to be a lycanthrope,' he steadied himself, 'the commotion is to do with the lunar cycle – it is the first night of the full moon.' The librarian finally managed to get out.

'Shit. Thank you, brother. Now calm yourself, we will handle this,' Carstair assured the librarian and placed a firm hand on his shoulder to further emphasise the gesture. 'Go back to your work.' With that he wheeled towards a group strapping weapons to themselves.

The Librarians of the order were the Order's collators and analysts. Some were made for fighting, others for research, but all could find a place in the Order. Those who were not born to fight joined the ranks of the Librarians and it was their task to study the arcane and the supernatural as well as to collect the reports filed by the watchers. They spent their days reading through books and finding ways to continue to keep the city safe. In the great reliquaries of the citadel, the order had amassed a great number of artefacts and literature on all that was unnatural and from these great repositories of knowledge, they forged the weapons the Order carried into battle and found the knowledge they required to keep evil things at bay.

Carstair approached a group of the Order's soldiers as they prepared to leave. There were four in total and Carstair recognised only one by name. Nestor was a promising soldier and enjoyed testing his martial skill in the field, but he was young and inexperienced beyond the walls of the Citadel too. The group had already donned much of their war gear. They all wore the familiar garb of the Order's soldiers; black leather trousers that disappeared into bulky boots that came up over their shins, offering both practicality and protection in the hunt. Some had knives strapped around their thighs and all had a sword hung at their waist. They each had a cream tunic that was tucked into their trousers and displayed the ankh motif of their order in jet black. The ankh ran from their chest to their belly buttons and spanned much of the tunic's width.

Carstair eyed the soldiers, they were all young and eager, but that was not always the best, especially in an unusual occurrence like this, 'Nestor, you and him are coming with me, you two go and find the watcher that submitted the report.' Carstair spoke with a commanding voice, he was a senior officer of the Order and the soldiers knew who he was and instinctively followed his command.

The other boy going with Nestor was Gideon, he had not long reached the rank of solider and was keen to prove his worth, although his boyish looks and long, golden curly hair suggested a juvenility that could not be covered up with bravado alone. He grabbed a bandolier of pistols and hung them at his waist before throwing a long black leather coat over on. The coat was shiny and bore few scars of battle or even of weathering. It reached to just above his knees and he pulled the belt across himself and buckled it, closing the cold leather around himself tight. The other two did the same and they ventured into the night to find the Watcher.

'He gonna be alright?' Carstair questioned Nestor about Gideon, not wanting to be babysitting an inexperienced soldier on what could be a dangerous mission.

'Gideon looks young, but he has the heart of a lion and he's smart too, he won't hold us back,' Nestor replied, defending his friend.

'Good!' Carstair said as much to himself as Nestor, 'strap up then it's going to be a long night.'

Carstair paced to the gatekeeper to log their exits; a custom of the Order to make sure someone would come looking if you didn't return. While he filled the gatekeeper in on their plans, his hands felt around his back, checking for the appearance of his knives and pistols. Nestor slung a brace of pistols around his shoulders so that they hung across his ribs and he two threw a black leather jacket on, though his was more weather worn than Gideon's. Carstair met the two young soldiers at the gate pulling on his own black coat. It had once looked like Gideon and Nestor's they were sure but now was so scratched and riddled with bullet holes and cuts that it resembled a butcher's apron more than a coat of the Order. He pulled the belt tight and buckled it around the waist. The coat, amazingly, hugging his form as the others did, rather than falling apart.

'Don't let looks deceive you boys,' Carstair warned as he pushed the doors of the gatehouse open and looked into the dismal night. Darkness now gripped the city fully and a downpour had moved in from the sea. The wind causing the oil lanterns that lit the streets to flicker and fight to stay lit. As the trio stepped into the murky evening, the rain pummelled into them and the wind bit at their ears, causing them to pull their high collars up to the night for protection. It was a stark contrast of the day's weather and sadly one the people of Uvrenmouth were more accustomed to.

As the party made haste through the streets to the last sighting of the entity, Carstair began to think on how strange the events of the day had been. An unusually warm day followed by a storm on the night of a full moon, the feeling he was being watched, the Grand Master's trancelike allure to the books of the Savage Dawn, and now the first lycanthrope to make it into the city in longer than he cared to remember. Carstair began to feel like something big was heading their way but had no time to dwell on such feelings now.

'This was the last place the watcher recorded the entity sir,' Nestor reported to Carstair.

The small group surveyed the narrow, dingy alleyway they had arrived at, but found no sign of anything, let alone a dangerous monster. The group made their way down the alleyway, looking for clues of the monster's identity or whereabouts. The alley stretched a long way behind a row of closed businesses. Carstair was grateful it was night-time; this job was infinitely more difficult in the daylight with people everywhere. As they neared the edge of the alley where it split into three different offshoots, it was becoming evident that the monster had not turned as in such a small space it would have left some sort of mark. They would soon have to make a choice of which offshoot to pursue or to split up, but Carstair did not relish the thought of sending the inexperienced soldiers off alone.

All of a sudden, the decision was made for them.

The sound of a woman's scream pierced the night and alerted the group immediately. Racing down the maze of alleys behind the town's main streets, the group desperately tried to pinpoint the location the scream had risen from. They were beginning to lose hope when the faint, muffled sobs of what could only have been the woman who screamed could be heard a little way off. Approaching the sound, the group slowed and became more acutely aware of how easily they could be walking into a trap, hemmed in as they were by the grimy walls of the alley to one side and the towering fascias of the rear side of businesses to the other.

Rounding the corner of the alleyway and spilling into one of the smaller side streets of Uvrenmouth, the group were confronted by a grim sight. In the centre of the flagstone street sat the young woman whose banshee-like scream had alerted them, though Carstair was pleased that it was only them it had alerted. Crumpled in a forlorn heap, quite overcome by shock she cried into a shawl at the mess in front of her, soaked from the rain that was mercifully receding somewhat. The mess was probably a friend or lover but barely recognisable through the blood and gore that she had been reduced to. As the group eyed the decimated corpse and its griever, Carstair reacted first.

'Nestor, cover that god awful mess and see to the poor woman. Gideon, you need to go get help now. Tell them I'm on a werewolf's trail, we'll need to dispose of some bodies.' Carstair's orders were taken in and the boys set about their duties like good soldiers.

'What about you?' Nestor enquired foolishly.

'I'm going after the monster you bloody idiot!' was all the reply he got.

As Carstair made his way along the street as fast as his frame would allow, he followed the remnants of the werewolf's attack. Blood and gore left an easy enough trail to follow, but they made their way over the wall of the street across the streams that bordered the western fringes of the town and headed into the woodland that followed, making it more difficult for Carstair to keep up.

Undeterred by this, Carstair leapt the wall and splashed down into the stream below, the water no higher than his ankles at this point. The water had washed much of the gore away but there were still some small traces to follow. He found the trail as some of the bushes and reeds at the streams edge had been pushed through and left in an unnatural pattern. Carrying on the pursuit, he entered the dark woodland that led from the stream.

In the trees, the air was cold and damp but the ground drier than the streets. The thick canopy that protected the ground from the brunt of the rainfall also kept most of the moonlight out, which made it difficult for Carstair to see any significant distance. Unable to rely on his sight he was forced to follow the disturbed flora, hoping not to be caught unaware. The air was eerily quiet in the trees and barley a rustle of leaves disturbed the stillness. So overgrown was the woodland, picking a path through branches and nettles it was a slow process; it seemed Carstair's quarry would be long gone at the pace he was achieving.

As it seemed there would be no end to this nightmare, Carstair finally saw the glimmer of hope as moonlight began to pierce the green armour of the woodlands edge. Spurred on by this he made good headway to the fringe of the wood and surveyed the land. He had arrived in the back of the great cemetery of Uvrenmouth cathedral. Great was a word that did not do it justice, the cemetery was immense, littered with gravestone after gravestone and interspersed with crypts and magnificent mausoleums, it was a breath-taking sight. Yet in the cold damp night, with his lungs burning from the pursuit, Carstair was far from inspired.

He slowly made his way into the graveyard, his walk slow and purposeful; he crouched a little to try to hide his form among the dead markers. Vigilant as always, he stopped again to try to see any movement. That is when it caught his eye; to the far side of the cemetery something stirred. Carstair carefully manoeuvred himself around the large gravestone he had found to conceal himself and watched as the movement found form in the shape of a great beast. Hunched over and ravenously devouring what part of the poor soul he had managed to tear off with, Carstair felt a mixture of sickness and anger rise in his gorge. He read the landscape to pick out the best approach to catch the beast unaware; his pistols would be too inaccurate at this range.

As he decided on a course, he made no more than two steps before something alerted the beast. It could not have been Carstair; his steps silently precise, his breathing controlled and reduced. The beast rose from its haunches and sniffed the air, its full scale now visible. It stood around seven feet tall, its shaggy coat rustling in the breeze, its long humanoid arms hung listlessly at its side, concealing the great power they held. The creature sniffed at the air, something visibly disturbing it.

That was when it came. Out of nowhere, a shadow, for that was all it seemed, struck the creature in its maw with a kick that sent the beast reeling before it lashed wildly in anger. The shadow began to take form as the outline of man became visible to Carstair. His long flowing hair melting seamlessly in and out of his form as he moved in graceful steps, a long coat not dissimilar to Carstair's own billowed around his movements as little winks of moonlight reflected from the edge of a small brass blade. The whole show enraptured Carstair momentarily until he realised his opportunity to close in on the beast.

Moving quickly, no longer worried about the element of surprise, he zig-zagged between head stones and crypts closing in on the fight. The stranger continued to attack the beast, making precise and swift movements, the beast lashing out in feral rage. The stranger was unable to land a decisive strike on the creature, but as one parry of a cruel and feral swing of the wolf's vicious claws by the stranger's blade managed to draw blood as it bit into the beast's flesh, it turned to run.

The creature, now on all fours, was exceptionally quick but in the confining ruins of gravestones, its lack of grace and agility slowed its movement. The stranger gave pursuit, leaping from stone to stone, running over crypt and mausoleum as though it were second nature. Carstair struggled to keep up, partly through fatigue and partly because the showdown was transfixing him.

Panicking at the swiftness of his pursuer and baffled by the maze of tombstones, many of which now lay derelict as the beast had crashed through them to get away, the cornered creature turned to face its assailant. The stranger never broke stride; manoeuvring himself close to a great oak that stood at the edge of the cemetery, he advanced on the beast with malevolent purpose, slowing only to pick up a long branch that lay at the mighty oak's feet. Pressing on only metres from where the beast had decided to make his stand, his run turned to a determined stride just feet away from the slavering jaws of the monster, the stranger held the branch out in front of him and crashed through it with his leading foot, not breaking his stride, but now wielding two batons of branches about a foot and half in length.

As he closed the distance on the beast, it lashed out with a wild haymaker, claws outstretched ready to tear into the stranger's flesh, but he was far too quick to be caught by such a wild swing, no matter the ferocity of it. The man ducked under the creatures blow and delivered both batons across the creature's chest driving them home with great power that shattered one into splinters. The beast reeled at the impact but was barely slowed. The stranger followed through his attack and spun to face the beast once more, his coat twirling around him, the baton spinning in his hand as he prepared another assault. The creature lunged at the stranger, but he pre-empted it and with both hands drove the remaining baton horizontally into the chest and up into the throat of the creature. The creature was driven back at first, but soon slowed its attacker's momentum and buried its claws into the shoulders and back of the stranger. The many layers of leather the stranger was wearing was not enough to protect him from the razor-sharp talons that pierced through each layer and sank into the pallid flesh beneath. Finally, having dealt its assailant damage, the wolf flung the stranger with ridiculous ease, releasing its grip and sending him hurtling straight into a tombstone which shattered at the impact. Reeling, the stranger slumped to the ground amidst the rubble.

Exhausted and wounded from the great tussle that had just unfolded but still transfixed on its attacker, the creature had not noticed that Carstair was now in close range of the two of them. As the creature made its final attack on the stranger, Carstair drew one of the ornate pistols that hung at his back; slowing his run, he rested the beautiful weapon on his left arm, cocked the hammer and took careful aim. Even at close range, the beast moved so quickly it was no easy shot but Carstair released the trigger and a silver bullet emerged from the barrel. The gunshot causing the beast to turn its head and slow its charge, but it was far too late for that. The bullet bit into the monster's calf and drove through the shinbone, splintering it and causing the monster to stumble and crash to the ground with force, barrelling straight for the stranger.

Almost instantaneously, the stranger rolled out of the way and in seconds was upon the beast, straddling its back and pinning its arms with his knees. With his back to Carstair, he reached into his boot and withdrew a curved and decorated silver blade, the handle bound in silk. The stranger prepared to sink the blade into the beast's back, aiming to pierce the heart from behind.

'That's enough, vampire!' Carstair called out calm and collectedly. 'If I wanted it dead, I wouldn't have aimed for its leg!' Carstair raised the second pistol, pointing it at the strangers back. The stranger held his hands out, the blade still in his right hand, the left bare save for an ornate gold ring with a ruby gem set in the centre.

'Drop the blade and get off the beast.' Carstair ordered still calm. There was a notable hesitance from the stranger and so Carstair cocked the second pistol. This seemed to be enough. The stranger threw his dagger into the slick mud, out of reach should the creature get up. But it was clear it was in pain; its laboured breathing detectable to the one who sat atop it.

The stranger rose slowly and turned to face Carstair. The man was handsome, his pale features framed in black hair that reflected the full moon's glare. His clothes, though covered in dirt and mud from the fight, were clearly better than many could have afforded in the city and fitted his form perfectly. The two faced off for a while before Carstair broke the silence by throwing a set of handcuffs at the stranger's feet.

The cuffs fell with a heavy thud and the stranger could see that they were silver, inlaid with runes carved around them.

'Put them on the beast,' Carstair ordered firmly.

Again, the stranger hesitated.

'I know what you are, now put them on the beast or join him on the ground,' Carstair demanded, still pointing one ornate pistol directly at him.

Reluctantly, the stranger picked up the cuffs, the silver burning the flesh of his hands as he did so. Not wishing to give Carstair any satisfaction, he winced only briefly and turned to face the creature. As he did so, his eyes ran bloodshot at the pain and his fangs elongated as he grit his teeth. He bent to the beast and administered the cuffs as quickly as he could, breathing a sigh of relief as soon as he could let go. As they locked into position, the runes glowed a light blue hue momentarily and the beast howled in pain. As the howls turned to grotesque screams, the form of the beast contorted into that of a human with ruffled blonde hair and an intimidating form not that dissimilar to the beast it had been moments ago.

In the noisy commotion of the monster's change, Gideon appeared with two more senior soldiers of the order. They appeared to the back of Carstair, weapons drawn. Carstair signalled to take the prisoner who had once been the rampaging beast and without hesitation the two senior soldiers of the order hoisted the man from the ground and dragged him off out of the cemetery, hurling him into the back of wagon to return to the citadel.

'So, what now?' the stranger enquired. Carstair still had a pistol still drawn on him while Gideon looked on confused.

'We go back to the citadel,' Carstair responded, 'you can decide how.' The finality of the words Carstair had spoken suggested that the only options were amicably or by force, and as there was a gun drawn on him, the stranger conceded that there was little use trying the latter.

'Very well, lead the way.' He offered and Carstair

lowered his gun.

Carstair, Gideon, and the stranger retraced the path they had taken, returning to the street where the attack had happened to find Nestor still comforting the shaken woman. The street was cleaner than before though; Nestor had done well to bury the remains of the mutilated corpse at the edge of the stream and the light rain had washed much of the blood away. What remained could plausibly be explained away as the remnants of a brawl or animal attack.

Pleased by the scene he had entered and Nestor's quick thinking, Carstair saw the night's proceedings drawing to a close. 'Nestor, Gideon, escort our friend here back to citadel, I will follow when I have made sure this young lady gets home safely.' Carstair gave his final orders for the night, but before he let the three of them go, he whispered into Nestor's ear, 'Keep a gun drawn on him at all times, but don't make it obvious.' With that, he let them go and picked the young woman up from the floor. He took off his coat and placed it around the young girls quivering shoulders to try to keep her warm.

'That thing...' she stammered, still visibly traumatised by the whole ordeal.

Carstair shushed her soothingly as they made their way to the stream where Nestor had disposed of her companion's remains.

'You don't need to worry about that thing anymore.' Carstair said with reassuring certainty.

'You killed it?' she ventured optimistically.

'That's not what I mean.' Carstair replied more bluntly, almost devoid of emotion now. The woman had not seen the pistol he had drawn and pressed gently against his coat. Glancing back to ensure they were alone, the gunshot echoed down the empty street and the bullet pierced her heart. Carstair let her fall onto the muddy bank of the river and holstered his pistol.

Chapter 4

The citadel of the Order was grand. Outside, the great, white limestone bricks extended hundreds of feet into the air. The ornate brass work at the gates and window frames had been painstakingly crafted by hand. The wood of the doors was the finest oak; as solid and unyielding as the Order itself. As Nestor and Gideon led the stranger through the gates and up the fine marble stairs to the entrance to the Citadel, even the rain that continued to fall did not stop the new arrival from staring up at the immensity and grandeur of the building, and the symbol of hope it represented.

Nestor spoke with the sentry and soon ushered Gideon and their guest along with a gesture of his hand. Passing under the great archway of the citadel's entrance, the trio were greeted by the warmth of several fireplaces and illuminated by the oil lanterns that hung at intervals either side of intricate tapestry's depicting the Order's heroics in battle, as well as majestically framed paintings of some of the former Grand Masters of the Order.

The stranger continued to stare around the room, his eyes darting from place to place. It unnerved Nestor who could not tell if the stranger was in awe or it was some animalistic search for a way out. Either way, they were not alone for long. Descending the stairs from the main tower, the Grand Master entered the great hall, preceded by two soldiers wielding ceremonial but deadly halberds. Two more soldiers appeared at each of the exits and although none of them had noticed, the door behind them had long been closed on them.

The Grand Master waved at the soldiers in front of him and they took sentry at the foot of the stairs. Despite his advanced years and frail frame, the Grand Master cut an imposing form, crossing the hall to meet them. A long, rich red gown extended down to the floor and flowed around his feet as he walked across the exotic rugs that lined his procession. He bore a cane in his left hand, though the stranger noted he did not seem to be reliant on it to walk. The cane was wrought of an ebony wood and the head was the familiar looped cross of the Order, cast in silver and bulbous on the top to fit the aged hand of the old man. The hand that entwined its way around the cross was pale and bore a silver ring which was large, especially on the Grand Masters bony fingers. It was clearly not made for him and bore an unusual rune that the stranger had not seen before; a cross emblazoned in a ring of fire.

'It is not our way to take in urchins from the street, but you know that, do you not?' the Grand Master questioned Nestor and Gideon but there was a lightness behind the words.

'We were... that is to say...' Nestor stumbled for words and Gideon was too afraid to come to his aid.

'Perhaps then this is not an urchin at all,' the Grand Master poised, 'so he is our guest? Prisoner?' he continued to offer options to the soldiers, but they remained rooted.

'I came here voluntarily,' the stranger spoke up in a

soothing tone that relaxed Nestor and Gideon but surprised the Grand Master.

'You came here because you had no choice,' the Grand Master retorted with a wry smile, the first time any emotion had entered his voice. 'Volunteers do not enter these halls with a gun loaded with silver trained on them, and looking at the state of your clothes, even though at some point I imagine they were quite fine, are torn and soiled from a fight. No, creature, you may have allowed yourself to be brought here but you are no volunteer.' The Grand Master turned his back on the three and made his way back towards the stairs he had made his entrance from. The finality of his words lingered in the air; Nestor looked embarrassed, Gideon fearful, but the stranger gave no emotion away save for the sardonic smile that twitched the corners of his mouth.

As the guards filed away and the hall began to empty once more, the stranger bore a glint in his eye as he continued to survey his surroundings. His arrival had been almost a spectacle that night but one that quickly faded, the glint faded more quickly as it was extinguished by the butt of a halberd that was brought down on the back of his head and the mysterious stranger slipped into darkness.

The stranger came to in a dank, dark concrete cell, awoken by the screaming of some sorry soul in another room. The only light that crept into the room through the gaps in the bars of the small window in the door. The dim light didn't bother him at all, he was used to it, but his wrists burned with a constant dull fire. He was bound by silver cuffs that in turn were chained to the wall. No doubt the same cuffs he had been forced to administer to the werewolf earlier that evening. He could not see his hands as they were tied behind him, so could not tell if they were just silver or magically imbued as well.

The screaming continued as the stranger evaluated his options. The cries of anguish were coming from a similar cell only a few feet away from his, a cell that contained the werewolf they had captured that night and a large set man in a sweaty, ill-fitting shirt and leather apron that hung to his knees. In the Werewolf's cell, Carstair was trying to extract information from the creature, still in human form.

The creature's name was Silas, that much Carstair had extracted, but as Silas continued to fight against his bonds, Carstair had been unable to prise anything else from the creature's mouth. As Carstair pushed another silver spine into Silas's flesh, he cried out in agony, the skin crackling and burning as the silver entered his body, blood spilling from the deep wound.

'Struggle all you want those cuffs are silver and the magic in them will stop you turning,' Carstair growled, visibly frustrated by Silas's will. 'This will end if you tell us where you came from.' A cheap trick that Carstair doubted would work but it never hurt to try.

'Go to hell!' Silas spat, blood and drool pouring from his mouth as he continued to lurch forward in his constraints trying desperately, but impotently to get at Carstair.

Tired of the slow game and unsure if there was anything to be learnt from Silas anyway, Carstair began to insert more and more spines of pure silver into Silas', arms, legs, shoulders, midriff. He no longer took his time to inflict suffering but quickly filled silas's body with searing pain as he brought him to the edge of his mortality. Silas' whole body burned and ached and the pain would not subside while he was peppered with the silver spines, blood now pouring from dozens of punctures.

Carstair, no longer seeing any worth in the questioning, picked up the tray of torturous devices that lay on the small shelf that was the only furniture in the desolate cell aside from the single oil lantern and made his way to the door. As he wrenched the heavy door open and began to leave, Silas offered up only one piece of information in the hopes of a quick death.

'I never entered the city undetected,' he wheezed 'I am of this city,' the last gasp the effort of a desperate man. 'Now kill me!' he pleaded; the pain unbearable.

Carstair stalled in the doorway and took in the semi cryptic information Silas had offered, then he continued on his way. Never looking back, he extinguished the lantern and the heavy oak door mournfully closed on Silas' quivering, bloodied form as his world became dark.

In the hall outside the prisoner's cell, Carstair signalled for the soldiers on guard to lock Silas' room and open the other. They did as they were instructed and with a groan the heavy oak door of the stranger's cell opened, flooding the tiny room with light from the hallway that caused his eyes to narrow acutely to adjust. His head slumped so that he stared at his feet, the long locks of dark hair fell around his pale flesh.

Carstair entered the room, walked to the shelf and placed the metal tray down. It clattered a little but it was obvious it wasn't intended to startle the stranger. He moved to the lantern and lit the oil using a match from his pocket. Carstair looked at the limp form the stranger sat in; he had been afforded a chair, unlike Silas, but it was of no comfort. Carstair eyed the stranger up and down assessing if he was unconscious, asleep, or maybe just playing dead.

'Rise and shine!' Carstair boomed, pretty sure the

stranger was aware of his intrusion.

Bound and restrained, the stranger slowly lifted his head so that he could meet Carstair eye to eye.

'Morning already?' the stranger puzzled, the wry smile re-emerging on his lips.

'Cute.' Carstair responded as he picked up a silver spine and looked down its length as if inspecting for imperfections. He slowly made his way to the stranger who could feel Carstair's eyes probing for where to insert the spine. He settled on the thigh, just above the knee. Slowly and purposefully, he drove the spine through the meat of the stranger's leg until it reappeared on the other side. The skin burnt where it entered and exited, but it was clear to Carstair that it was not as painful as it was with Silas. That or the stranger had a greater control of his emotions.

'Funny how you react to silver differently,' he mused out loud. 'Silas, that's our friend from earlier,' he interjected, 'well, Silas found it quite unbearable.'

'There are many things your people do not understand, despite your halls of learned men,' the stranger suggested provokingly, 'perhaps in time I can show you.'

'You're more talkative than the other one that's for sure, vampire.' Carstair used the word to try to elicit more response. 'Who are you? How did you get here? And what are you doing?'

'We want the same thing, are we not friends here?' the stranger began to enquire.

'You are not my friend, monster, I kill things like you, I do not befriend them.'

'Remove the pin from my leg and I will tell you what you want to know... friend,' the stranger bargained, flashing a smile up at Carstair.

Carstair thought on the deal and, seeing nothing to lose as he could easily put a hundred more in if the stranger did not give him what he wanted, agreed and removed the spine from his leg, even if he was irked by the use of the word 'friend' for a second time.

'Very well monster, tell me your tale,' and with that Carstair drew back a pace or two so that he could lean against the wall, crossing one foot over the other and folding his arms.

'Thank you,' the dulcet tones returning to the stranger's voice now that he was no longer in pain. 'Well you clearly know what I am,' he continued watching every reaction in Carstair's face. 'My name is Azerrad Gdalicanu, in another life I was a nobleman, but now I am a… guardian of sorts.' For the first time, he seemed like he could not find the right words.

'Guardian of what?' Carstair questioned, his curiosity peaking.

'Of the arcane, the damned, of things that stand between this world and another darker more bloodthirsty one, of mankind.' Azerrad allowed his words to sink in and noted the quizzical look that washed over Carstair.

'You are a vampire, you feed on mankind, you are the very manifestation of the dark, bloodthirsty world you speak of.' Carstair was drawn into the story and found any malice draining from him as he listened entranced to Azerrad's words.

'It is a delicate road I tread, between the living and the damned. But in my 238 years, I've learned to walk it well,' Azerrad let the revelation hang before he continued. 'I feed on animals, not humans. It is enough to slake the thirst I feel and allows me the control to keep a part of my humanity. My curse is my gift, there is no better guardian than a creature who barely needs to eat or sleep and possesses the power to destroy most men.' Azerrad sounded almost regretful in revealing this information.

'Then why are you here if you are a guardian of

somewhere? I know you do not guard this city.' Carstair continued his line of questioning desperate to know more.

'I'm here because people from your city purchased a set of rare books from a vender who should have known better. You brought them here to your master, I believe.' Azerrad continued, 'These books are dangerous.'

'If they are so dangerous, why did you let them out of your sight?' Carstair scoffed, no less intrigued.

'I did not,' the response came, 'I travelled with the books. By the time I caught up with them it was too late to them back from that rust bucket ship, so I stole aboard and journeyed here with them.'

'That damn fool, Rangehorn!' Carstair cursed, interrupting the tale.

'Once I learned of their destination aboard the ship, I decided to follow them and see if perhaps this is not a safer place for them to rest.'

'This is the safest place in any land.'

'Then I see no reason not to let them age in the vaults of this citadel, but as I said, they are dangerous, and need to be protected.' Azerrad finished his sentence with an air that suggested he was about done talking while bound in the dungeons.

'We do not use arcane power to harm, we only use it to protect and if these books are here this is the safest place for them,' Carstair responded, 'and we found the missing book from the inner chest pocket in your coat. Not such a safe place for it.' Carstair eyed the vampire for his response.

'Without the book, you would not have found much use in the ones you have. To make full use of the books you would need that key, too.' Azerrad's revelation sparked a degree of truth in Carstair's mind as he recalled Gallion talking of a key, yet he questioned the motives of the monster sitting before him. Why was he so willing to tell him about the book? Unless he realised Gallion would know its use regardless.

Satisfied he had learned all he needed, Carstair pushed himself away from the wall, walked steadily to the tray of implements and picked them up, looking remorsefully at them and the wasted opportunity to use them. He turned, pulled at the handle of the door and left to remove the blood-stained butchers apron he still adorned.

Azerrad remained bound in the chair but had suffered a better fate than Silas so far. He sat and thought about his next move. He had been relatively open and honest with Carstair hoping that the Order was something he could trust in; he had heard about this dusty old place on his travels and most people spoke of them as protectors of peace. Nothing had penetrated their walls in centuries, and no one was certain what ancient secrets were held in their deep vaults away from the evil who may wish to use it.

His wrists still burned, and he shifted them uncomfortably, but found he was beginning to tolerate the pain to a degree. He looked around the room in the diminished light, searching for a way out, but it was designed to keep creatures such as himself in. He relaxed back in the chair as best he could and thought of the love he had been forced to leave, all those weeks ago when he boarded the ship.

Memories danced in his mind as he thought of the chestnut hair dancing around her beautiful face and the wicked smile that could bring cities to ruin. He longed for her embrace and her crystalline eyes that pierced his very soul. As the memory played out like a well-worn record, he marvelled at the duelling elements of her existence; the raw passion and fiery love he knew and the magnificence and martial fury that lay just below the surface.

Serenity began to overtake him before he was rudely awakened by the creaking groan of the old oak door swinging open. Two soldiers appeared in the light, one holding a similar halberd to the one that had struck him down that night, the other jangling a chain of keys that were anchored to his belt.

'If it was one of you that hit me earlier, we are going to be having words.' Neither of the soldiers responded but shot each other a worried glance.

The second soldier fussed to find the right key, as he did so he navigated his way around Azerrad cautiously and knelt to see the cuffs. Unlocking them and allowing them to fall to the floor with a clang, the two soldiers looked on nervously. Azerrad rose from the chair and soothed his pained wrists in his hands as he stretched out his muscles.

'I assume the Grand Master awaits!' Azerrad chirped, pleased at the turn of events and strolled out the cell door, much to the relief of the soldiers.

Chapter 5

Azerrad was followed out of the dungeons by the two soldiers who had released him, though they kept a purposeful distance between themselves and the vampire. He made his way up from the depths of the citadel's dungeons and found himself in an unfamiliar hall. He was ushered into an antechamber by the guards at his back. The room was small, much smaller than the great hall at the citadel's entrance, yet it was no less lavishly decorated. One wall bore the stern faces of several of the Orders Grand Master's, as had the great hall. Azerrad paced gently, taking in the craftsmanship that had gone into the paintings as he waited for the guards.

'Please, wait here a moment,' one of the soldiers said as they emerged from the stairs. They crossed the flagstone floor and departed through a curtained archway to the room's far side. Azerrad was content to look upon the faces of old while the soldiers arranged what he assumed would be another audience with the Grand Master.

He slowly continued his tour of the paintings that hung around the room; one a cruel scene depicting a band of mounted warriors chasing down a pack of wolves in the twilight of the moon, their lances felling the beasts; another a serene scene of the city bathed in glorious light, a curious juxtaposition of the two sides of this world. Finally, he came to the largest and most imposing painting that depicted a great man clad in ceremonial armour, his dark eyes burning from where they hung, the frown a manifestation of determination, the white moustache proud and no less stern. Azerrad read the small gold inscription that sat at the base of the picture; 'Grand Priest Julien Uvren, Founder of the city, saviour of its people'.

After a short while, another soldier appeared at the curtain, dressed less formally than the others he bore no visible weapons and wore a tunic of cerulean that sported a golden ankh in the centre. He was carrying clothes which he dumped onto the floor.

'The Grand Master thought these would benefit you,' the soldier said calmly. 'When you are ready, make your way this way.' The soldier turned and departed through the curtained doorway and left the vampire alone. It dawned on Azerrad that in all the commotion of his capture and his pleasure at his release that he was still dressed in the ruined clothing of the evening's adventures. He made his way to the pile of clothes and picked up each garment to inspect it. Not his first choice, but he could tell his soiled clothes were beginning to smell.

He carefully removed his boots and disrobed, his muddy and torn trousers falling in a heap, his leather jerkin and stained shirt following suit. As Azerrad stood freed of his clothes he let the moonlight bathe him as it entered through one of the great windows that adorned the eastern wall. In the light of the moon, his skin seemed to radiate a ghostly blue as the paleness reflected the moons light undiminished by any imperfections. The piercing wounds of his back where the beast had caught him had healed and left no lasting mark with which to identify their battle, even the skin of his wrists and the site of the silver spine's intrusion were mere blemishes already.

Azerrad picked up the white shirt he had been brought, the cotton material fell effortlessly as it hugged his form, a good fit he thought, though a little ostentatious. The ruffled collar and elaborate cuffs more than he would have chosen. Buttoning the shirt, he bent to pick up the trousers. More inconspicuous than the shirt they were simply black and leather but fitted as well as the shirt. Seeing no alternative, he picked up his scuffed and dirty boots, hammering them together to remove any debris he could and replaced them on his feet. Noticing the pile of mud and debris he left on the ornate carpet, he looked around quickly to see if anyone was around to notice before pushing it under the thick curtain of the window with his boot. He ran his hands through his silken hair like a rake and pushed his hair from his face as he made his way beyond the curtain doorway.

The doorway led into a corridor that was carpeted in a well-worn, but expensive and patterned manner. More paintings and tapestries hung on the walls and there were more curtained entrances interspersed on the right running down the corridor's length. At the end lay two heavy looking doors with huge hinges and handles to match. To the left a solitary archway that was not curtained at all. As he ventured down the hall, Azerrad began to understand that the Order was steeped in traditions, partly from the images that hung on the walls and partly that they hung there at all.

The hallway was brightly lit by many lanterns on either side, the air in the hall was still and the slight flickers of flame caused interesting shadows to be thrown around here and there. Azerrad thought it strange that there were no guards to be seen but continued his methodical advance along the hall. Soon, sounds of movement could be heard; the footfall of busy workers and the dull hum of chatter came from the open doorway. Upon passing it, he peered through and could see rows of desks each with a candle stand, the green leather of their surface contrasting with the deep brown of their frame, the room was bordered by great bookcases that towered into the rooms ceiling space, ladders were needed to reach the top shelves. In there, there were easily twenty people moving about from shelf to shelf or working at some tome on a desk. Those desks being used were further lit by a candle in the holder that each desk had. The workers were studious and ceremonial in their appearance, leading Azerrad to assume they were the librarians of the Order. His passing went unnoticed but the gentlest of breezes and lightest of rustles spiked his senses and he turned to see what it was.

It was an armed guard in similar blue regalia to the man who had brought Azerrad clothing earlier, but this one had a sword sheathed to a thick leather belt that entwined around his waist. The guard's right hand stretched across his body to grasp the hilt of the sword that dangled to his left side, keeping the weapons movement in check. He offered out his left arm, dictating that Azerrad should enter the curtain covered room from which the man had appeared. The lack of doors made the place eerily quiet and unnerving to move around in, and Azerrad wondered if that was by design.

Azerrad took the man's offering silently and swept aside the curtain to enter the room that adjoined the hallway. As he disappeared through the velvet screen, the soldier took up post guarding the outside. The room was just as elaborate as the others Azerrad had witnessed, but instead of paintings and tapestries hanging from its walls, there were mirrors; equally ornately framed as the portraits. There were lanterns all around bathing the room in a warm, pleasant light and a fire roared in the hearth at the right side of the room. In the centre of the room, an imposing dining table stood, eight chairs arranged arounds its edges, only one unoccupied.

At the head of the table sat the Grand Master. He looked gaunter than before and a tiredness had crept into his features. To the left of the table were two soldiers, stern and grim faced, between them was the unoccupied chair. At the other end of the table, a man dressed as those Azerrad had passed in the great library. He held a quill in one hand and a book lay open on a fresh page. On the right side were the two soldiers who had brought him here, flanking Carstair who sat impudently in his chair, seemingly uncomfortable with the formality of proceedings. He sat opposite the empty seat, one of his guns lifeless on the table in front of him. As he made his way to the empty seat and slowly lowered himself into it, Azerrad's form made no disturbance to the image reflected by the mirrors and as he sat, he had no doubt that Carstair's other gun was trained on the chair under the table.

'So,' began the Grand Master, 'you are Azerrad Gdalicanu.' His pronunciation impressed the vampire.

'I am.'

'Well, I am Grand Master of the Order Guilherme Gallion. You know Carstair, those are brothers Roderik and Hector,' he gestured at the two soldiers to his flanks, 'those are brothers Gideon and Nestor, I guess you know those too, and that is brother Alden, one of our librarians here at the Order.'

'I would like to say it's been a pleasure,' the vampire jested.

'Quite,' Gallion replied, 'Carstair has told me of your

tale, and my what a tale it is. A vampire that does not feed on the living and dedicates his life to protecting books of the damned. A noble undertaking.'

'There are plenty who would use the books for unspeakable evil, and others who might unleash something they cannot control. They need protecting.' Azerrad spoke, not letting an emotion enter his words. 'But here, perhaps they can find a better sanctuary.'

'You would leave the books in our vaults?' Gallion questioned.

'You seek to protect the world from the evil it harbours as do I, are we not friends united by a common goal?' Azerrad questioned back.

Carstair continued to look uncomfortable and fidgeted with his gun, the librarian scribbled down words and the soldiers kept their professionalism, keeping quiet and still.

'So, vampire, what is it you would ask of us?' Gallion no longer used vampire as an insult but merely an accurate address.

'I have heard of the wonders of your vaults and would very much like to spend some time there.'

'He cannot enter our ranks, he is not human,' Carstair complained.

'I do not wish to be part of your Order,' Azerrad interjected.

'Wish it or not Carstair is right' Gallion agreed.

'He is still a monster, he cannot be trusted,' Carstair pressed his dislike of the events home and gently let his thumb cock the hidden pistol. Only Azerrad caught the gentle metallic click and the subtle movement of his muscles.

'Restrain yourself,' the Grand Master instructed in Carstair's direction, making Azerrad wonder if he too had caught the brute's subtle threat. 'Perhaps we can be of use to each other. There are plenty of treasures in the library and the vault we are yet to understand.'

'I will help in any way I can,' Azerrad replied, pleased to have found a way into the vaults and possibly an ally in the Order.

'Excellent, we will keep the books safe,' the Grand Master replied, 'Carstair will see you have accommodation and will arrange for a librarian escort to work alongside.' His words were spoken in a way that all but signalled the end of this meeting. With that, he rose from his seat slowly and laboured. His hand grasped his cane as he left the table, Nestor and Gideon rising and following him from the room.

Carstair looked put out by the Grand Master's request but slipped the hammer of the pistol carefully down before he holstered the gun he had been holding under the table. rising himself and picking the other gun from the table he holstered that too. He threw a subtle nod over his shoulder at the other soldiers indicating that they should see to the fire before they left, before taking his leave.

'I will send for you brother vampire,' he called mockingly to Azerrad, though his back was already turned, and he had nearly left the room.

Azerrad sat in the chair a while longer, taking in the events that had just occurred. The soldiers put out the fire in the fireplace of the room out and left without acknowledging him at all. Through the great arched windows that had been at Gallion's back, Azerrad could see the sun begin to rise. He smiled at the symbolism of a new dawn washing away the night.

It was more than an hour before Carstair returned to the room. As he entered, he found Azerrad stood at the window watching the comings and goings of the courtyard below. Carstair watched curiously as the morning sun bathed the vampire in light, though he cast no shadow across the room, he was resplendent in its warmth.

Sensing Carstair's appearance, he could guess what the soldier was thinking. 'The sun does not hurt my kind, you know. It is your kind that taught them to fear the light,' he said with a dignified grace as he turned to face Carstair.

'Something you would do well to remember, perhaps,' Carstair shot back. 'Your room is ready. Follow me.' He didn't wait to see if the vampire acknowledged him but turned on his heel and departed the room as quickly as he had entered it.

Azerrad followed suit, the speed in which he chased after Carstair causing his ruffled collar to flow in the generated breeze, but he had no issue matching his pace. He followed Carstair down the hallway to a staircase that led to the second and third floors of the citadel; the dormitories of the Order. Ascending to the top of the stairs, the air began to cool, and the frequency of lanterns diminished leaving the windowless climb in semi darkness. As they reached the third floor, they departed the stairs, though there was no other choice, and entered a similar, dimly lit hallway. The walls were bare; however, an oil lantern gave a slight respite to the gloom; no pictures hung here only cold wooden doors hanging in gaps in the sullen grey stone of the corridor. At the end of the corridor one door lay ajar, a stream of light emitting from it.

'We'll call when we need you, stay here until then,' Carstair said, his arm pointing in the direction of the open room.

'Very well,' was the reply, courteous as ever.

Carstair left Azerrad to enter the room alone. It was small, much smaller than the vampire was accustomed to, but not unhomely. To the left as he entered lay a small, wooden cot to sleep on, made with fresh linen. At the foot of the bed a simple wardrobe that looked like it may fall apart if it were shook too hard. On the other side sat a small desk not dissimilar to the ones in the great library and a fireplace that had a small bundle of firewood by its side. There was a single oil lantern on the wall and at the opposite end of the room to the door stood the source of the light that had radiated into the hallway; a grand arched window, the panes delicately divided by wrought black lead in a diamond pattern.

Azerrad made his way to the window and peered out. He saw the same courtyard he had spent hours watching earlier, suggesting he was on the same side of the building as the room downstairs. He could not see the city though, only open farmland and pasture leading to the dark and desolate looking mountains that bordered them. He tried the window to see if it would open, it did and the cool breeze that flowed in through it passed over Azerrad and once more filled him with memories of the life he had left behind. He moved to close the door to his quarters and fell on the bed with a crash, kicking off his boots and sliding his arms behind his head under the pillow. It was mere seconds until he fell asleep and dreamt of his love once more.

When he awoke, the sun was almost gone from the window, its last rays hugging the horizon as it seemed to try to hold on for a few more moments. Azerrad rose and pulled the window shut, the evening breeze beginning to nip. In the obscurity of dusk, he lit the lantern on the wall, its flame quickly illuminating the small room and pushing the shadows away. On the floor by the door a note had been pushed under the oak entryway and he bent to pick it up. It was from the Grand Master:

Azerrad, I hope you slept well. I have left something for you
at the door.
Tomorrow, you can introduce yourself to the librarians and
help them with some translations they are working on.
Gallion

Curious, Azerrad opened the door to see what it was that Gallion had left him. To his surprise, he found a silver tray with a beautiful crystal decanter and a matching tumbler. The decanter was filled with a ruby red liquid that caused Azerrad's senses to flush. He pulled the sleeves of his shirt over his hands and picked up the tray, turning quickly to put it on the desk in his room. He released the sleeves from his hands and stared longingly at the fluid as it settled from the movement. Apprehensively he removed the stopper from the decanter, the rich iron scent wafting into his nostrils, his teeth sharpening subtly in his mouth. He breathed a fairly large sigh of relief; it was not human. He poured a glass and took a deep draught of the invigorating liquid.

His first meal in days rejuvenated Azerrad and he decided to take a wander around the citadel. He passed many dormitories similar to his, some lay in darkness, others a stream of warm orange light peered from under the door. The air in the building was warm, the result of several fireplaces he assumed as he descended the stairs. Eventually he found himself in the hallway he had been in earlier that morning. He had yet to see any other lifeform, but the number of dark dormitories suggested that the citadel functioned round the clock.

He found the library he had seen earlier; it was much quieter than it had been and there were only small flickers of light that emitted from the few candlelit desks that were occupied. He made his way in silently, the aroma of dusty books and ancient pages a welcomed memory for him. His entrance so stealthy and quick he did not disturb the two librarians working at their desks as he wandered through the aisles, his senses illuminating at the wonders to be found. He entered the stacks; a slender, pale yet powerful hand rising to the books at waist height, the fingers trailing across leather bound tomes and fabric novels. Passing seemingly unnoticed by those around him, the silence of his footfalls almost eerie in their absence.

Towards the back of the stacks, the books began to become more ancient. Old books that had not seen light for many years, bound in many manners; some framed in gold, a few more macabre tomes framed in bones. He reached to touch the craftsmanship of one such repository of information when his solace was interrupted.

'They are something else are they not?' a young voice posed from a ladder near to where Azerrad stood. He had been so entranced by the allure of the ancient books that he had failed to notice the librarian quietly going about his business.

'Quite so.' He replied his tone giving no indication that the intrusion had startled him at all. 'Full of power, I feel it emanating from them even here.'

'They are older than anyone in the Order can remember,' the young librarian continued enthusiastically. 'Pardon the intrusion but, you're him, aren't you?'

'Him?' Azerrad returned in a playful confusion.

The boy blushed at his forwardness and fought to get out any words, 'the um... well you know... the uh...'

'Vampire?' Azerrad almost whispered still playing his part in the show. 'I'm Azerrad,' he broke the tension and offered his hand to the boy.

The librarian descended the few steps of the ladder, almost tripping, and gingerly took the hand offered by the vampire. It was cold to touch but he did not recoil as he had expected to. Azerrad too sensed the unusual reaction and firmly shook his hand.

'It is an impressive collection of literature and lore you have here...' Azerrad let the end of the question hang to prompt the boy into offering his name as he had failed to do so in his awe.

'Brother Edryd,' he replied apologetically. 'It is my honour to be the one who will assist you in your work for the order,' he continued enthusiastically.

'Very good,' came the reply, 'Are you often working from dawn until dusk?'

'I like the books, and I am quite junior in my ranks amongst the librarians. Rarely do I get to do anything of import around here, just returning the books when they are left and to study some of the less intriguing texts,' Edryd said, a hint of melancholy in the tone he now used. 'But perhaps that will all change now.' The young librarian clearly saw this opportunity as an honour, when Azerrad knew he was merely on babysitting duty that no senior member wanted to deal with.

'I think it will young Edryd,' Azerrad reassured the boy. 'But for now, I take my leave.'

'Until tomorrow,' Edryd replied, a smile beaming from ear to ear as he grasped the vampire's hand once more before he made his way out from the stacks.

Edryd watched him leave, the graceful manner of his departure as alluring as the delicate tone of his voice that still echoed in the young librarian's head. Once the form of Azerrad had melted away, he found he had drawn the disapproving look of one of the senior librarians that sat at a desk not far from where he stood. The smile began to fade from Edryd's face, and he returned to the work he was in the middle of.

Azerrad wandered down the corridor and eventually found his way into the main hall of the citadel. It was not busy, but soldiers moved from one doorway to another and congregated in small groups at regular intervals. He sat on a great oak bench that backed into one of the corners of the hall, a preposterous tapestry of the priest Uvren fighting off a full-grown werewolf with his bare hands hung behind him. From the bench, he watched the comings and goings of the order, quietly logging the usual occurrences of the day. Occasionally Carstair would cross the hall and throw him only the briefest of nods in acknowledgment, seemingly the only one who noticed him.

He began to think of what role he might play here. He liked the boy he had met in the library and was pleased he would be able to find out more about the Order's understanding of the arcane powers in the world, but he had been a warrior as long as a scholar and he questioned whether this secretive fraternity of soldiers had more in store for him.

Chapter 6

The days seemed to come and go at will following Azerrad's housing in the Order's citadel. He no longer paid attention to day or night, mealtimes or sleep. The Order was still supplying him with animal blood to keep his vigour and there was always someone around, there was always movement in the citadel.

In the days he had spent there he had learned of the comings and goings quite quickly. Guards swapped shifts with military precision and librarians took shifts transcribing dusty tomes or cataloguing and trying to understand the arcane relics housed in the vaults. Occasionally someone would come in cloaked and veiled in mystery, they would present pieces of paper with written reports to one of the senior soldiers of the order, more often than not Carstair. These were the watchers, he soon learned; the silent guardians that stalked the streets and reported back on what they were seeing. They were almost delicate in their own deadly way, the way their cloaks and clothing hung close to their bodies yet moved as though leaves of a tree in a gentle breeze at even the slightest nudge.

Azerrad was aware how dextrous and smooth their

un-gloved hands were and once caught a glimpse of one pushing a golden lock of hair back into their hood and behind their ear. Perhaps this is the role women played outside of the libraries, he surmised. The watchers' identity was to remain a secret for their own stealth and protection, but he wondered how many others knew or had realised they were women at all.

As he made his way into the library to find Edryd, the sun was almost at its apex, meaning it was close to midday. He had gone to the markets as soon as he could to purchase some new clothes, he was not particularly fond of the ones he had been donated by the order. As he moved down the hallway, his close-fitting trousers and boots seemed to appear and disappear as he moved between shadow and light. His shirt much less ostentatious and neatly tucked into his trousers was done up to its collar; simple, white, and carefully pressed. It was concealed in an equally form fitting blazer, whose golden buttons caught the sun and winked like tiny eyes.

Entering the library, he was greeted to the usual enthusiasm of his young friend and the quiet disgruntlement of many of the other patrons to the library. As he moved to a desk next to Edryd and entered into polite pleasantries, he was admonished by an older woman in grey robes, her pallid features wrung in a scowl at the noise and disturbance the pair were making.

'That is sister Agatha, she is one of the top librarians here in the order and not an advocate of your help, I'm afraid,' Edryd explained to Azerrad.

'She does not look capable of advocating much beside deathly silence and a grim work ethic,' Azerrad replied, garnering a snicker from Edryd. 'Perhaps we should take a look into what the vaults can offer us?' he asked, 'Sadan's deamonologie will still be here when we return,' he continued, sounding almost downbeat at the prospect.

'I do have a few friends in the vault, perhaps we can assist in their work for a while,' Edryd conceded.

Edryd packed up his work and placed it neatly into the desk he was working at to return to it later. They then quietly left the library, Azerrad making a mocking bow to sister Agatha as he left, a small smile appearing on his face, a faint redness descending over hers.

They made their way to the oak doors that had remained shut at the end of the hallway. Edryd opened the great doors and entered, Azerrad was surprised it was unlocked. They descended a small set of carpeted stairs and found themselves inside a vaulted room. The ceiling stretching into the sky and the great stone pillars that held up the rest of the citadel imposed on the room like a mighty ruler of old. There were stacks on either side of the room that housed an innumerable number of boxes, chests, reams of papers, and everything and anything in between. The centre was lined with desks similar to the library but more kitted out to work with tools. They littered the floor where they could around the great pillars and people sat at them, most busily working on contraptions, or reading scriptures.

'Edryd, you old scoundrel,' a cheerful voice bounded from the bustling work stations.

'Elijah, it is good to see you, old friend,' Edryd returned equally cheerfully.

Elijah rose from his desk and hastily made his way to greet the pair as they continued to marvel at the goings on in the vault. Shaking Edryd's hand, the other librarian eyed Azerrad up and down. Amongst the uniform appearance of the librarians, Azerrad stood out in the way he was dressed and the way he held himself. Standing at over six foot in height, he could not blend into the background here. As Edryd introduced Azerrad to his friend, the librarian offered his hand. Taking it firmly, the chill that passed into Elijah sent a curious look across his face, but he did well to mask any discomfort.

'So, what brings you down here?' Elijah asked curiously. 'Run out of books?' he joked and laughed.

'Showing Azerrad around, thought he might like to see the trinkets you play with down here,' Edryd said in a joking tone, but Azerrad could see he wasn't comfortable at jesting like this.

'Perhaps I could see what you are working on?' Azerrad interjected to save any embarrassment.

'Certainly, I have a new 'trinket' I am deciphering at this moment,' the mischievous grin eased Edryd, and Elijah led them to his workstation.

On the desk lay a curious item; it was stout and cylindrical and made entirely of brass. There were words in a language that Edryd could not read beautifully etched into its surface.

'Came in with a bunch of things from the Savage Dawn's last voyage,' Elijah noted picking the item up and rotating it in his hands. 'Never come across anything like it before and can't read the inscription either,' he mused, a little hint of annoyance crossing his words.

'May I?' Azerrad asked, holding out his hand to receive the brass cylinder.

'Sure,' Elijah responded, almost immediately relinquishing hold of it to Azzerad's surprise. He clearly didn't see the value in the relic as Azzerad did.

Turning the cylinder in his hand himself a few times, Azerrad made a few 'hmmm's' as he inspected the artefact, even going as far as to put his hand to his chin as if deep in thought for several moments. The librarians watched the pantomime awaiting a response. Finally, Azerrad depressed a small button almost hidden in the cylinder's mechanisms. As he did so, the cylinder expanded into what resembled a telescope as each part of the item moved outwards. Once it was extended, there were several coloured lenses that could be moved in and out of the telescope's focus; one an emerald green, another ghostly purple, and a final glinting blue one.

'For those who wish to see what others seek to hide,' Azerrad read from the cylinder he held. 'It's written in my native tongue. What you have here is an occulum,' he continued with distinct certainty. 'It is a way seeing what there isn't, hexed items or magical binding and such.'

The two librarians stared at the vampire in awe, in seconds he had been able to identify something that otherwise would have taken months to decrypt and even then, may have taken many more to work out its use. For the next few hours, Elijah and a few other intrigued librarians brought scrolls and artefacts to Azerrad for inspection. Azerrad whiled away the afternoon translating inscriptions and scrolls for the librarians, carrying out more work in a few hours than would have been possible in months for the Order.

As well as translations he sat and showed a few librarians what some of the relics were. Some were weapons concealed and deadly others navigational aids and a few were simply beautiful ornaments. When Azerrad had had his fill of entertaining the librarians with his skills he melted into the shadows to indulge his own curiosities.

The vampire wandered the stacks of chests much as he had done the library a few nights ago, trailing his hand here and there as though by touch he could tell the many miles or centuries the objects had travelled, though in reality, they merely reminded him of his homeland.

As Edryd and his friend eagerly worked together on the occulum, Azerrad found a quiet corner away from the eager librarians and took a particularly old looking box down from a stack. He had to wipe away the dust to see what symbols it bore. As he did so, the cloud of departing dust revealed a dead language he could not read, though some of its symbols seemed familiar. Opening the chest, a small puff of dust was expelled at the hinges. Peering in, unsure what to expect, he found only a few pieces of aged parchment. The writing on the parchment was undecipherable to Azerrad and he wondered if it had been worked on at all, or simply put aside as a failure. The thought of the information it could contain disappointed him as he thought of it going unread and unused.

Rifling through the parchments, he came across a piece written in a different hand and by the looks of the red penmanship, it had been written in blood. He paused, but its information was lost to the passage of time. He replaced the paper and returned the box to its place on the shelf, resigning it to obscurity. Watching the day draw to end, he wondered how many other chests and how much more information had been lost to this world in some other dusty vault.

During the nights, Azerrad had taken to wandering the streets of Uvrenmouth, learning its streets and walkways little by little and exploring all the hidden secrets it had to offer. More and more he was finding his feet at the Order and could began to see a place for himself working with them for the good of mankind. Finally, he decided it was time to collect the small box of belongings he had brought with him and stashed away in an abandoned house, just in case he needed to make a quick escape.

Azerrad approached the building cautiously as he always did, not desiring to alert anyone to his use of the derelict house. He brushed through the overgrown garden, his gentle movements barely disrupting the vegetation. He moved around the side of the building to where he had loosened a board that stood as a barrier to the downstairs window and slipped into the encompassing darkness of the home.

Even in the day, it was horribly dark inside—a few rays of light piercing holes and gaps in boards—but at the dead of night, it was oppressively dark. The gloom seemed to cling to Azerrad as he moved through the house. The stale air he was used to seemed distorted he thought as he ascended the stairs, a faint trace of sweetness cut the air and elicited his senses.

He moved more cautiously as he reached the top floor. Even in the darkness his sight was keen enough to make out the lay of the walls, though he knew them without needing sight anyway. He entered the bedroom where the small crate of belongings lay, hidden in the back of an old rotting cupboard that was the room's solitary decoration. Stealthily he crossed the room, his footfalls silent as he knew which boards not to disturb. At the window he picked up a small white candle that was almost at the end of its life and, taking a match out of the inside of his jacket pocket, lit the candle.

Despite the candle's modest flame, the absence of any light made it glow like a beacon in the sea of black. Azerrad opened the cupboard doors and placed the candle in a small tin holder on the cupboards base, curbing the light and lighting the vampire unnaturally as he crouched to retrieve his things. He reached in and lifted the box before freezing; something disturbed his senses, a gentle scrape of something against the wooden floor downstairs, the tell-tale sign of someone who was not accustomed to the building's nuances. He silently replaced the box and expertly moved away into the recess of a corner, the shadows enveloping him. There he waited patiently, slowing his breathing and watching for an intruder, but none came. The house returned to its silent slumber and the candle danced wickedly as it clung to the last embers of the wick.

Wanting to remove the box before he lost the

candlelight, he drifted back to the cupboard, bent down and pulled the box out, this time he was more focussed on haste than stealth. The gentle sounds of the crate being moved and the old, worn drape that had concealed it sliding to the ground like a snake slithering into the darkness dulled his impeccable senses. By the time he was alerted to the presence of another, the cold steel of a blade's edge was pressed menacingly against his throat. Crouched on the floor, crate in both hands and under the blade of another, Azerrad felt more mortal than he had in a century. He froze looking for a way out as his assailant slammed a boot down on top of the box he held, causing it to crash to the floor. The resultant disturbance ended the flames valiant fight to remain lit, but in its death throes he could see the beautiful nature of the boot that struck down on his things. The black leather an abyss in the already darkened room, the brass buckles that ran from ankle to knee, shining like cats' eyes in a beam of light, the thick sole and gentle heel revealing more of his attacker's identity.

Alone in the sea of darkness, death biting at his heels, Azerrad smiled.

Chapter 7

Relinquishing the blade from Azerrad's throat, the assailant backed away. The delicate footsteps familiar to Azerrad's ears. 'You have become complacent, Azerrad,' the mysterious figure remarked, but the beautiful accent and gentle tone were unmistakable to Azerrad, and his heart leapt.

'You have been missed, Katerina,' he replied fondly.

The two lovers laughed as Azerrad rose to his feet. Staring through the blackness at each other, Katerina dropped her blade, the sound echoing through the empty room, though neither paid its clamour any heed, then threw her arms around Azzerad's neck, her thighs wrapping around his waist. Azerrad pulled Katerina close into him, feeling the soft touch of her lips as the two kissed, the weight of his longing for her finally lifting from his shoulders in that moment.

After the lovers fell from each other's embrace, Azerrad questioned Katerina of her voyage and of news from their homeland as relit the candle stub and collected his belongings. The voyage had been quick from Jatrador to Uvrenmouth and without any incidents, to his relief. She had stowed away on a merchant ship journeying back from Jatrador along the trade routes established by the Savage Dawn. Since the books were removed from Jatrador, there was little for her to do, so news of Azerrad's safe journey and possible new location to keep watch had been welcomed by Katerina.

When the pair had caught up on all that had happened in the weeks of their being apart sat in the dim candlelight of another dying candle, Azerrad explained how he had met with the Order, how he now was staying there and helping in their work. He left out the part about his capture and almost torture; Katerina was strong willed, much more so than he, and may well have advocated retribution rather than working alongside them, and so Azerrad kept his own council on the matter. She enquired if the Order knew what the books were or if they were planning on trying to use them, but so far, he had not questioned in detail on this matter.

'If you are staying with the order, then why are you hiding things here?' Katerina asked her lover, confused as to why he would keep things at risk away from where he was staying.

'I had to be sure they were trustworthy; you know the delicate line we tread between our world and theirs.' He replied

'And are they?' she continued with the questioning.

'I think so,' he hesitated, 'some of them are at least, their leadership is still shrouded in mystery, but they try to be protectors of some sort, that I am certain of. The books will be safer there than we could ever keep them in Jatrador.'

'I trust your judgement Azerrad, but this place calls out, you must feel it too,' she spoke honestly and for the first time it caused Azerrad to think about the last few weeks.

'Yes, I have felt it too,' he admitted, 'but what it is, I do not know.'

'The city is calling the unnatural to its gates, there is

something else at work here, something that the Order may not know about,' she spoke gravely and Azerrad understood that the time for translation and discovery in the citadel's libraries and vaults may soon be at an end.

'Yes, it is the primal urge in me that has led to my desire to stay,' he mused, 'but there is so much good we can do here. You should see the vault of relics they keep hidden with little knowledge of their true power.'

'I agree,' Katerina replied, 'this place will need our help.'

Azerrad collected his crate of possessions and led Katerina out of the derelict home. They made their way back into the streets using the house's back entrance to make sure they were not seen, but Azerrad no longer worried about disturbing the vegetation as he had no intention of returning here now.

They walked through the quiet streets, occasionally passing someone returning home from work, or a latecomer leaving for one of the taverns. They made a courteous acknowledgement as they passed but neither sought to engage anyone in conversation.

Katerina had stowed her belongings at the docks and come straight in search for Azerrad, so they made their way back to the harbour where the journey had begun for Azerrad to collect his lover's things. There were few people working during the night at the harbour, so going unseen did not prove to be an issue. Katerina's possessions were where she had left them, under a mass of nets and rigging, though she was visibly displeased that several boxes of fish on ice had been left to melt around her crate.

The pair slunk out of the boatyard quietly, hugging the shadows and slipping away. Back in the lantern lit streets they reminisced of old times and talked of the future here in another city. As they passed the glow of one of the city's packed taverns, the riotous chorus that cascaded out into the peaceful night caused them to slow, watching the toils of the workers as they told tall tales and complained about anything and everything they could.

The tavern was awash with every aspect of society, there were grizzled dock workers mixing with well-dressed socialites and entrancing women who caught the eyes of not just the young and eligible but the older, more seasoned gentlemen, too. Azerrad recognised several of the soldiers of the Order among them; although they no longer wore the livery of the Order, he had seen them in his comings and goings. A night off he suspected, but it seemed strange to see them mixing with regular folk.

As they moved out of the enrapturing glow of the tavern's windows, still carrying the meagre boxes that contained all they had, both felt eerily at home here. Nearing the citadel, Azerrad suggested that Katerina should find a more discreet entrance until he could formally introduce her to the Order the following day. He took her crate from her, and she kissed his cheek gently as she swiftly disappeared into the darkness of the night, her scent lingered with Azerrad though and he was glad it did.

Making his way through the gates and into the main hall Azerrad was not interrogated on the contents of the boxes he carried as he expected, the truth being enough for the night watchman without further inspection. The hall was warm and brightly lit as ever; several groups bustled around, a few more in plain clothes and Azerrad wondered if they were off to one of the city's watering holes as well. Most likely, he thought, probably the one he had passed; the Order seemed to keep to itself even when it was outside the remits of the citadel.

Just as he was about to leave the hall and continue to the dormitories, a voice caught his attention. It was

Carstair's. Glancing over he saw that he was talking to Edryd and Elijah, who he had met earlier that day. He moved into the hallway and stashed his and Katerina's things out of sight and returned to try to hear what was being said. Carstair was quizzing the boys and a mild annoyance drew over Azerrad as he wondered if he had been too hasty in accepting the Orders seemingly genuine hospitality. From his concealed spot, Azerrad listened as best he could to the exchange between the three members of the Order.

'What is he up to?' Azerrad heard Carstair question Edryd. 'Is he helping with your work? I heard you went into the vaults today.'

'He is helping, he knows some of the languages far better than any of us, he worked out what Elijah's relic was straight away,' Edryd replied somewhat defensively.

'Did you suggest visiting the vaults or him?' Carstair continued accusingly.

'Well, he did, but our research was dragging, I welcomed the change of scenery,' Edryd protested.

'They were more than welcome–' Elijah tried to add but was quickly cut off by a silencing finger from Carstair.

'Thank you, brother, but that is all,' Carstair dismissed Elijah, not needing his input any further. Understanding it was not his place to argue, he regretfully left his friend to deal with Carstair alone and ventured off to find some food. Carstair waited until Elijah was out of earshot before turning his attention back to Edryd. 'I know you were told to keep an eye on the vampire and the Grand Master is keen to use his skills, but remember this,' Carstair spoke slowly and purposefully as he held Edryd's stare, 'he is more dangerous than any book or artefact in this building. Do not be so quick to forget that do you understand?'

Edryd nodded sullenly, feeling like a scolded boy.

'Report back to me in a few days,' Carstair added before he was interrupted by a soldier in full regalia.

The soldier handed Carstair a piece of paper and the senior soldier read it quickly, his eyes darting across the page as he took its contents in. There was a brief interchange in hushed tones that the vampire could not make out, but he could tell there was no panic in any of those involved voices or expressions. Towards the end he did make out '…shit's getting weirder' which came from Carstair. Without waiting to be seen by anyone, he disappeared into the hallway and made his way on the now familiar trek up to his quarters collecting his belongings on the way.

Carstair dismissed the soldiers he was talking to and glanced around the room, despite him not glimpsing the vampire, he felt he was around, and the hairs stood up on the back of his neck at the thought of someone eavesdropping on his conversations. He smoothed them down with a wide palm and made off in the direction of the stairs that led to the Grand Master's study and quarters.

Carstair rapped the door and waited patiently to be summoned in. When he was, he was cautious to shut the door, not slam it. In the field, he was a fine soldier, but in presence of Gallion he found that he was intimidated. By what he could never narrow down as the old man was brittle enough to snap across his thigh and welcoming enough toward his guards.

Gallion was sat in his ornately carved oak chair at a desk that took up far more of the study than was required. The emerald green leather that topped it reflected the flicker of the lantern flames as the Grand Master leafed through a huge, aged book. Carstair could see that the book was bound with red leather that was turning brown with age and could be locked with metal clasps, the dull sheen of the metal suggested it was lead or something similar.

'It is no use Carstair,' the old man said without looking up at Carstair, 'I need the key to unlock the book's secrets.'

'What secrets might they be sir?' Carstair said, realising the stupidity of the question as he said it.

'The people of this city are kept safe by the blood of our kind, Carstair,' Gallion started and Carstair knew it would be a long conversation, so he calmly pulled out a chair to sit and listen. 'For centuries, we have been tasked with keeping the monsters from this city, and we are so effective at it that barely anyone outside our ranks even remembers that there were monsters to be saved from in the first place.' Carstair nodded listening intently. 'Does it seem fair that we must bear the brunt of this responsibility?'

'It is the duty we have chosen, sir,' Carstair said and Gallion believed he believed it.

'Duty, pah, we are burdened by the knowledge we possess and yet shackled by it. The world around us moves on as we hide in the shadows to protect them from themselves. I believe there is a better way, a more enlightened way, and the answers lie in this book. With them, we can free our people from their burden and release them from their thankless duties,' as he rested Carstair noted that Gallion had become quite animated in his oratory.

'Then ask the librarians to look, or... the vampire.' Carstair suggested, though he was hesitant to suggest using Azerrad. 'The librarians say he has knowledge of the ancient languages.'

'The librarians have their uses, but they dither. And the vampire cannot be trusted with this task, not yet, not until his loyalty has been tested, not until his humanity has been tested,' Gallion corrected, the cryptic nature of his words taking Carstair by surprise.

'Humanity?' the soldier quizzed.

'You of all people know that we make difficult decisions for the greater good, Carstair. There may come a time when we need a monster, not a hero.'

'Speaking of which, our men took down another werewolf on the outskirts of the town,' Carstair finally got in the reason for his visit.

'Good, that is their job is it not?' Gallion replied, his eyes drifting back to the open pages before him.

'Well yes, of course it is,' he replied respectfully, 'but it is the second one this week and the third this month if you include the one, I brought in. Something is changing.'

The Grand Master took a pause before answering, his responses usually so quick it unnerved Carstair to see him select his words more carefully. With a gentle sigh he gave Carstair a response, 'Yes, I have been concerned for some time. The dark energy of this place is growing stronger. Drawing more and more creatures to our doors. I will need my loyal soldiers for the times ahead may be difficult. I need people like you that I can trust. But for now, you need to trust me.'

'I do sir, of course,' the loyal pup replied.

'It is perhaps time you took the vampire out for a field test,' Gallion scribbled something onto a piece of parchment by the book before rising from the chair and passing it to the seated Carstair. He poured out a glass of brown liquor from the crystal decanter that stood on the edge of his desk, briefly glanced at his loyal soldier to check he understood what had been ordered and turned to the window to watch the town slowly drink itself into the next day. The cloudless sky was dotted with stars that winked as they were watched, and the crescent moon waxed high in the starry night sky.

Carstair departed the room and made his way to his own quarters to find some solitude. He thought about having to work with the vampire and test his humanity, whatever that meant. Sometimes the old man speaks in such riddles, he thought, would it not be easier to come out and say what he means. As he rounded the corner of the hallway that branched into the senior soldier's dormitories, there was a brief section that overlooked the great entrance hall. He paused and marvelled at how much quieter and tranquil it was at night. The two guards stood to attention at the doorway, the gatekeeper reading in his cubicle, the light's glow steady in the windless room.

The serenity was broken as a watcher entered through the door, visibly tired even from the distance Carstair watched from. He saw the watcher present a sheaf of paper to the gatekeeper, and Carstair knew it was a report. Tired and weary himself he weighed whether he should go down and check it out or leave it to one of the senior soldiers still on duty. There appeared to be no urgency in the gatekeeper, the guards, or the watcher, so he turned back towards his room.

Carstair unlocked his door with the unnecessarily large key that his door took, evidently the sacrifice for the largest of the senior rooms. Though his was by far the largest room, it was not large by any means. Just like Azerrad's room it had a single wooden bed, a wardrobe for his clothes, a desk, a fireplace, and a respectable window, but Carstair's room also sported a hand basin and a bedside cabinet that bore an oil lamp as well.

Carstair lit the lamp at the bedside, the dimmer glow of the smaller lamp failing to scare off all of the shadows in the room. He began to run water in the basin and using a washcloth that hung at its side, he washed his face, letting the water rush from it and onto his shirt. The cool water refreshed him somewhat, but his eyes were still darkened at their base and were beginning to become bloodshot. He slumped onto the bed and ran his hands through the dusky, hazel hair that was beginning to grow out of his control and fell backwards, sinking into the well-worn mattress, bunching the pillows under his head as he did so. The light glowed low and cast the room in a pleasing, warm orange hue.

As he watched the night sky begin to cloud gently through his window. As his eyelids became heavier, he could not shake the unsettling feeling that the moon's gaze gave him, but slowly his thoughts drifted away, and he finally slept.

On the other side of the building, Azerrad entered his room to find the alluring form of Katerina draped across his bed. She had removed her boots and jacket and lay in skin-tight trousers and a flowing lacy shirt that subtly hinted at her intent. The window lay open and the cool evening breeze that rushed into the room caused the lantern to flicker and the curtains to dance for the two of them. Dropping the boxes to the floor, Azerrad let the jacket he was wearing fall unceremoniously to the floor as he slid his boots off. Keeping her gaze, he blew out the lantern and slowly climbed onto the small bed next to Katerina. Even in the darkness, he could feel her eyes locked on him and finally felt peace that she was here. He slowly put his finger to her chin and pulled her face to his, kissing her gently. Katerina smiled and pulled Azerrad's face to hers more firmly, sliding her arms around his neck and pulling him close. The vampires intertwined like creeping vines as they gave in to their passions, watched on by that same crescent moon that had caused Carstair such trouble.

Chapter 8

The dawn arrived and flooded the citadel with light. Carstair was awoken from a deep sleep he had sorely needed. The night had brought an uneasy sleep, the moon's unwelcome glare had caused Carstair to dream of strange occurrences and dark places. As he sat on the edge of his bed, his eyes still adjusting to the light, he thought of what field testing the vampire entailed. Then he thought of the report that had come in last night and the strange things that had happened over the last few weeks. Gallion had become increasingly distant and cryptic recently and he felt that things in Uvrenmouth were shifting. He didn't like to be kept in the dark and not knowing how to prepare made him uneasy.

Carstair's head swam with all the thoughts circling in it. Perhaps finding out what report came in last night would help him assemble the thoughts into place. But coffee first, he thought, he needed something to bring him round. Dressing quickly and stopping only to splash water onto his face, not wash properly, Carstair left his quarters and headed to the refectory to find some refreshments.

The sun was beginning to round the corner of the citadel and lapped playfully at the window's edge. The curtains had ceased their dancing and lay dormant at the open window. Still led on his bed, Azerrad opened his eyes to find Katerina sat at the small desk leafing through a book from her things and eyeing it intently. She was draped in the shirt from the night before, but nothing else and it clung delicately to her form. Azerrad watched her for a moment, mere minutes, but so lost in his love for her that it seemed like an age had passed when he came round to the quizzical look from his lover; her eyebrow raised inviting the question of what assistance one could be.

He rose from the bed, pulling the linen sheet with him to hide his naked form, and drifted across to where she sat. He gently placed his hands on her shoulders and bent down to kiss her neck, taking in the sweet scent he knew so well.

'It might be best if I broach the subject of your arrival on my own to the Order first,' he mused half expecting some resistance.

Seeing the seriousness in the features of his face, Katerina replied understandingly, 'if that is what you think best.' She continued, 'did something happen last night?'

'I overheard one of the soldiers quizzing one of the librarians about my intentions here. It seems my standing in this place is not as certain as I had thought it to be,' he replied.

'They fear us, they have hunted our kind for centuries. It still baffles me why they didn't just kill you on sight. Perhaps they will come to see our true nature,' she tried to reassure her paramour.

'I thought this could be a safe place for us, for the things that need protecting,' he replied almost ruefully.

'Do not despair yet, my love,' came the soothing response, 'Things change. In time, this Order here might come round to what it does not understand.'

'I will speak to Edryd today and talk to the Order of your arrival.'

'I will find my own way out, spend a little time in the town and get a feel for the place.'

The pair dressed and kissed each other goodbye. Azerrad departed through his quarter's door, Katerina through the open window. Despite the dark nature of the clothes she wore and the height of the dormitory window, she scaled the side of the building swiftly and agilely, entering the courtyard unseen before slipping out into the city. It concerned her how easily she could make it past the guards unnoticed and briefly questioned just how safe this fortress could be.

Azerrad descended the stairs and thought about what to do first. Finally deciding to confront Edryd.

The refectory was busy as those working the morning ate and roused themselves over coffee. Carstair sat alone nursing his second mug of coffee, the rich aroma filling his nostrils and preparing him for the day. As he sat watching, another senior soldier by the name of Gould caught his eye and made his way over to him. Trying not to look like Gould's intrusion was unwelcome, though it was, he kicked out a stool beside him so that he may sit.

'You hear about last night?' Gould said as he gratefully took the proffered stool.

'No, enlighten me,' the irritable response came.

'Watchers marked another wolf entering town yesterday evening, a team caught up with it a few hours ago,' Gould replied.

'Caught up with it? They took the guy in?' Carstair enquired.

'Put it down, but not before it ripped through three bodies. The clean-up teams are having a tough time dealing with this one.'

'It wasn't a full moon last night,' Carstair replied confused.

'No, but it was not the work of a man that shredded those poor bastards last night and the team claim it was a wolf they took down.'

'What the fuck is going on here?' Carstair grumbled in a hushed tone so that his annoyance would not alert the others in the refectory. 'Leave it with me, I will speak to Gallion again, see if he has answers.'

Gould nodded and stood, sliding the stool back under the table with his foot. He understood that keeping this on the quieter side might be in everyone's best interest. Carstair watched Gould leave the refectory, pausing only for a cursory chat with a librarian as he left. Draining his mug with one gulp, he stood to leave as well, dropping his mug at a cleaning station as he went out. Rubbing his eyes with his hand, he bore the look of a man with the weight of the world on his shoulders. He decided he should change before confronting Gallion so returned to his chambers to do so.

Out in the streets of Uvrenmouth, the city was stirring into life; maids and cleaners bustled around heading to their places of work to prepare for the morning traffic, vendors and sellers were making their way to the market to set up their wares, and dockworkers trudged mournfully as they prepared for another day of toil at the shipyard. The sun shone between breaks in the cloud, but it cast no warmth on the streets of Uvrenmouth that morning. As Katerina moved quietly amongst the growing crowds of people, she heard whispers of the events of the night; rumours flying of a terrible beast that stalked the city's streets.

She kept to the shadows as best she could as she

heard the different rumours that were abounding the populace. By the time it was midmorning she had already heard that many tales that to try to identify or trace this monster would be nigh on impossible. Some said it was huge, seven feet tall with terrible claws and lupine features; others that it was some form of large cat that had escaped a menagerie; others that it was a deviant man that was performing some sort of ritual. It seemed that the town had long forgotten the evils that haunted its past, she thought.

She continued to watch the city ebb and flow until she decided to sit outside a small café that overlooked some of the harbour. She ordered coffee and although it had no effect or purpose for her, the taste reminded her of a different time, before all this. She sat and watched the rolling wave's crash into the sea wall, spray erupting in theatrical fashion as she sipped her coffee. A group of young women walked past chatting and Katerina caught elements of the stories she had been hearing all day. Soon, a group of dock workers made their way past on a break, also gossiping about the night's events. News travelled fast around the city it would seem and almost everyone was talking about it.

As she thought about moving on, an elderly lady appeared at her side and inquired if she sat alone. Katerina told her she was and offered a chair to the women who graciously accepted and sat down. Not wanting to seem rude, Katerina decided she could while away a little more time to keep the lady company. As they sat, the waiter brought the old lady a pot of tea and all its accompaniments, while topping up Katerina's coffee.

'It is a comforting spot when you are not used to the city,' the old lady said, staring out at the sea wall as well.

'Is it so obvious that I am not one of you?' Katerina

playfully replied.

'Perhaps not to many of these younger folks, but I have seen much in my time, and I recognise the look of a visitor.'

'I can see why you find peace here,' Katerina offered the old lady, both their gazes on the crashing waves.

'Have you heard the news?' the old lady enquired.

'I have heard many rumours, but it seems no two people can tell the same tale,' Katerina smiled as she replied.

'No,' the old lady agreed, 'there are few that even remember the tales of the creatures the Order drove off, and none old enough to actually remember those dark times.' The statement was almost rhetorical in its delivery, but Katerina decided to pursue it further.

'Do you?' she asked.

'Remember those days? My dear, how old do think I am?' the old lady jested not waiting for a reply. 'I remember my mother telling tales of her mother and father and their entanglement with a monster. My family was one of the unlucky ones. But they are all but myth these days. That is why no one truly believes what ever happened was unnatural. But we know different, eh?' The knowledge the sentence held hung in the air for a while as Katerina digested what it meant.

'I am sorry, you lost someone?' she managed in reply, unsettled by the old lady's words.

'My grandfather, though I was not yet born. My mother would tell tales of his heroic actions, there were few willing to listen and fewer still willing to believe her.'

'It can be a cruel place this world,' Katerina spoke from experience.

'It can indeed,' the old lady replied finishing her tea. 'Thank you for indulging an old lady and talking for a while,' she added as she made her move to leave. The lady left without any more interaction and Katerina paused for a while thinking about the strange encounter. Finally, she departed the café, leaving two gold coins for her drinks, including a sizeable tip, and made her way towards the market stalls. It was here she believed she would understand how the city ran.

At the citadel, Azerrad found Edryd at his usual stall in the library; the desk an array of books, some very old and others new, his ink still drying in the open book in front of him. Azerrad entered the library in a more subtle manner than usual. His face was still chiselled and smooth, but there was grim determination it. His posture and demeanour suggested business. Even sister Agatha averted her usual stern gaze when she saw him stride in.

Edryd noticed him enter but tried to keep his focus on his work, unsure how to act following his interaction with Carstair the evening before. As Azerrad approached, he noticed that Edryd was more unkempt than usual; his hair messier, the golden locks frayed and out of place, his eyes glassy and sleep deprived, complimented by the bags that lay under them. Even his attire was not as neatly pressed as usual. The young librarian's image softened Azerrad's mood a little and he took a lighter tact than he thought he would have.

'Edryd,' he acknowledged him in a single word greeting.

'Azerrad, how are you this morning?' the boy feigned interest back at him.

'That will depend,' came the ominous reply Edryd had been dreading.

'I am no spy!' Edryd blurted out, catching the vampire completely off guard. Whatever he had expected Edryd to say, this was not it.

'Spy?' he quizzed back.

'I saw you yesterday, I know you overheard what the soldier Carstair said to me,' he said almost accusingly, not wanting to be drawn into a game of cat and mouse.

'I see, well you can understand how this all seems then,'

'When I was told I would be working with you I was overjoyed, the chance to do something meaningful for the Order, for humanity, but Carstair came to me and told me to keep an eye on you. I assumed in the 'you're a vampire I could be in danger kind of way', but no, apparently he wanted actual reports of your behaviour,' Edryd rambled on, Azerrad taking in every word as he watched the features on the boy's face for signs of untruth. 'I was honest with him on the work we have been doing, but I also told him that you have been nothing but helpful.'

Azerrad saw no lie in the boy's face, 'I believe you Edryd,' he relented, 'but it seems my position here is under false pretences.'

'How so?' the boy asked.

'I am not a guest of your Order if it is having tabs kept on my conduct and movements,' he suggested back.

'I think that the order is distrustful of something it has spent its duration trying to get rid of. But there are those within our ranks who can see this for the opportunity it is, myself included,' Edryd spoke truthfully. Azerrad did not know if he truly shared the young librarian's optimism.

'Give Carstair a report on me, it will look suspicious if you do not. For now, though, let's work on these damned books a little more,' Azerrad slumped into the chair beside Edryd, picked up the glorious, leather-bound book he was working from and began to translate it for him, the young librarian struggling to keep up with the vampires rhetoric.

Carstair had donned clean and ironed trousers and a casual shirt over which he wore a black waistcoat. The clothes looked a little ill fitting, possibly due to their age, but Carstair cared little for what most people thought of his appearance. He had washed and pushed his hair back from his face before leaving his quarters for the second time that morning. As he made the trip across the landing to the stairs leading to the Grand Master's quarters, he paused as he had the night before. The great hall was busier than it had been the night before, librarians going about their work moving books from one place to another, soldiers chatting as the performed their tasks. Nothing seemed out of order though and this calmed Carstair a little.

He entered Gallion's study, once beckoned to do so, and found the Grand Master as he so often did pouring over an open book. He instinctively took a seat near the desk where Gallion sat, but he always took one of the less regal looking ones out of habit. There he sat patiently waiting for Gallion to speak first.

'Carstair, I was not expecting you this morning, to what do I owe the pleasure?' Gallion asked barely moving his eyes from the open book but sounding genuine.

'There was another report of a wolf attack last night, I am told a team suppressed the incident, though not without cost,' Carstair answered.

'Your information is correct, is that all you came here to ask?' came the reply, a hint of irritation now edging into the Grand Master's voice.

'No,' Carstair returned, a hint of irritation in his voice

too at the trivialization of his statement. 'Does it not seem odd? Four wolf attacks within months of each other? This one not even during a full moon. It almost as if...' he trailed off unsure how to proceed.

'Go on?' the Grand Master encouraged.

'It's as though something has awakened in this city,' he finished his other thought.

'Exactly,' Gallion remarked, pleased at Carstair airing the thought, 'as though something has awakened. I sense it too, it is why I have spent so long on this literature, I think something big is coming and if we do not find a way to stop it, I fear it may be our undoing,' the Grand Master spoke slowly and purposefully, gaging the soldier's reaction to the news he was hearing. 'Do you know what necromancy is?' he poised at Carstair.

'Dark magic?' he replied a little confused, 'The Order suppressed the use of it centuries ago.'

'They did, but I am fearful that someone, something, has found a way of using its dark power. That is why I sent for these books so urgently. I believe they can tell us what dark power is being summoned here.'

'What does that mean for us?' Carstair asked worriedly.

'I do not know yet, but we need to test the vampire's loyalties sooner rather than later. There is no time.'

'How do I do that sir?'

'Take him out on patrol, see how he reacts to orders,' Gallion proposed. 'I am sure that the time will come when we get to see where his loyalties lie,' the certainty with which Gallion spoke unnerved Carstair a little.

'I have business with a watcher today, I will arrange a patrol in the coming days,' Carstair ceded, rising from the chair and making his way to leave, assuming the discussion done.

'See that you do,' was all that Gallion added, his attention back to the ancient books on his desk. As

Carstair made to leave he saw the Grand Master's free hand gently thumb at a small pocketbook that looked remarkably like the one he had locked away once he had removed it from the vampire in the dungeons.

Carstair left the Grand Master and headed out from the citadel to catch up with watcher who had brought the information in last night. As he entered the street, the brightness of the sun forced him to shield his eyes, yet he couldn't help but notice the unfavourably cold wind that blew in the city streets that day. He knew he would find the watcher in position on the outskirts of the city and so began the journey to get more answers.

It was dusk before Carstair returned to the citadel. He returned through the main gates, anticipating the warmer atmosphere of the main hall. From a side street, Katerina watched him as his outing came to an end. She decided to wait until darkness fell fully before trying to contact Azerrad.

As Carstair entered the great hall, the noise of its patrons washed over him as the warmth of the fires eased his chilled bones. He saw Azerrad leaving the library and making his way towards him.

'Carstair,' Azerrad greeted the soldier.

'What is it?' was he all he got back.

'I have something I must discuss with you and the Grand Master urgently,' the words fell like unwelcome rainfall on Carstairs ears. He had little appetite for disturbing Gallion again, nor to do anything at all for that matter.

'Urgent?' Carstair asked imploringly, begging for Azerrad to say it could wait.

Sensing the desperation in his tone but feeling

unsympathetic to his feelings, Azerrad chirped back, 'quite so.'

With a huff and dramatic tilting of his head towards the domed abyss of the great hall's ceiling, he ran a weary hand over his wearier face and beckoned for one of the guards to approach. The soldier came close enough for Carstair to whisper something in his ear and then departed in the direction of the Grand Master's staircase. Carstair summoned Azerrad to follow him and they entered the refectory to wait on a reply.

Carstair went to the counter and returned with two mugs of coffee still steaming as he placed one in front of Azerrad and cradled his own. One of the refectory orderlies brought a solitary plate of food and placed it in front of Carstair. They both sat silently, Azrerad visibly impatient, while Carstair watched the red haze of the sunset fade to the blackness of night from the imposing window as he shovelled pieces of food into his cavernous jaw. After some time, the soldier returned and whispered something back to Carstair. Draining his mug and grasping Azerrad's, which was surprisingly empty, he returned them to the cleaning station along with his plate before leaving without suggesting the vampire follow. He did anyway and Carstair led him from the great hall into the corridor he was familiar with and into a smaller room not too dissimilar to the one where he'd had his audience with the Order not too long ago. As they entered, already seated at the head of the table was Grand Master Gallion.

Chapter 9

The look that Gallion bore was not one of pleasure. Carstair was a little surprised that he had even agreed to meet this evening and not set a time for the following day, something he felt the Grand Master only did because it was the vampire that had requested it and this thought caused him a pang of jealousy. Disliking the feeling the meeting was giving him, Carstair took a seat next to Gallion quickly, hoping that the quicker the vampire said what he had to say the quicker the ordeal would be over.

Sat at the head of the table, the Grand Master's slight form seemed almost regal in the formal robes he was wearing. The beautiful emerald green cloth fell from his shoulders and crossed hands in regular pleats, the intricate gold stitching glinting in the receding light. Though he wore no hood and the silver hair he had was neatly pressed to his head, shadows crossed the Grand Master's face, though neither Azerrad nor Carstair could tell where they originated. It gave his stern expression a new sinister complexion and Carstair struggled to look in Gallion's direction.

Azerrad made to take a seat, following Carstair's example but Gallion quickly waved him away.

'I trust this will not take long, you may remain standing to address the room,' Gallion advised, explaining his gesture. Azerrad surveyed the room in a little confusion, for it consisted of only himself, the Grand Master, Carstair and the guard at the door. He also questioned whether this matter could be quickly resolved but kept that thought to himself.

'Grand Master,' Azerrad began respectfully, 'in order to be completely transparent with you and the Order, my kinsman has made her way to Uvrenmouth.'

'Kinsman?' Gallion quizzed, 'Jatradorian?' he again questioned, 'or vampire?' he finished.

'Both,' came the reply, 'she is my partner, we were tasked with the books' protection and once I arrived, I sent word for her to follow.'

'But chose not to divulge this information to us until she has already made footfall on Uvrenmouth's land?' Gallion posed, 'this does not seem at all transparent, nor safe for your 'compatriot',' he continued, emphasising the word Azerrad had used moments ago.

'Perhaps not but I had to be sure that leaving the books here was the safest idea. I was not sure of that at the time,' Azerrad defended his actions.

'And now?'

'I am certain they are well kept here, Master,' he replied, seeking to bring some civility back to the conversation before it headed in any other direction. 'If I am to work with your Order, then Katerina must too, and she did not seem to find any issue entering the city,' Azerrad slyly interjected

'Let me remind you, you are a guest here as long as we deem it that way,' Gallion spoke in a measured tone that suggested that Azerrad needed to tread carefully. 'Must is a rather demanding word to use in the hospitality of others,' the words came out as lethal as any blade and it was clear to Azerrad that the Grand

Master was capable of cutting any foe down with them despite his usual gentle appearance.

'I meant no disrespect,' Azerrad backtracked, 'but as well you know, the contents of those books must be kept safe, we wish to work with you to that end.'

'And where is this companion now?' Gallion asked.

'Taking in the city, learning its habits.'

'Spying?' Gallion accused.

'You distrust my kind, I understand that. For thousands of years you have been raised on slaying monsters like Katerina and I, but unlike the wolves, we can have control, surely I have demonstrated this to you in my short time here. Have I not been asset so far?' Azerrad found himself in a strange position of pleading a case to which he had never pled before and found he did not care for it much.

'You are right. Thus far you have been useful, but there may come a day where you pose a threat to our order and that I cannot overlook lightly.'

'Should that day ever come I would welcome the swift vengeance your kind would wrought upon me,' the vampire replied, knowing full well they wouldn't get very close.

Gallion's expression changed, softening at the contriteness in Azerrad's voice. He had been an advocate for using the vampire's knowledge and, if he could be controlled, his speed and strength in the field as well. Gallion silently observed him for what he saw him as, a valuable asset that could solidify the Order's place as protectors against the dark. Balancing the weight of probabilities in his mind, he finally broke the silence.

'Very well, we will find a place for your companion within our walls, but she will be subject to the scrutiny placed upon you,' Gallion offered. Azerrad wondered if he was outright telling him he was being spied on or if he somehow knew Azerrad knew what had conspired between Edryd and Carstair that night.

'Grand Master?' Carstair's silence had been almost unnerving, but he was quickly shut down.

'I do not need your council Carstair, though your objection is noted,' Gallion said, quashing the notion of objection quickly. 'Next time we have need to go out, take Azerrad and his companion with you, see how they fare, the rate that we have had incidents lately I do not doubt it will be long until then.'

Carstair nodded curtly, already knowing he was to take the vampire out at the next opportunity, and rose from his chair, assuming that concluded the meeting. Azerrad did not make a move to suggest he was ready to leave yet, and as the thought that he and Katerina were to be tested sunk into his consciousness, he loosed one last gambit.

'You mentioned the rate of incidents,' Azerrad's eyes flashed wickedly as he dangled a morsel of bait out for Gallion.

The Grand Master held his hand up, a rigid finger extended, suggesting that Azerrad should wait. 'Leave us,' he directed at Carstair who looked visibly put out by the statement but did as he was told like the loyal hound he was.

Carstair drew the curtain across the room's entrance making sure that it was well covered. He dismissed the guard and instead took up his own silent watch as he listened in on what was being said in the room, the curtain hiding his form impeccably.

'Do you know why there have been so many more sightings of monsters?' Azerrad asked Gallion.

'I have an inkling that someone is trying to draw the unnatural to the city again,' Gallion replied monotonously, his tone giving no clue to his feelings. 'It has been attempted more than once in the past.'

'The city calls to us,' Azerrad half whispered, the

theatricality of his narrative polar opposite to the Grand Master's. 'It is drawing beings such as I and the spate of wolves you've had to it.'

'But who could awaken such power, and why?' Gallion replied with genuine curiosity.

'Those are the questions indeed,' the vampire continued, 'the power in those books you moved could awaken the city, there is endless power contained in them, but they are safely under lock and key'

Gallion took in the truthfulness of Azerrad's words, 'I have no doubt there is no one within these walls with enough power or malice in their heart to wield the dark power the books hold.'

'It would take a powerful necromancer to control the power of the books, and it is possible there are more books like them out there. To fully utilise their power would take great personal power, but to inadvertently turn the city into a beacon to the unnatural significantly less,' Azerrad suggested, finally taking a seat at the far end of the table as he thought aloud.

The Grand Master sat opposite him, his elbows resting precariously on the table edge, his spindle like fingers supporting his chin as he took in what the vampire had to say.

'If there is someone behind the recent incidents then I doubt that this is anything but the start of things to come,' the vampire continued, his tone now warning in nature.

'What about you?' the Grand Master asked, taking Azerrad by surprise.

'What about me?' he replied.

'Could you read the books? You have spent years protecting them, surely you know what they contain,' the accusation had never been contemplated by the vampire and he bore a look of genuine amusement at the thought.

'Indeed, these books have been under my protection

for many years, but I have never read from their pages. I was warned about the terrible power they contained long ago, and I never cared to learn it for myself,' Azerrad admitted.

'You said there could be other books of their kind?' Gallion posed, moving quickly on and seemingly content that the vampire had told the truth of his knowledge of the contents of the books.

'Hypothetically, of course, but if there are I do not know of their existence.'

The Grand Master looked burdened by what he had learned from Azerrad, 'I see dark times ahead yet what our roles are I cannot see.'

'To protect the city and its people,' Azerrad suggested, feeling he knew less and less of the Order's role within it.

'Protect the city and its people,' the Grand Master echoed, 'by our blood are the streets kept safe.' The bitterness the Grand Master spoke with reminded the eavesdropping Carstair of the words that Gallion had spoken to him previously.

'I think it best that I continue to work with Edryd, try to figure out what could be happening here.' Azerrad suggested.

'Edryd? That boy is too green for this, I will see that one of my senior librarians is available,' Gallion returned, unnerving Azerrad with the use of the word 'my'.

'Edryd is stronger than you think,' the vampire insisted.

After a little time lost in thought, Gallion relented and rose from his chair for the first time since their meeting. As he rose methodically from the throne-like chair at the end of the table, he turned to peer out into the twilight of the courtyard below. Night had fallen and the lonely lanterns on either side of the walls lit by the guards before anyone entered the room cast a warm glow in the now poorly lit room.

'Funny how we fear the night,' Gallion spoke into the darkness without turning to face the vampire. 'So peaceful compared to the bustle of the daytime.'

'You know as do I the things that haunt the darkness. Do not forget it was you and your kind that made those things fear the light.'

'Indeed, I do,' Gallion said, sensing the conversations death. Gallion returned his gaze to the room and in the warm orange haze he looked frail, yet simultaneously powerful; the two aspects juxtaposing in his stance as though one were hiding the other, but which way round Azerrad could not quite tell.

Finally, Gallion made a move to exit. He swept passed the seated vampire, his robe billowing at his feet as he did so. Just before he drew back the curtain he paused and left a parting sentiment. 'Be ready when Carstair comes for you and let your companion know of the arrangement.' With that, the Grand Master swept back the curtain and disappeared into the hallway. It was empty save for the dancing shadows of the lantern's flickering light.

Gallion made his way back to his chambers where the fire in the hearth still blazed; new logs had been added while he was absent. He took off the ceremonial robe and hung it on a stand in the corner of his chamber. The close-fitting purple shirt and black cotton trousers made him seem almost like a silhouette due to his lithe form. The shirt buttoned to the neck and held at his wrists by golden cufflinks was immaculate and the silver filigree that wove mazy patterns across its surface was entrancing.

He made his way to the small table in the corner that held an ornate decanter of golden-brown fluid and poured a glass of the liquor, holding the crystal glass to his nose to take in the bouquet. Replacing the glass on the table briefly, he uncuffed the shirt and rolled the sleeves up his forearm before grasping the glass once more and taking up his favourite spot in the great window of his chamber that looked out across his beloved city. He contemplated there for a while before sitting at his desk, strewn with books, and seamlessly picked up where he had left off before he had been interrupted, his hand once again wandering to the small leather pocketbook.

Down on the street, concealed in the darkness of the twisting alleyways, a figure watched the Grand Master's window as it had gone from empty to occupied and empty again, the firelight causing the shadows to move around the form of Gallion like a macabre marionette show. In the shadows, Katerina kept vigil for now on the citadel, waiting for news from Azerrad.

Carstair was in the refectory making his way through a tankard of ale. He had made a hasty exit following the closure of the conversation between the Grand Master and the vampire. It had been so hasty, that had the Grand Master not paused to leave a parting statement he would likely have seen Carstair skulking off. As he finished the ale and ordered another, he wondered at all that was going on in the Order and where it was heading. All he knew for certain was that he was loyal to Gallion and if he wanted the creatures' tested for their loyalty, he would be the one to do it.

Azerrad had remained seated alone in the meeting room. Though he did not feel it himself, the room had become quite cold without the fire to heat it, the miserly lanterns not providing any warmth to note. He thought of the words Gallion used in their encounter; he chose his words carefully when he spoke to him and there were certainly hidden meanings and veiled threats in them, of that the vampire was sure.

Finally, he rose from his contemplation and exited the room, extinguishing the lanterns out of courtesy before he did so. He too found the hallway desolate and thought about returning to his quarters, before deciding he should seek out his lover. Pulling the collar of his coat up to shield his neck and ears and running an immaculate hand through his shining black hair to push all the errant strands back into place, he entered the great hall and quickly glided across it to make his exit from the citadel.

From his well-positioned seat in the refectory, Carstair caught a glimpse of the vampire as he melted away across the great hall towards the building's entrance.

As he entered the night, a cold wind blew across his face and Azerrad turned his back to its source before entering into the quiet streets that surrounded the citadel. It was not long before he picked up Katerina's scent, though she was far too clever to have left it unintentionally; she was luring him to her. As he stood at the entrance to one of the city's winding alleyways, staring into the abyss the walls created as moonlight struggled to pierce its veil, he got the feeling he was being watched.

Turning on the spot he could see the Citadel in the distance, its great spire rising majestically at its heart, and he could see the blazing light at its biggest window as shadows crossed in the flame's movement. Turning back to enter the alley, he stopped dead. A shrouded figure stood in front of him a blade now gently pressing into his breastbone. The figure was hooded and all their features were well concealed, but Azerrad did not flinch at the impending death that was being promised for the scent the mysterious figure bore told him all he needed to know.

'Still fond of games?' he said as he pushed the blade away from him.

'Always,' the figure responded removing her hood and revealing her identity.

Azerrad told his lover of the meeting that had transpired between him and Gallion; that the Order was willing to take on board their help but that they were guests, or prisoners to an extent. That their loyalty would need to be demonstrated and that the Order were aware that something was amiss in the city, but what they did not know.

Having heard all Azerrad had to say, Katerina had only one question for her love, 'Do you trust them?'

'There are those in the Order who are trustworthy, Edryd and some of the other librarians, Carstair is a lapdog whose loyalty is to Gallion and no one else.'

'And Gallion?' she replied

'I believe he is aiming to do the best for the Order, but I do not know exactly what that means.'

'Then we will allow them to hold their ridiculous loyalty test and see where it leads. But for tonight, you are mine,' Katerina spoke with determination, grasping Azerrad's hand and leading him off into the city to walk for a while.

Chapter 10

The sun rose on the two lovers who had walked all through the night, finally settling in a spot that overlooked the harbour. The ocean waves gently lapped into the boats that sat restlessly on the bobbing tide. Every now and then a larger wave would spray water up over the rocks at the harbour's edge, causing a salty aroma to drift on the clam breeze that came in from the sea. Watching as light began to spread across the twinkling waves, Katerina nestled further into Azerrad's arms as the two sat leaning back against a stack of crates.

The gentle warmth the sun brought to the morning dispelled the chill that had descended on the city at nightfall. The pair rose from their spot and made their way back to the citadel, passing the last stumbling remnants of the previous night as they did so. Upon entering the citadel, Katerina marvelled at the artwork and tapestries as Azerrad had on his first encounter. Crossing the great hall to more stares than usual, owing more to Katerina's beauty than anything else, they were expectantly met by the lumbering form of Carstair.

He was waiting arms folded in the relative darkness near the hallway, where the light from the windows had not yet reached. He was smartly dressed in clean trousers and a shirt that was pressed and tucked in; the ankh he wore at his neck visible where the shirt was not fully buttoned to his neck. Azerrad was surprised to see him up so early, but he thought perhaps his absence following the meeting with Gallion had gone more noticed than he had intended.

As the pair approached him, he pushed away from the wall he was propping up and met them in the dusky light that was filtering into the hall as the sun rose further.

'I take it this is your kinsman,' Carstair said curtly as they met, 'I am Carstair, one of the senior soldiers of the Order and personal assistant to our Grand Master. I am told to make you welcome.' His tone remained forced and he awkwardly held out his hand.

Katerina took it and shook it delicately. 'Thank you, Carstair,' she replied with a mocking half curtsey.

Carstair grunted at the faux courtesy and felt intimidated by the new arrival; she had an unnerving presence that made him feel robbed of his strength. He found it was all he could do not to stare at her and had to concentrate hard to force himself to speak. Azerrad noted his discomfort and smiled to himself as he let his eyes wander around the hall, internally laughing at the juvenile response to his lover.

'You can continue your work with Edryd as arranged with the Grand Master last night,' Carstair shot at Azerrad without so much as a glance, 'miss, you are to follow me, I will take you to meet the librarian you will be aiding,' his tone softened a little when he addressed Katerina and she had to stop herself rolling her eyes. She was used to men falling at her feet, but she thought the guardians here at the Order might have slightly better control.

Azerrad nodded and ventured off to find his librarian

companion. Carstair turned on his heel and headed in the same direction once the vampire was a little way ahead, not wanting to walk alongside him. Katerina followed him, observing all the citadel had to offer.

As Carstair and Katerina entered the library, Azerrad had already found Edryd and was selecting some books with him to work on. Sat at one of the desks was a librarian in the usual garb of their role. She held herself up with great posture, her neatly braided hair tied back out of her face. She was leafing through a book that she seemed to have little interest in other than to pass the time as she awaited the arrival of Carstair and Katerina.

As they approached, the librarian put down the book she had been browsing and stood to greet the pair. She politely nodded at Carstair as he approached and quizzically eyed Katerina, excited to have been tasked with something more important than cataloguing the dusty old books.

'Gaasis, this is Katerina, show her around, will you?' Carstair ordered in the softest tone he could muster. With that, he turned and left the library to find solace in some other task.

Gaasis held out her hand and Katerina shook it, the warm touch of Gaasis stark in contrast to her chilled flesh. The librarian felt a tingle run up her arm but did her best to disguise the discomfort of the encounter. 'It is nice to meet you Katerina,' Gaasis spoke in an enrapturing voice.

'And you,' she replied, pleased to find this librarian had more confidence in her presence. 'So, if we are to work together here, perhaps you would be so kind as to take me on a tour around the place, my partner has not been courteous enough to do so yet,' she joked playfully, gesturing with her head in Azerrad's direction. The men too engrossed in their books to take any heed of what was said.

Gaasis rose from the desk and took Katerina by the arm, wheeling her around towards the exit. The two of them left with little commotion but could not avoid the distinct disapproval of Sister Agnes who rolled her eyes as the two of them departed. Katerina overheard the faint mumble of 'great, now there's two of them' come from under the Sister's breath, but she let it pass.

Gaasis toured Katerina around the Citadel, showing her the great hall and all its wondrous paintings, telling her about the artists and depictions as they went. It was clear to Katerina that Gaasis was smart and knew a lot about the Order's long history, something that may come in useful in an ally. They wandered the halls where the paintings of previous Grand Masters hung and watched over the newer entrants. They chatted about the different roles in the Order and what they would be doing together.

It seemed Gaasis was also a younger member of the librarians like Edryd, and Katerina prodded at her with questions to see if their pairing was a babysitting role or more of an apprentice type one. 'Your guess it as good as mine.' Was Gaasis's only reply, and Katerina felt it sincere.

Finally, Katerina was shown into some of the vaults, but it appeared that Azerrad's appearance in previous days had taken some of the spectacle of a vampire entering them, as few were curious enough to introduce themselves. Once the tour of her new workplace was complete, the two of them made their way to the refectory to get refreshments. Gaasis ordered food and the two drank coffee while she ate and they spoke more of the work they would be doing, under the scrutiny of stares from some of the Order's soldiers.

As Katerina whiled away the day in the pleasant company of Gaasis, even if she could sense an air of hostility from the martial branch of the Order, Azerrad had been hard at work with Edryd searching some of the older catalogues of the library for more information on the unnatural occurrences that had been increasingly visiting Uvrenmouth in recent months.

Azerrad had confided in the young librarian some of what had been said during his meeting with Gallion the previous night. He had explained about the awakening the city was experiencing and his fears of what this could mean. He trusted the young librarian was loyal to the betterment of mankind and saw no reason he could not trust him with this information and in turn, the librarian felt honoured to have earned the vampire's trust.

The pair spent hours poring over books that might have some lore or talk of the kind of unnatural things that had been happening, but many were written in archaic languages that even Azerrad could not read or were too vague. As Edryd worked his way through the catalogue for a group of centuries old texts, Azerrad would pull the identified tome from the shelf and peer through it, searching relentlessly for an answer or a clue or even just a start.

Over the coming days the pair spent almost all of their time in the library researching and making their way methodically through the back catalogue of the citadel's library. While Katerina and Gaasis worked in the vaults deciphering some of the treasures, artefacts and weapons that had been collected over the centuries by the Order, the men persevered in their goal.

It was coming to the end of their fourth arduous day when they finally came across a breakthrough in the research. In an old, decaying book that Azerrad thought may have contained pages made using anthropodermic practices—though he kept the thought to himself as he didn't want to frighten his young companion—he found reference to activating the power held within a city.

'Edryd,' Azerrad called, halting the young companion's work, 'I think there is something here.'

'Really?' came the excited reply, relieved to have maybe turned a corner on this accursed task.

'Here, listen,' said Azerrad as he began to translate the ancient language, 'there is power held within many of the cities of this world that can repel or draw those most sensitive to them – sounds promising don't you think?'

'What language is it in?' Edryd enquired eagerly.

'I think it is an ancient form of Asquillan, my city has many books written in similar script, many of the symbols and letters used in it can be found in Jatradorian, I can make out roughly what it is saying.'

'Well thank goodness for that, my arms were going numb from carrying around these heavy old books,' Edryd continued, pleased.

'Don't count your chickens yet, this will not be easy to read and may not contain what we want it to,' Azerrad warned, staring intently at the book's pages.

Over the course of the evening, Azerrad worked to translate the ancient book and Edryd hastily scribbled down what he said, making notes where there was ambiguity in what the text may be saying. By the fall of night, they were beginning to see a bigger picture forming.

'Perhaps that is enough for one night, Edryd, there is much we must digest,' Azerrad's suggestion was not open for discussion, Edryd could tell that from the way it was delivered. The young librarian was a little disheartened to have gotten so close to completing their task but without Azerrad's translations it was futile anyway.

'Very well,' he conceded beginning to pack up the translations and catalogues for the evening.

As with most of their time spent in the library, the

pair were not disturbed by many other patrons as the light began to fade. Those transcribing or archiving materials had long since fled when their time was ending. As Azerrad watched the forlorn figure that Edryd cut as he cleared away their things, he threw a small lifeline to him.

'Perhaps Edryd, we should get a drink and talk with Katerina about what we have learnt today,' the vampire suggested.

'I don't really leave the citadel much to be honest,' Edryd admitted.

'Then what better chance to see the city? We will meet you in the great hall at nine,' with that, Azerrad left the library before Edryd could protest.

When Azerrad returned to his quarters, he found Katerina drinking a glass of crimson fluid she had poured from the decanter on his desk. As she smiled to see him enter, it looked as though her ruby lips were melting into her mouth with the way the liquid lingered on her teeth. He met her as she rose and the two kissed, the taste of blood still on her lips. It invigorated Azerrad and he pulled her closer, savouring the sweet taste. He poured himself a glass and recounted to Katerina what he and Edryd had learned that day. She harboured a worried look as the crinkles of her frown blemished her perfect skin. Hating to be the cause of her concern, he told her of the plans he had arranged for them.

'Would you object if I invited Gaasis?' she asked. The two had bonded well over the course of the week and she felt that the more people they could trust and bring into the fold the better.

'You trust her?' Azerrad hadn't meant the question to sound as accusing as it came out.

'As much as you trust the boy,' she fired back.

'Very well. We leave at nine,' Azerrad finished.

Katerina made her way to Gaasis' quarters amidst

plenty of disapproving stares and some friendly faces, mainly from the librarians she was familiar with now. When Gaasis answered the door, she was dressed in her casual trousers and a loose-fitting top. She was surprised to see Katerina at her door but was pleased to have received the invite. Like Edryd and many of the other librarians, she also did not leave the citadel very often.

The quartet met in the great hall and exchanged introductions and pleasantries for a while before they made their way out of the citadel and on towards the busy taverns closer to the market and the harbour. They settled on the one Azerrad and Katerina had passed on her first night in Uvrenmouth and mad their way in.

The bar was busy and noisy and although it seemed to quieten a little at the strangers' entry, it soon returned to a rapturous din once more. Edryd and Katerina found a table, while Gaasis and Azerrad made their way to the bar. Azerrad ordered a bottle of red wine for himself and Katerina, Gaasis asked for a tankard of beer and Azerrad decided that Edryd would have one too. When the bartender returned with the drinks, the vampire left a small pile of gold coins on the bar. Quickly the bartender took them and put them into the till but kept one in his hand and marvelled at such an unusual sight in a city famed for its silver. Pleased that the pile more than covered the cost of the drinks, he deposited the final coin into his pocket and went on to serve a group of citadel soldiers who had warily watched the vampire and the librarian order drinks.

Azerrad and Gaasis sat at the table and dished out the drinks. Katerina took a sip from her glass and the way the crimson wine held on her fangs reminded Azerrad of the way blood had hung there in their room earlier. Gaasis took a long draft of her beer, while Edryd looked almost intimidated by his, but drank from it before it became obvious.

'So,' Katerina began, 'tell us of this book.'

Edryd and Azerrad retold the tale of their weeks work and the ups and downs it had brought, they spoke of the ancient book they had found that seemed to hold dark secrets of what the city could draw to it with the right incantations.

'The troubling part of this whole story,' Azerrad said, 'is that the things that are possible with the right magic are catastrophic, and I think the first part has already happened.' His audience watched and listened to his words as he spoke to them quietly so no one may overhear. 'The book speaks of being able to turn the city into an unnatural beacon.'

'What do you mean, beacon?' Gaasis questioned, 'what is it pointing to?'

'It's not pointing to anything, it is drawing something in. Katerina and I have already felt its call,' he replied. 'The city is drawing the unnatural to it. That is one of the things the book says can be done, but there are far more worrying outcomes. Someone with the right knowledge can control the unnatural things that are drawn to it, even create more and raise the dead to fight the living.'

The librarians looked afraid at the thought of someone able to wield that power.

'It would take someone powerful and schooled in the necromantic arts, I can only assume that there is some necromancer in the city and that they awoke the city, which is why we feel the call,' Katerina added.

'Do you think they plan to wage war on the city?' Gaasis asked.

'I do not know yet, it could be that they mistakenly did it, or that they do not possess the knowledge to do anymore but keeping the books your people took from our shores safe is paramount at the moment, for the destructive power they contain could well be what your library book speaks off,' Azerrad warned.

The four continued to drink and discuss the possible issues that might arise from what they discovered, and how much about they should say and to whom. As they hashed out the potential ifs and buts, from the far corner of the room, almost completely cast in shadow and further concealed by the constant movement of the tavern's inhabitants, Carstair quietly slugged from a tankard and watched the conclave chatter.

Chapter 11

Dawn rose on the city of Uvrenmouth, and its people went about their usual routine. At the harbour, the dock workers began another day of lifting and moving crates of goods to and from the vessels moored in the harbour. The market traders unfurled their stalls to begin displaying their wares, from clothing to fruit and vegetables to antiques and books, you could find anything in the busy stalls of the market. Cafes began opening and the taverns were cleaning from the night before. Everywhere the city swarmed, blissfully unaware of the dark revelations that had been made the night before.

The citadel awoke just as the city did, and quiet halls with few soldiers began to teem with librarians and other workers as they made their way for breakfast or to relieve the night shift. Even though it was early, Azerrad and Edryd had already set up camp in the library and save for the sister who kept eye during the night, they were alone in their study.

Edryd had continued to scrutinise the catalogue, hoping to find more literature of a similar nature to the one they had come across the day prior while the vampire continued to translate the work they had. In the vault Katrina and Gaasis set to a task on a blade etched with unusual runes but spoke in hushed tones about who were loyal to the Order's true purpose. In the Grand Master's chamber, Gallion and Carstair conspired.

'You followed the vampires last night?' Gallion asked, his frail fingers stirred a silver spoon through the cup of coffee that sat on his desk. He had not yet dressed for the day and instead sat at his desk in a robe of crimson, trimmed in black and tied at the waist with a sash. On the Grand Master's lithe form, it looked baggy and unflattering, but it was comfortable, and the Grand Master cared not for how he appeared to Carstair.

'Yeah,' Carstair responded, visibly tired from the late night and early start, his hair askew and a stubble visible. 'They were there for a few hours with the two librarians, I couldn't hear anything that was said but it didn't look all that casual.'

'Do you think they have uncovered something?' Gallion continued his questioning, simultaneously trying to figure out the best course of action.

'They have found something,' came the reply, 'Edryd will tell me when he reports.' Carstair sounded extremely certain of that fact.

'News came in this morning from one of the watchers in the northern part of the city, seems we might have a chance to test the vampire's loyalty soon,' Gallion casually remarked as he leafed through the mornings newspaper that had been left on his desk for him, paying it little attention as he did so.

'Shouldn't we be getting ready?' Carstair asked a little anxiously.

'Do not fret, the watchers think they have found a pack of wolves holed up in an abandoned warehouse in the district there. They are keeping an eye, but it is midway through the lunar cycle and there have been few sightings of them venturing far from the warehouse. You will take a team when darkness falls, the vampires included, and confirm the intel,' Gallion instructed.

'Very well,' Carstair responded, but could not help thinking about the wolf that had turned when the moon was but an infantile crescent. With that he rose from the chair he had occupied and made for the door. His movement was lethargic, and the Grand Master wondered if Carstair did not approve of his plans, not that it mattered, he was a loyal servant and would see that the Grand Master's will was enacted.

Carstair made for the library to inform the vampires of the plan; how much he was willing to divulge he had not settled on but thought he might as well get it out of the way. He found Azerrad with Edryd at their usual haunt in the library, busily working on some book that Carstair couldn't even pretend to care about. He told the vampire not to expend to much of his energies on books today and that they would be following up on a potential sighting later that evening. When Edryd looked worryingly at Carstair, he assured him that his services would not be required outside of the citadel.

Once he had addressed Azerrad, he didn't hang around long before setting off to find Katerina. As he swiftly sauntered off in the vault's direction, Azerrad and Edryd watched him, as if expecting to find some ulterior motive given away in his demeanour or actions, but none came; he proceeded in his usual, un-agile way.

'So, he's taking you on missions now?' Edryd accused, the delivery of which seemed more like a scorned lover than worried companion. The bemused look Azerrad threw his way made him reconsider the way he had said it. 'I mean, do you think you can trust him?' Edryd added hastily.

'Apparently so. The Grand Master told me he thought it would be good if I went on a few missions with the soldiers, I guess he found one. It is most likely they want to test me and Katerina to see if we are on the Order's side or the monsters.' Azerrad noticed the worried look etched on Edryd's face and changed tack, 'I don't trust them,' he continued, emphasising the word them, 'but you cannot blame them for not trusting us either.'

'That's good to know,' Edryd said quietly thinking that this might be a bad idea.

Carstair found Katerina in the vaults with Gaasis and explained as he had with Azerrad the plans the order had for them, although he had to quell Gaasis' desire to join them, rather than reassure her she wouldn't be required as he had with Edryd.

"I am just as competent as any of the soldiers here in the field, I can be of service to you!" Gaasis argued, her attention focused on Katerina as she spoke.

"I have my orders and you have yours Gaasis," Carstair replied in a threatening tone.

"This is ridiculous," Gaasis responded her arms flailing wildly in the air.

"It seems our hosts wish to test our abilities," Katerina interjected, breaking the tension a little, "a test not needed of you, my friend."

Gaasis sighed as her arms returned to her side. Her fiery nature had not taken the news well, but she also knew the role her job demanded of her.

When the day ended, the librarians were told to go about their evening normally by the vampires and that they would all meet up again the following evening to privately discuss the events, away from prying ears. They all retired to their quarters and the vampire's awaited news from Carstair that they were leaving.

In their quarters, Azerrad and Katerina prepared for

their outing. They dressed in dark leather trousers with thick soled boots, Katerina's coming up almost to her knee, Azerrad's just above his ankle. Katerina donned a skin-tight jacket that buckled up at the front and despite its appearance, left her remarkable mobile. Azerrad wore a leather jerkin over a dark grey pull over, the jerkin crossed in parts with belts holding an array of weapons that would be concealed by the large over coat that Azerrad dressed in finally. Katerina wore a belt at her waist that held a pistol and a hunting knife, but Azerrad knew there were more concealed blades somewhere on her person.

Once they were ready the two shared a glass from the blood-filled decanter and spoke of what they might encounter. It was light-hearted as they joked about perceived inabilities of the mortals that would accompany them, but it was also underscored with a hint of hesitation at what events might unfold as the evening passed.

It was closing in on midnight when a gentle rap at their door roused them from their talk. As Katerina opened the door, she found a skittish messenger waiting on the other side. He all but recoiled to come face to face with the vampires, kitted as they were, 'Mister Carstair request's your presence in the rear courtyard. You are to follow me.' With that, the messenger turned and headed down the hallway not waiting for a response, his brown cloth shirt and loose trousers flowing as he did so.

The vampires shared a bemused look before following him out of their room and down the hallway to a staircase they had never used, nor even noted before at the far end of the corridor. It spiralled narrowly, almost vertically and was poorly lit with only few small windows and no lanterns. They emerged in the courtyard that Azerrad had watched on several occasions when in the meeting rooms of the citadel. The messenger was dismissed with a nod from a fully geared up Carstair and promptly vanished into another doorway in the courtyard.

Azerrad and Katerina looked at each other as both sensed the reason for the secretiveness. They approached the gang of soldiers that Carstair had mustered; they all wore the Order's robes but concealed them fairly well beneath jackets of differing lengths and shades of brown. Azerrad recognised the two boys who had brought him in on the night he fought the werewolf with Carstair, both of whom looked almost apologetic as they nodded to his arrival. There were two more equally young-looking soldiers with them who eyed the vampires suspiciously as they approached.

The motley group was rounded out by two older men who looked more akin to Carstair in both looks and attire. They wore the ankh of the Order around their necks but were dressed in plain clothes, not the uniformed regalia of the other soldiers. They barely took any notice of the two vampires as the approached.

The group had horses ready and there was a larger doorway to the far end of the courtyard that led out into the city. As the vampires approached, Carstair introduced them to the men and the men to them, the four soldiers more forth coming than the two attendants in saluting them. Carstair briefly explained that the attendants were essentially librarians employed in the field to help with non-military matters.

'We don't tend to announce our departure on this kind of mission,' Carstair said, sensing the new member's curiosity at all the cloak and dagger movements that were happening. 'There is much happening in the citadel at most times, and it is needless to worry too many people when we go out on excursions of this manner.' With that, he climbed onto his horse and made his way swiftly to the gate. The others followed suit as did Azerrad and Katerina who had been handed the reins of two spare horses. Once saddled the group made its way out of the courtyard gate and into one of the streets that ran alongside the Citadel. It was quiet, hedged in mainly by farmland and a lone house that glowed with the light of the fire that roared within.

The group rode silently and quickly to the site where the possible pack of werewolves was supposed to be holed up. They rode for the better part of half an hour; the city's northern peripheries were quite far from the citadel, and they had taken a route that would lead to the least amount of encounters with the city's inhabitants. As they approached the rusting iron mesh fence that surrounded the industrial sector of the area, Carstair held up his arm to inform the riders to stop.

The group obeyed the signal and waited as Carstair dismounted from his horse, handing the reins to an attendant at his side. He walked towards the fence and traced a hand across some of it as looked on at the warehouses beyond. From here, they looked quite small, but they were much bigger up close and a deathly maze if you were not careful.

'What's he waiting for?' Azerrad leaned over and whispered to Katerina.

'Them,' she replied as two forms emerged from the undergrowth that surrounded the other side of the road.

Two forms appeared as if out of nowhere and strode across the road. When they came toe to toe with Carstair they lowered their hoods revealing their faces. The first watcher had long curly blonde hair and her porcelain features seemed to glow in the moonlight; the second had much darker skin and straight black hair that flowed around her shoulders like a river. Both watchers cut alluring forms and the soldiers could barely avert their gazes from them. It began to be obvious why the watcher Azerrad had seen in the citadel had remained cloaked the whole time.

The watcher's conversed with Carstair, handing him a piece of paper that must have been a report of some kind. When he was happy, Carstair pleasantly dismissed them, a change of tact to his usual manner, and returned to the group to relay the information.

'Right lads, the watchers reckon there are four bodies in there, probably all wolves. They haven't left the warehouse for two days so they must be running low on supplies, so watch yourselves,' he instructed.

'Is this a capture or murder mission?' Katerina asked almost sarcastically.

'It's a do what we have to mission,' Carstair snapped back angrily. 'If they attack, we will put them down, if not maybe we will take them in for questioning.'

'Doesn't sound like you expect them to lay down for you,' Katerina continued to press Carstair.

'They're monsters, they never do,' he replied with a finality to his voice. He may not have been the smartest amongst the group, but he knew how to drive home a message and Katerina and Azerrad felt that they might end up the same way as whatever lay in wait for them if they would not follow orders.

As the night drew in around them, Carstair formulated a plan while the watchers took the horses to a safe distance. The soldiers all drew a pistol save for Carstair as they made their way toward the building; Nestor and Gideon were to go around to the rear entrance and make their way in that way, the other two soldiers were to secure the perimeter while the attendants kept an eye out for any breaches. Carstair, Azerrad and Katerina would then enter from the building's main entrance, cutting off all escape routes for the werewolves hiding inside.

Each group did as they had been instructed; Nestor and Gideon silently breached the warehouse from its rear exit, making their way through a group of offices that looked like they had been turned into dormitories. There were clothes and empty canisters of food scattered around and the place smelled awful. Pistols at the ready, they continued to make their way quietly through the office area when Nestor spotted something moving in the corner of the room, hidden by blankets on a makeshift bed of some sort.

Nestor signalled for Gideon to cover him while he approached it to find out what it was. Each footstep Nestor took was slow and purposeful to not make a sound and disturb what lay beneath the blankets. Once he was within arm's reach of the bed, he drew his silver dagger from within his cloak and used it to slowly peel back the blanket.

The colour drained from his face when he realised what it was. A young woman laid on a stained, broken mattress, barely able to breathe. She was a sickly pale save for several red wound marks around her neck, arms, and breasts. She lay in dishevelled, tattered clothing and the shallow intake of breath she could muster made her seem almost dead.

Nestor reeled when he realised what was happening and found Gideon with an equally horrified gaze. Following his stare, he found a second woman in an equally poor state lying on the floor, clinging to life by the merest of touches. She too had deep, bruised bite marks scattered across her emaciated flesh.

'What the fuck?' Gideon whispered to Nestor. 'That's no werewolf victim.'

'No,' Nestor replied ruefully, 'but they are,' he continued, his outstretched arm and the dagger it held pointing at the ruined forms of several humans in the corner of the room behind Gideon.

Neither could really tell if they were men or women or even children as the mess of bone and viscera no longer held much form at all; just a pile of bone, limbs, and torn pieces of flesh remained and the vibrations of flies that circled it. The pair looked at each other and made their way more quickly now into the main space of the warehouse.

They moved between a set of drapes that hung at the doorway into the warehouse and surveyed the expanse before them. To the sides of the room were large crates and the packing machinery for them. They cast billowing shadows to all four corners of the room and the high vaulted ceiling was barely visible beyond the rafters.

Carstair and the vampires entered from the main doorway into the building which was a huge metal shutter that had been propped open by a couple of wooden crates and scrap metal. They all had to duck to enter, but where the vampires found this easy, Carstair could not follow suit and almost had to roll to get his frame through the gap. Once they entered, they could just make out the form of the two soldiers on the other side of the room as the emerged from the rear exit.

The air was stale in the warehouse, but it was still, too still for any of their likings and the three proceeded with caution, wary of an ambush. The crates to the edges of the space made the room darker and more enclosed which put the three on edge. Carstair reached to his sides and withdrew his beautiful pair of pistols. Azerrad drew a small silver blade and Katerina withdrew the sabre that had hung at her waist from its scabbard, the silver metal gleaming even without a light source.

When Nestor and Gideon saw the three, they bolted across the warehouse to tell the others of their gruesome discovery, but they barely made it a quarter of the way across the distance before they were sent flying from their feet by a huge werewolf that had burst from the crates to their left. The beast hit them full on, but Gideon had taken the brunt of the attack. He flew 15 feet across the dusty floor, dropping his pistol as he did so. Nestor had a millisecond more to brace for the impact and had shielded himself to an extent using Gideon. He had still been thrown to the ground and was winded, but he held onto the pistol and dagger he had been carrying.

Carstair took the centre flanked by the Vampires, Azerrad to the right and Katerina to the left. He kept his guns trained on the floored soldiers on the other side of the room to offer them a degree of protection if the beast re-emerged, Katerina traced her sabres tip along the floor creating a piercing sound to try to draw out whatever lurked in wait for them, and Azerrad drew a second blade as he stalked forward, covering Katerina as she moved across the room.

The room settled momentarily before it erupted in violence. The beast emerged at the boy's right side, feral and furious; Carstair took aim and fired but at the distance he narrowly missed the beast's head, grazing its shoulder instead. The beast cried out in rage and pain, halting its advance in time for Nestor to return to his feet to protect Gideon. Having bought the soldiers a moment, Carstair turned to give the vampires orders, only to see them both being brought down by humanoid creatures that were dressed like humans but had mutated faces with long, yellowing fangs.

Both Katerina and Azerrad knew what was assailing them; they were feral vampires. Their hands more like talons now, their features distorted and eyes blood red from feeding on human victims. The creatures lashed out at the pair; they had caught them off guard, crawling down from the shadowy ceiling. As the brawl escalated, the two found their composure and fought the creatures so they could regain their footing. The feral attack would have slain a mortal, but the talon scratches had barely broken their skin thanks to the abnormal reflexes the pair owned. Azerrad ducked a wild swing and plunged one of his blades into the vampire's midriff, causing it to squeal with pain as the silver bit and the skin began to sizzle. It swung its arm violently backwards the way it had come but Azerrad seamlessly swayed backwards out of its arc before driving the other silver dagger into the creature's heart. The action caused the monster to cease moving and drop to the floor in a broken heap, the wound smoking slightly as the heart combusted.

Azerrad had dispatched the creature with little effort; though these feral vampires looked grotesque, they were too thirsty to mount any sort of planned attack. On the other side of the room, however, Katerina's duel had been more theatrical. Having regained her footing, she sent the creature from her with a kick to its chest, delivered by her long, powerful leg. As it surged forward to attack again, she gracefully spun her body, the creature's talons missing her torso but her trailing blade cutting into its thigh. The monster cried out but driven by feral ferocity, attacked once more, again missing in its attack and receiving another cut for its trouble, this time to its shoulder. Over and over the creature attacked, each time losing a little speed and power and over and over Katerina's sabre bit into its flesh. Finally, with time pressing, she dodged another attack but this time she kept her blade close spinning it in her hand as the feral vampire passed her, before thrusting it though it's back and out its chest, piercing the heart as it did so. As it slid from the blade to the ground, she looked at Azerrad, the smile on her face showing the pleasure she took in the kill.

While the vampires had been fighting, Carstair had closed the gap on the two young soldiers as Nestor had tried to keep the beast at bay. He stood over Gideon to shield his injured friend, but the beast rained blows down on the soldier who slowly began to crumble to his knees, unable to match the power the wolf had. The wolf saw its opening and raised a clawed hand to deliver the killing blow, Nestor shut his eyes anticipating death, but it never came, the sound of a gunshot bringing him to. He opened his eyes to see a silver bullet enter the beast's skull and explode out again, Nestor looked up to see Carstair aiming his pistol over his bent elbow.

'Get up!' Carstair yelled to Nestor as he reeled to see what was happening.

From the shadows where the first beast had attacked stood three more hulking in the gloom and on the crates ahead, more shadows moved. The werewolves attacked first, Carstair firing another bullet through the chest of one, bringing it to its knees. Katerina advanced on another close to the crates, as it raised its arm to strike at her, a blade flew through the air piercing its palm and pinning it to the crate. The beast tried to free itself, but Katerina was too quick and severed the beast's arm from its body in swirling display of swordsmanship. As the creature turned to face her once more, she danced back the other way severing its leg at the knee, causing the monster to fall to the ground in a gush of blood, where she dealt the killing blow.

The final wolf had made its way to finish the two boys who both were still crumpled, Nestor giving his last to protect Gideon from any of the blows. Busy with the other wolves, Carstair and the vampires were unable to slow its progress. It bounded into Nestor and hit him a back hand that sent him sprawling in the air towards the crates at the side of the room. The beast then struck at Gideon, its claws piercing into Gideon's ribs causing his whole body to explode in pain as he cried out. Nestor screamed out, watching his friend being killed and feeling useless to stop it. The wolf raised Gideon from the ground bringing his face towards its gaping maw ready to feast on his flesh when it let the soldier fall to the ground. Through pain and blood and drifting in and out of consciousness, Gideon saw the creature holding its ruined stomach. Azerrad forced his foot into the back of the monster's knee causing it to fall to the ground before plunging his dagger into the creatures back.

As Azerrad's duel played out, more crawling shadows emerged from above the crates. Carstair counted at least four feral vampires and looked on in horror. They raced towards Azerrad and the soldiers as Carstair drew a beat on them as they paced. He fired several rounds that all hit home in several places on the creatures, but barely slowed their advance, the silver causing barely noticeable discomfort.

'You know so little of the tools you are given,' Katerina scolded Carstair as he looked at her in utter confusion. She paced towards him, withdrawing one of her leather gloves and running the edge of her blade across her palm as she strode, blood spilling from the wound. When she reached Carstair she placed her wounded hand over one of his pistols and let the blood drip into the mechanics.

Carstair recoiled the pistol in horror, 'What the fuck are you doing?' he cried.

'They're blood reaper pistols, imbecile,' she remarked as she tried to close ground with Azerrad and the vampires.

Carstair looked on still visibly horrified at what just occurred, but as the blood worked its way into the workings of his gun, he saw it light up momentarily in a dull blue glow. Still confused but realising his soldiers were in danger he took aim at the advancing vampires. The first of his shots hit one of the vampires clean in the chest, the next two struck another in the stomach and leg. To his surprise, unlike before, the vampires stopped their assault dead and dropped convulsing to the floor, a foamy blood appearing at their mouths as they shook before falling silent.

Carstair looked at his pistol in disbelief. He raised it once more, but the final two vampires were fighting in close quarters. Nestor had managed to crawl back to Gideon and begun to drag him to towards the exit of the warehouse while the feral vampires were occupied. With the soldiers relatively safe at that point, he slowly made his way across watching his vampires fight the feral ones. Azerrad caught the furthest most vampire by the throat as it had lunged at him but before he could deliver his blade the creature sank its talons into his shoulders causing him to drop the knife and fall to one knee as he struggled against the monster's power and the pain in his upper body. Nestor looked up to see Carstair casually making his way over and scrabbled at the floor to find his blade. His head spun but he felt the cold metal and grasped it. With all his might, he threw himself at the feral vampire that was clinging to Azerrad's shoulder with its elongating fangs and plunged what turned out only to be a piece of strewn metal into its chest. It was enough to cause it to release its grip on Azerrad who drew another blade from his coat to dispatch the monster.

The final vampire was heading Azerrad's way before it was distracted by Katerina's whistle. Caught between going after Azerrad, Katerina who had distracted it, or Carstair who was now closer, it froze momentarily which was all that was needed. As Katerina lunged her sword towards its heart as she leapt forward, Carstair fired the last bullet loaded in his pistol. The sword pierced the monster as its body shook from the bullet's impact. Katerina smiled as she felt the kill was hers, but as the body on the blade started to convulse and froth red blood at its mouth, Carstair smirked before making his way to Gideon and Nestor.

Chapter 12

Nestor didn't remember much of what happened after he had come to Azerrad's aid. His head was ringing from the blows he had taken, and his mind raced painfully as he tried to get Gideon out of the hell hole they had walked into. He was aware he had most likely saved Azerrad's life by distracting the feral vampire long enough, but after that all he had thought of was saving his friend. With the melee still ongoing, he had gripped Gideon's tunic and dragged him with all the might he could muster out of harm's way, unsure if he was even still alive.

When the room finally fell quiet, he had managed to prop the poor soldier against a crate that lay at the building's extremity. Having finished his pissing contest with Katerina, Carstair ran to the young soldiers to inspect the damage. Katerina helped her lover to his feet and the pair inspected their wounds and gathered their arsenal; the bite on his shoulder was deep but already beginning to heal.

Azerrad turned to the two soldiers huddled over their comrade and as he replaced the final blade within his coat, made to join the trio. Katerina caught him by the arm and stopped him. With the two conscious soldiers with their back to them she whispered to Azerrad. 'What the fuck was that? I thought it was a small pack of werewolves and it's the middle of the lunar cycle,' she said placing her hand now on his shoulder.

'You think they meant to have us killed here?' he replied grimly.

'Well they've lost one of their own in doing so,' Katerina spoke almost mockingly.

'I don't think he's dead yet, but I don't think it would cause them to lose sleep if he was,' Azerrad continued, his sombre tone unwavering.

The pair gave each other worried glances and headed to join the three humans. Gideon did not look good; the impact from the werewolf had seemingly shattered several of his ribs and he was sputtering blood with every wheezing breath. Scratches and grazes covered his arms and face from skidding across the rough floor. He lay limply in the arms of Nestor, who was trying to stop the bleeding of the deep claw marks that had pierced his chest.

'Poor bastard's done,' Carstair remarked, seemingly done with the conversation, but as Gideon's heaving chest continued to blow, Nestor refused to give up.

'Come on Gid,' he said, his eyes raw with tears as he pulled his arm around his shoulder and trying to raise him from the ground. The poor boy yelped in pain as he was hauled up. Azerrad could see the struggle in Nestor's face and swiftly moved to the other side of Gideon to take some of the weight and support the boy. He shot Carstair a cold look as he and Nestor tried to move the soldier outside. Before they left, Nestor told the others of the gruesome discovery they had found in the back.

Dragging poor Gideon away, Azerrad and Nestor made for a small doorway in the corner of the room, hoping it would open and be their quickest exit. Katerina and Carstair made for the back to see for themselves what Nestor had described. Carstair stared at his beloved pistol, now covered in Katerina's blood, and holstered it gingerly. He wasn't keen to be putting the gun smeared in blood into the relatively clean leather, but it had spent its payload and he saw no reason to reload it. Katerina went ahead, using her sabre to slide the drapes to one side she leaned to the side to get a better look through the doorway before she stuck her neck out and went in. Seeing no obvious disturbance, she disappeared seamlessly through the drapes that rustled gently as they fell back into place. Carstair looked at his other pistol momentarily before following her through.

The sight that met them was as disturbing as the young soldier had described. There were the ruined remains of bodies to one side and the barely conscious women on the other.

'They gonna turn?' Carstair asked Katerina looking upon their fouled forms as they lay clinging to life.

'No, I don't think so,' Katerina replied, 'they were being fed on, no point in creating more hungry mouths.'

A short grunt was the only reply she got as Carstair continued to ponder their fate.

'They might survive this,' Katerina offered, 'physically anyway, what their state of mind would be I couldn't say,' she backtracked. 'They were lucky in a way.'

'Lucky?' Carstair scoffed, 'they have been used as a food source for monsters and cling to life by the barest of slivers, what luck is there to be found in that?' His words fell like crashing waves.

'Those monsters we just fought were turning, it would not have been long before they ended up like the poor souls behind us,' Katerina pushed back.

'This is no better a fate,' Carstair replied coldly, 'I will get a team in to clean this wretched hole up. Come on,' as he spoke, he gestured with his arm that they should leave through the back door.

Katerina paused for a second, looking on with pity at the two almost dead women on the floor. She was almost certain Carstair's clean-up crew would not be taking them to the infirmary to heal, but there was little she could do for these poor souls. She turned to head out of the exit, leaving the girls to the final fate of the watchers.

When they emerged, they could see that Nestor and Azerrad had managed to get Gideon to the place where they had left the attendants to keep watch. They tried to comfort the fallen soldier as best they could. As Carstair approached, the watchers re-emerged from their vigil and spoke with Carstair. He told them what had transpired and that when the soldiers were gone, they were to clean up the warehouse and destroy what remained of the monsters. The watchers nodded in abeyance and made for the warehouse to begin their task. Carstair instructed the soldiers who had waited patiently outside for their return to help with the clean-up. Night was halfway through, and they would not have a lot of time to work under the cover of darkness.

'Can he ride?' Carstair asked Nestor.

'I can ride with him,' the young soldier replied respectfully, still wary of Carstair trying to leave Gideon behind.

'Get the horses,' Carstair barked at the attendants. They disappeared into the wooded area the watchers had appeared from and were gone for a few minutes before returning with the horses. The vampires helped load Gideon onto Nestor's horse with him before climbing into their saddles. Carstair hoisted himself into his own and gestured for the group to leave. As the party cantered away, Carstair paused and looked down at the attendants he was leaving to help with clean up.

'You know what needs to be done,' he said firmly.

'Sir,' the attendants replied acknowledging their superior.

With that, Carstair spun his horse and galloped off after the group, his coat tails billowing in the wind as he rode, dust spitting up from the horses' hooves into the calm night air. The two attendants looked at each other and made their way to the warehouse, following in the footsteps of the watchers. The four of them dragged the carcasses of the monsters and the remains of their victims out into the night, piling them high in a pyre of flesh. Once they had removed them all that remained were the two girls who lay so perilously on the brink of death. The attendants entered the building once more, but the watchers remained outside, knowing what was about to happen.

Inside, one attendant drew his gun from its holster, but was stopped by the other who gently held the first's arm to stop him bringing the weapon to bear on the girl.

'The noise,' was all he whispered to his friend.

He nodded in understanding and the two drew small blades from their waist and cut the girls throats in a simultaneous act. Their bodies writhed momentarily but little blood fell from their wounds; there was little left that they could give. As the thread of life they hung to was severed, the attendants looked on seemingly trying to decide if what they had just done was cold or merciful, but it was not their place to question the methods of the order, only carry them out. When the girls fell motionless, they heaved them onto their shoulders and carried them out to the funeral pyre they had built and tossed them on top.

The watchers looked on, saddened by the reckless waste of life that had just occurred. One of the attendants wrapped a rag around a piece of wood that lay strewn in the warehouse's grounds and dunked it in a small oil spill nearby before lighting it with a flint he withdrew from his jacket. As the torch caught light he watched for a while, making sure that the flame was well established then threw it on top of the mound of bodies. The flames soon ignited the clothes of those in the pile which would eventually become a smouldering heap of ashes and misfortune.

As the pyre slowly began to burn away, the mournful figures of the watchers and the dutiful ones of the attendants returned to the inside of the warehouse to eliminate any sign of the fight that took place not long ago.

Meanwhile, the rest of the group continued their ride back to the citadel. The journey was longer than before as Nestor had to carry the burden of his fallen friend which slowed them down considerably. They still took the quieter route but could not make the haste they had in arriving at the northern territory. The night held firm as they rode, but they were unable to return completely unseen, here and there a door would prise open or a shutter lift so that the occupants might catch a glimpse of the riders. This did not go unnoticed by the group, especially Carstair who feared that gossip may begin about their purpose.

When they arrived at the gates to the citadel, the rain began to pour. It started slowly but by the time they had managed to get inside the courtyard where their evenings adventure had begun it was raining substantially. The five were soaked; their hair clung unceremoniously to their heads, the soldier's cloth uniforms hung desperately to their forms, and the horses gently whined to be out of the downpour. Azerrad and Katerina helped Nestor get Gideon from his horse while Carstair called the stable boys to get their mounts.

Once down, Carstair instructed them to get Gideon to the medical building so that he could be seen to by one of the doctors, but he warned them to try not to make too much fuss getting him there. A task that seemed easier said than done; they were all but dragging him as he couldn't keep consciousness to walk properly.

As the three of them hauled Gideon to the medical ward, Carstair looked on, droplets of rain falling from his hair and running down his face. His grim demeanour and unwavering pose made him look like a statue in the courtyard. He wondered what his conversation with the Grand Master would be like; they had not expected the outing to be anything other than run of the mill but the information was flawed. He couldn't help but wonder if that was the watchers' fault or if it was just not possible to have known there were more things in there.

The rain continued to beat down and the distant figures of the soldiers and vampires were hazy and almost out of sight, but Carstair had not moved, still deep in thought as even his thick coat struggled to keep the weather out. The Grand Master would no doubt ask about the vampires as well and he thought of what he might be able to tell him. They had followed orders as much as he was able to give them, but it had been such a confusing encounter that he hadn't really given any. They had killed the monsters, but they had been attacked first. They had shown him the true purpose of his weapons and effectively increased their chances of dying at his hands and helped to bring home his wounded soldier when he would have readily left him, injured as he was. He guessed they had passed any test that might have been laid out and yet he could not bring himself to trust something he had been trained to hate, trained to hunt, trained to eradicate.

Carstair's silent vigil was finally broken by the noise of horses approaching the gates to his back. As the stable hands opened them, the two attendants trotted in, equally as soaked as Carstair was. He watched them approach and dismount before making his way to meet them.

'Is it done?' he asked.

'Aye,' one of the attendants replied, 'the lasses and the monsters went up before the rain fell, we left the watchers to finish up when the rain began so we wouldn't leave too many tracks and traces of our presence.'

'Good work, lads,' Carstair responded nodding his head as he spoke, 'go get changed and get something to eat, I have to see the Master.'

The attendants gratefully nodded and made their way into the building through the doorway the vampires had emerged from earlier that night, followed by Carstair who drew the heavy oak door closed behind him, sealing out the stormy weather.

In the infirmary, Nestor helped a nurse get Gideon out of his robes and onto a bed. Gideon's body looked worse when they undressed him, his skin a patchwork of deep lacerations and bruises. When the doctor had seen to him and administered some pain relievers, Nestor took up a seat by his bed, extinguished the oil lamp next to it, and sat in the darkness watching over his friend, praying he would pull through.

Up in their room, the vampires undressed and dried themselves off before donning loose fitting robes. Azerrad took up a seat at the desk and stared out into the gloomy morning while Katerina sat on the bed watching him, the lantern light playing across her face. Neither said anything but simply sat in the warm glow of the lanterns flame and dwelt on the events of the night.

In his quarters, Carstair dried himself and washed his face, hoping to wash away the night with it. He removed his holster carefully and placed the pistols on the dresser top. He looked down at them, one glinting and pure the other smeared with her blood. He could not decide if it was a good thing he now had a new weapon against his enemies or if something he had held sacred had been somehow tainted by her intrusion.

A loud rap at the door startled Carstair from his trance and he answered the door with a visible look at annoyance etched across his face. 'What is it?' he asked the intruder impatiently.

'Sir, pardon the intrusion, but the Grand Master wishes to speak with you,' the messenger replied meekly.

'Very well,' Carstair responded shutting the door on their conversation and returning to his dresser to put on fresh clothes. He threw on a casual jumper and trousers, tried to tidy his messy hair a little, and opened the door to leave. The messenger had taken leave and was already gone, so Carstair made the short journey to the Grand Master's chambers quietly and alone.

Chapter 13

As the sun rose the next morning the town buzzed with news of secretive riders in the night. Some posited that they were outlaws fleeing the authorities, which many pointed out must have been false as they were seen heading into the city not away from it; others suggested that the order was carrying out some secret work involving the mining facilities to the north of the city, but very few suggested that they were out monster hunting.

The vampires rose with the sun and dressed as normal, but both felt that the circumstances surrounding the previous night were anything but normal. They drank from the decanter and made their way to find Edryd and Gassis to tell them what had transpired that night. The halls of the citadel seemed eerily quieter than they were used to, which came as a surprise to the vampires as their excursion had primarily been kept quiet as far as they knew.

They both headed to the library thinking it would be better to talk to the others as a group. Edryd was sat at his usual desk, studious as ever, books that he and Azerrad had been poring over strewn in front of him. To Azerrad and Katerina's surprise, the alluring form of

Gassis was sat next to him, flicking though the pages of a dusty old book, but seemingly uninterested in its contents. It appeared that they had all deemed it wise to meet together.

Azerrad sat at the desk next to Edryd and exchanged pleasantries as did Katerina and Gassis, but none of them felt particularly comfortable talking about the night's happenings under the scrutiny of the library's patrons. Instead, they agreed to meet that night and discuss what was going on. Katerina and Gassis left to take a look at what treasures the vault may offer whilst Azerrad and Edryd tried to find a way to stop any necromantic powers that were being cast on the city, though it was becoming clear to Azerrad that the library didn't possess books anywhere near as powerful as the ones he was charged with protecting.

Upstairs in the Grand Master's chamber, a weary Carstair sipped at the brown liquor contained in the glass he rolled in his hand, the decanter next to him almost empty. He had retold the tale of the evening's events to Gallion, who had listened intently despite the early hour he had been roused at. The Grand Master seemed older today, Carstair thought, more decrepit in looks and yet he was full of life, almost sprightly as he had moved about the chamber. Carstair wondered if spending his days reading those magic books was beginning to take its toll on the old man.

'The only thing that bothers me,' Carstair began, and the Grand Master looked at him patiently, interested in the revelation that was about to be revealed, 'was how the watchers were so unaware of what was in the building.'

'As you have noted before Carstair, there are strange things at work in the city, they cannot be held accountable for an anomaly like this,' Gallion replied.

'I am not blaming them, but this was a huge mistake,'

'Those vampires could have been holed up in there long before the watchers spotted the wolves moving in,' Gallion posed.

'That's another thing, vampires and werewolves holed up together? I have never heard of it,' Carstair protested, unable to process the anomaly of the evening.

'When our people first began cleansing the city of their wretched kind, many monsters sought shelter together, necessity makes for strange bedfellows sometimes,' the Grand Master continued.

Carstair rubbed his tired eyes and ran his hands through his ragged hair before holding it in his hands as he tried in vain to process all that had transpired.

'You completed your task with minimal fuss and loss even in adversity,' Gallion spoke in soft tones to try to ease the burden of Carstair's mind. 'That is all the Order expects of you – loyalty. In the grand scheme, things went well. You protected the city and it turns out there may be a use for the vampires beyond deciphering archaic books and long forgotten trinkets.'

Carstair raised his head from his hands to look at Gallion. 'Loyalty,' he whispered back gently nodding his head. 'Protect the city,' he continued quietly, 'we are but blunt instruments the Order wields to defend itself, to defend its people.' He spoke rhetorically as if trying to convince himself, but he thought of Gideon, who he was all too ready to leave to die with the rest of them.

'You are our sword and shield against the darkness, but that time may finally be coming to an end, no more will the streets need to be protected by the blood of our people, if we can use loyal monsters to kill the rogues, to keep the peace,' Gallion spoke passionately.

'You mean the two vampires? They're decent fighters, I'll give them that. But they're not going to be our personal guards.' Carstair retorted, a little annoyed at the insinuation that he needed any type of loyalty from anything but humans.

'You're not seeing the full picture, Carstair. These vampires have shown they can be controlled, used for the good of our people. With the city drawing more to our gates, what's to say we can't use more of their kind? Turn them into weapons to defend what we hold dear?' Gallion posed back, sensing the hesitation in Carstair's voice.

Carstair was thrown by what Gallion was saying, 'Controlling two is different than trying to control enough to guard the city, what if they turn on us? What if they decide they don't like killing their kind? What if—'

'Leave the what if's to me, Carstair,' the Grand Master cut him off as he began to ramble. 'You are my most loyal servant, there will always be a place for those loyal to me here,' the words came out seemingly friendly, but there was a hint of threat in the way they were delivered that worried Carstair a little. 'Go get some sleep my friend, you are exhausted and not thinking straight.'

Carstair thought about protesting, but he was exhausted, that he could not deny; his muscles ached, and his eyes burned, they had been open for so long. He rose from his chair, draining the glass he held and feeling the fiery liquid burn as it ran down his throat. He had no more to say so turned and left the room, shutting the door silently behind him.

In the infirmary, Nestor had struggled through the night in fits of broken sleep, worrying about Gideon. He had watched over him as the sun rose, his breathing steadier than it had been the night before, but he still looked pretty banged up, covered as he was in bandages and a sling. The nurse came in every hour or so to check on the pair of them and tried to tempt Nestor to return to his dorm to rest but he refused every time.

Early in the morning, the doctor had come in to check on him too. The doctor had seemed pleased with Gideon's progress overnight and that made Nestor's mood rise. He had told Nestor that much of the damage seemed superficial and broken bones and bruised egos would heal in time, but there didn't seem to be any internal issues that were beyond their expertise. He should make a full recovery eventually, Nestor was told, before being told himself to get some rest. But Nestor refused to move, wanting to be around when Gideon awoke.

Gideon did wake finally in the mid-morning, groaning as he did so. He looked at Nestor through glassy eyes, but as the pupils began to adjust and he came back to the world he began to thrash at the bedding and panic, seemingly fighting off a phantom attacker. Nestor struggled against his friend as he tried to calm him down, but his eyes had widened wildly and were panic stricken, he mumbled words as he tried violently to get away, 'Monster... Wolf... Corpses.' The distress had alerted some of the nearby nurses who rushed into the room to help subdue him, one wrestling alongside Nestor, the other filling a syringe.

As the pair managed to get Gideon under control, the second nurse administered the syringe to Gideon and after mumbling more about monsters and violence, he finally fell under the medicine's spell and settled back into induced sleep. When the nurses were happy, they left to inform the doctor who returned to check on the patient. After checking Gideon with the stethoscope, he told Nestor that he needed rest and that he had to leave. Although Nestor tried to protest, he was ushered away by the nurses and told to come back that evening.

Nestor did not want to sleep, still haunted by his ordeal. Instead, he got a cup of coffee in the refectory. As he entered, he saw Carstair draining a mug of coffee; he looked worse than Nestor felt. Nestor thought about sitting with Carstair when he had got his drink, but Carstair had already departed. Alone with his thoughts swimming in images of Gideon's terrified eyes, he stared out of the window and watched as the rest of the Order went about their daily rituals.

Carstair climbed the stairs towards his quarters sluggishly and when he reached the landing, he looked back over the rail to see the great hall as it began to teem with life once more. He sighed and turned to find a man in a long white coat approaching. He recognised him as one of the Order's doctors and tried to palm off his advance, insisting he was fine and just tired from the evening prior.

'You mistake my meaning, master Carstair,' the doctor said with a smile. 'I am not checking on your wellbeing I have come to inform you of the young soldier in our care.'

'Oh, Gideon,' Carstair brushed it off giving little interest now he knew what it was regarding. 'He doing okay?' he feigned.

'Yes, he should recover physically, but he awoke not long ago screaming about monsters and demons.'

Carstair grunted, annoyed at the disturbance, 'Leave

it with me. Thank you, doctor,' he said quickly before stomping off to his room before the doctor could say more.

The afternoon sun waned in the sky, its warmth quickly dissipating as it sank closer to the horizon. It had been another fruitless day for Azerrad and Edryd in the library, they had failed to find any meaningful way of stopping the city's unnatural beacon and Azerrad could feel it growing stronger by the day.

The girls had fared no better in the vaults and each were ready to down tools for the day. They had all arranged to meet in the tavern that they had some nights ago, but decided that it would be better if they made their way there separately this time, so they all retired to their dormitories to change and wait for darkness before venturing out.

The sun still beamed on the horizon as Nestor returned to the infirmary. He hadn't gotten any rest but hoped the nurses would think he had after being gone for a few hours. He checked in with the sister at the front and made his way towards the back where Gideon was sleeping in a small room off the main corridor. He gently pushed the door open so as not to disturb his friend if he was still asleep and as he entered, he found that his friend was still soundly asleep in his bed. Nestor shut the door and moved round to draw the drapes shut on the small window that was now letting in only a trickle of light. He lit the lantern on the wall and looked at his friend.

As he stood watching, a moment of horror passed over him. There was no movement at all coming from Gideon's form beneath the bed sheets. There was no movement of the sheet on his chest as it should have risen and fallen, no slight flaring of his nostrils as breathe was forced through them. In a panic, he grabbed for Gideon's uninjured arm to try to find a pulse but he could not, he tried in vain at his throat as well but there was no blood running through his veins. He leaned over his friend to feel his breath but felt nothing.

His head spun as the reality of the situation dawned on him and only then did he realise how quiet the room had been when he entered, how cold his friends skin had been to the touch. He burst out of the room calling for help and a nurse and the doctor from the morning came running to his aid.

'What's the matter, Nestor?' the nurse cried as she was running towards him.

'It's Gideon, there's something wrong... I think he's...' Nestor struggled to get the words out as tears welled in his eyes and his throat felt like it was closing, 'I think he's dead.'

The doctor got there first and calmly entered the room. He looked at Gideon and tried to find a pulse as Nestor had moments earlier. He used the stethoscope on Gideon's chest but found no sign of life and looked remorsefully at Nestor as he rose.

'I'm afraid your friend is gone,' he said soothingly but without compassion.

'Gone? You said he would recover this morning?' Nestor blurted out angrily as the nurse put her arm on his shoulder and tried to comfort him.

'His internal wounds must have been worse than we first thought, it seems that his breathing failed him,' the doctor tried to explain.

'Has anyone else been to see him?' Nestor asked as he shrugged off the nurse's touch, his anger beginning to grow at the thought of his friend being left to die.

'Carstair sent another soldier down to check on him a while ago, he was only in here for a few minutes then he left,' the nurse interjected, still trying her best to console Nestor.

The words fell on Nestor like a ton of bricks and his face began to redden as he digested them. He threw off the nurse's arm once more and stormed out of the room. As he half ran down the corridor, tears streamed from his eyes as he finally stopped and allowed his exhausted form to slide down the corridor wall. For the first time in his life with the Order, he felt totally alone.

The sun's final rays descended, and darkness enveloped the city. Workplaces shut and the bars and taverns began to open for their evening trade. Edryd and Gassis left the Citadel to go to the tavern where they would meet Azerrad and Katerina later. Edryd had suggested he accompany Gassis on the walk as it was night-time and rumours were doing the rounds in the Citadel of what really went on the night before. Gassis had accepted the gallant offer, although she was not afraid to walk alone and felt more like she was escorting Edryd.

The pair made their way down the winding lanes that led to the hub of the city's night life. It was quiet and they could hear their feet on the cobbled stones of the lane. The pair awkwardly conversed about work and life in the citadel before Edryd, who was rambling anyway, was silenced by Gassis. She put her finger to Edryd's lips, and he felt his cheeks begin to flush at the gesture.

'Listen,' she whispered as she took his arm at the elbow and led him along.

The pair commenced their journey but neither said a word as Edryd strained his ears to listen for what Gassis was alluding to. He thought at first, she must be on edge as he could not hear anything unusual as they walked, but the longer he listened, sure enough, he could hear it too. There was another set of footfalls echoing in the cobbled street, a little way off behind them. Edryd turned to catch a glimpse of their owner but there were only shadows moving in the street behind.

'Someone's been following us since the citadel,' Gassis continued to whisper, the words barely audible at all.

The pair stayed with their arms interlocked; Gassis preferred this as she could dictate Edryd's movements. They continued their journey, Gassis making sure they kept a steady pace and that Edryd continued to look forward and mumble nonsense at her so that their pursuer would not guess he had been made. As they neared the end of the road, they were faced with two options; the tavern was at the end of the road that spurred left, but the street to the right would give them a better chance to catch whoever it was that was following them.

When they reached the end, despite her desire to know who was trailing them, Gassis led Edryd left on their intended journey. They arrived at the tavern to find it already teeming with patrons. She sent Edryd in to get a table in the window while she ordered them two beers. When she returned, she placed the beers down and sat so she could see out of the window.

People came and went on the street outside, the pair drank their drinks, and Edryd continued to rabbit on about this and that, but quietly Gassis kept watch. Shadows moved as light from the street and drinking establishments became obscured and for a moment, she thought she caught sight of someone watching them from a darkened corner of the street opposite.

On the street outside, a hooded figure peered into the windows of the taverns across the way, noticing every movement of the punters inside. When the hooded figure saw Gassis get up and head towards the toilets, he stealthily departed the shadows and made for the tavern entrance. As he entered through the door, he barely made it across the threshold before a hand grabbed the back of his dark, tattered robe and felt the feel of something sharp press into his side.

'Why were you following us?' Gassis spoke softly but the tone suggested she meant business.

'Please,' the man pleaded raising his hands slightly, 'I am not here to hurt you.'

'Then what are you doing?' Gassis pressed the blade a little firmer into his side.

The man lowered his hood and Gassis recognised his face from the citadel.

'I am Nestor, I am a soldier of the Order,' the man revealed.

'Sent you to spy on us, have they?' Gassis asked regretfully, lowering her blade and releasing her grip.

'No,' Nestor insisted, 'they do not know I am here,'

'Then why are you here?' Gassis questioned him.

'You're meeting them, aren't you?'

'Who?'

'The Vampires,' Nestor said as quietly as he could, 'Azerrad and Katerina.'

Gassis thought about playing ignorant but instead turned him and ushered him to the table where Edryd sat.

'They will be here soon,' she relented and went back to the bar to get more drinks, as the evening darkened, Nestor explained a little of who he was, and the librarians returned the favour as they waited for their companions. Through the smoky haze of bodies jostling to and fro, in the same dark nook of the tavern he had watched them from before, Carstair drank from a stein of beer eying the trio.

Chapter 14

The evening drew in and more and more patrons frequented the tavern, rushing in from the blustery weather that was forming in the streets of Uvrenmouth. Amongst the windswept hair and red cheeks of those taking shelter from the condition outside, it was easy to spot when Azerrad and Katerina entered. Their hair fell seamlessly into place as they departed the blowing gale, their porcelain skin unblemished by the weather's assault, nor the change in temperature as they moved inside. Even though they had been living in the city for some time now, all eyes still followed them as they moved through the tavern, but most lost interest quickly.

They scanned the tables near to the entrance and found their comrades sat near the window, drinking with another. From behind, they could only see the cloak he was shrouded in and the greasy chestnut hair that adorned his hidden features but Gassis and Edryd were not alone. The vampires approached cautiously, unsure about the addition to their conspirators meeting. When they drew closer, Gassis waved them to hurry over, but the pair continued their cautious advance until her waving caused Nestor to turn to see what it was in relation to. The concern on Azerrad and Katerina's faces eased a little as they recognised the soldier that sat with their friends, but they were still unsure of why he was there.

The pair lowered themselves into the seats Edryd had loyally guarded with his life as the tavern had filled out. They warily eyed Nestor who felt uneasy under their gaze. Finally, he rose, trying to break the tension and suggested he bought more drinks. Though the vampires protested, stating that it was not necessary, Nestor would not take no for an answer and made his way to the bar. Once his back was turned and he was out of earshot, the vampires leaned into their friends who looked concerned.

'What is he doing here?' Katerina asked a little curtly.

'We never, uh...' Edryd tried to talk but found himself unable to.

'He followed us here looking for you,' Gassis replied for him, matching the curtness in Katerina's voice.

'Us, why?' Azerrad asked confused by Gassis's response.

'I don't know, ask him,' she responded truthfully.

Nestor returned from the bar with beer and wine for them and as Azerrad thanked him for the hospitality, Katerina moved straight to the interrogation. 'So why are you here, Nestor?'

'Something happened at the Citadel, I didn't know where to turn,' Nestor replied, taken back by the quickness of the question.

'What happened? And come to think of it, how did you know we were here?' said Katerina, firing off a volley of questions.

'I saw the librarians leave the Citadel after nightfall, I guessed it was to meet with you here again,' Nestor explained.

'You followed us here,' Gassis accused.

'No, I only saw you leave the citadel,' Nestor protested.

'Then how did you know where to come?' she continued.

'I was here the last time you all met, I guessed this was where you would be heading, so seldom do the librarians venture from the citadel.'

'But we were followed here,' Gassis insisted.

'Not by me, I promise you that,' Nestor said earnestly.

Gassis looked like she was going to continue to press the matter, but Katerina interrupted before she could, 'What happened at the citadel?'

'Gideon's dead,' Nestor revealed. It was then Azerrad understood his bloodshot eyes and hallowed appearance; he was grieving.

'The boy came second best to a werewolf attack, it was always a possibility,' Azerrad said as soothingly as he could. 'But we are not here to council you over the dead,' he added.

'He was murdered,' Nestor said in a quiet anger, glaring down at the table, 'one of Carstair's men did it.'

'How do you know?' Katerina asked.

'The doc said he would survive before I left, the nurse saw one of Carstair's men check in on him, and by the time I arrived in the early evening he was dead.' Nestor explained.

'That doesn't make any sense,' Azerrad mused, 'Why would they kill one of their own?'

'He woke this morning while I was there, it took three of us to restrain him. He was raving about monsters,' Nestor continued mournfully, 'I think that's why they killed him; he had lost his mind and couldn't be trusted.'

Azerrad ran a regal hand through his silky hair,

digesting the news Nestor brought. The vampires looked at each other and instinctively knew that they needed to bring Nestor on board. The librarians drank from their glasses and waited to see what the vampire's next move was.

'Nestor, we have been working with the order for a little time now, helping decipher the ancient texts and such,' Azerrad began.

'Yes, your work is not a matter of secret at the citadel,' Nestor replied quizzically.

'No, but over the last few weeks, we've been researching what has been happening in Uvrenmouth,'

'Happening?'

'Surely the amount of sightings and encounters with creatures has seemed abnormal to you?' Katerina interjected.

'I guess, but different teams do different jobs and it's not really our place to ask questions,'

'Well, there are necromantic powers at work in this city. Someone is using dark magic to awaken the city and draw creatures to its power. Katerina and I can both feel it.' Azerrad spoke, lowering his tone somewhat so that all the members around the table had to lean in a little and through the movement of bodies, Carstair watched on with interest. 'We fear that they are using the power contained in books similar to those we are sworn to protect and that they may actually try to steal them from the Order to complete their task.'

'Their task?' Nestor queried a little confused.

'Azerrad and I have found mention of ancient rituals that begin with turning a place into a beacon to the unnatural by tapping into its dormant power, then once the place begins to attract the unnatural to it to it, there are more spells, some to make more creatures rise and some to control them,' Edryd pitched in for the first time that night.

'What he says is true,' Azerrad added to counter the doubtful look on the young soldier's face, 'we fear that someone is going to bring down the order and it is too caught up in its own traditions to see it coming.'

'Last night our little adventure turned out to be a lot more than we bargained for, Nestor, and if what you say is true about your own kind silencing themselves, things may be worse than we thought,' said Katerina, picking up the conversation.

'It's a lot to digest,' Nestor admitted as his head swirled with talk of dark magic and subterfuge.

'Well, eat up,' Gassis added hastily, 'we don't have time to beat around the bush.'

'Come now,' Azerrad tried to interject.

'She's right, we are running out of time,' Katerina interrupted.

'Very well then, what course of action do you suggest?' He replied to his lover.

'We need to sound out those in the Order that are loyal to its course and not just its master,' she suggested back, 'if an unnatural attack comes, we need to know who we can turn to for help, not just a clean-up crew.'

'Edryd and I will sound out the librarians in the morning and gather those we know are loyal, but if the order closes ranks, we will need more than brainpower to stop it,' Gassis offered to the table.

'Katerina and I can deal with the Order if it comes to that,' Azerrad added defiantly.

'No, you can't,' the rueful voice that shot him down belonged to Nestor who had taken all the four had to say in and was making a decision on where his allegiance lay. 'The order is too big and well trained to go against it on your own, but there are many who are loyal to the beliefs it stands for, many for whom Gideon's death will not sit well with. I will sound out the soldiers for you, see if they believe what you are saying to be true.'

The table fell momentarily silent at this revelation from Nestor, none had expected him to join their cause, but he was filled with a grim determination to avenge the loss he had suffered at the hands of his own and was willing throw in his lot with theirs.

'Seems fate has thrust upon us an offering, we would be fools not to take it,' Azerrad spoke to his companions.

The five of them raised their glasses and drank from their drinks, toasting their newfound comradeship. As they spoke and drank long into the evening, Carstair drained his drink and looked over the rim of the empty stein with a grimace. He could not hear what had been discussed from his vantage point so far away but more and more he began to distrust the librarians and question the value of working with monsters. He left his glass and a small stack of silver coins and disappeared through a doorway at the back of the tavern before more patrons left.

Carstair turned his collar up to the still howling wind as it beat upon his ruddy face and made his cheeks tingle. He retraced the same path he had followed the librarians down earlier and made his way back to the Citadel to make sure he was there when the others returned.

The others stayed until there were few left in the tavern beyond the old drunks who would not budge until the bell sounded and the lights fell dark. Nestor and the vampires filled the librarians in on what had happened the night before and they all made plans of what they would do the following morning before leaving for the Citadel as well.

They split into two groups, the humans went first and followed the same route Carstair had taken not so long ago. The drunken haze had numbed Nestor's grief for a brief moment, and he began to feel a new place for him, albeit not one he had imagined in the Order.

The vampires decided to take a longer way home and made their way to the harbour where they had enjoyed the ocean breeze some weeks ago.

The night breeze was far fiercer than it had been before and the two found a spot by the edge of the harbour where they sat, their legs hanging over the ledge, sheltered by several shipping crates that were piled together ready to go onto a cargo ship in the morning. Where they sat the wind could barely penetrate, but their faces were repeatedly doused in the gentle spray of the violent waters in the harbour as the crashed against the rocks and sea wall.

Katerina cuddled into Azerrad and although she barely felt the cold, she enjoyed the solace she found in his arms.

'Almost reminds you of being human, the salty sea air,' Azerrad remarked, inhaling a great gulp of it. Katerina chuckled at the thought of being human.

'How many lives of humans have we watched over those books?' She questioned rhetorically. 'Two? Three?'

'I lost track decades ago,' Azerrad mused back at her.

'Do you truly believe the order can stop this necromancer?' Katerina asked, her tone turning more serious as she spoke.

'They are stronger than you think,' he admitted. 'And we have little choice but to trust them now.'

'They don't trust us though,' she replied.

'Deep down I don't think that they trust themselves, but they represent the best chance of keeping the books hidden and out of the hands of this nefarious power that is rising,' he said staring out into the black abyss of the open sea.

'Perhaps,' she said, 'come, we have lingered long enough.'

The pair stood and surveyed the harbour for prying

eyes before heading back into the city on their journey to the Citadel. The night was still bitter, and a biting wind nipped at the pair, though they did not really feel its effect aside from the chaos it wrought on their hair as they went.

By the time they reached the Citadel again, the city was beginning to quieten and there was little commotion in the great hall as they tussled and rearranged their hair, now out of the gusty wind. There were no sign of the others and so the vampires sought to slip away to their chambers unnoticed. They made their way quietly across the hall but to their surprise they found Carstair keeping watch on the proceedings of the hall from a secluded chair that had made him almost invisible at first glance.

The human's appearance caused the pair to falter slightly as they headed out of sight, not accustomed to being surprised like that. Katerina clutched Azerrad at the elbow and feigned a little difficulty walking as if to mimic being drunk, but the charade washed over Carstair who knew full well what they had been up to that night.

'Carstair,' Azerrad acknowledged the human as politely as he could.

Carstair merely raised his head a little, barely acknowledging the greeting and said nothing, but his eyes darted from place to place as he watched the few comings and goings at that time of night. Unnerved by his worsened demeanour, the vampires hastened off into the corridor that led to their room, vanishing instantly into the shadows that veiled the hallway from the great hall.

Chapter 15

The sun streamed into Edryd's room as he tiredly awoke. It was darker in Gassis's room; the sun had not yet risen enough to enter her window where she was washed and dressed and got ready for the day. In Nestor's room, the sunshine could not lift the gloom that surrounded the young soldier, his heart heavy with the loss of Gideon and burdened with the knowledge he had received that night.

The three headed down to the refectory in their own time, but as each one entered, they found the vampires already seated drinking coffee and drawing the scornful looks of much of the Citadel that was in there. Quietly, each got their own breakfast and joined the pair as they sat alone in a quiet corner, no longer worried about their allegiances.

Eventually, all five who had sat so similarly around the taverns table the night before had assembled around the refectory table to eat and discuss the day's plans. The vampire's eternal youth meant that the late night and early rise was unnoticeable on the perfect features of their skin, only their eyes ever showed their age and it was an age far greater than the tiredness of one evening. Gassis also bore no sign of the weight they seemed to be carrying, her ebony skin immaculate and her clothes perfectly pressed and form fitting. The other two, however, bore the brunt of the group's woes; both Edryd and Nestor looked drained, their hair messy, their eyes darkened, and their clothes hastily thrown on without much care.

The quintet chatted over breakfast, but the attempt to be more upbeat than sullen failed and the gravity of the times ahead weighed on them all. It was decided that first thing that morning the vampires would go to work as usual, Azerrad in the library and Katerina in the vault so as to arouse no suspicion. Meanwhile, the others would sound out a few of the order to see if they could widen the circle of friends they could rely on if the situation in the Citadel soured. Edryd and Gassis would then meet the vampires in the afternoon, and they would all meet that evening.

It was decided that somewhere with less prying eyes than the tavern might be a good idea, given Carstair's coldness upon their return the previous evening. Plus, Edryd couldn't seem to stomach the idea of being around beer for at least a few days.

Azerrad couldn't be sure, but he suspected that Carstair knew they were conspiring. He was certain he knew they had all met that night. It was decided that a secluded spot in the harbour would be their conclave's meeting spot before they all headed out on their duties.

Azerrad swanned into the library with his usual panache and even afforded Sister Agatha a wink in an attempt to thaw her icy demeanour, a gambit which partially worked as her cheeks turned a rosy colour and her scowl softened to a frown.

'No lackey to do your running this morning?' she remarked as she noted the time of his arrival.

'Under the weather,' Azerrad replied trying to charm her more, 'but I am sure he will surface eventually,' he finished, beaming a wide smile in her direction that caused her to return to the book that lay open in front of her.

Satisfied that he had thrown her off his trail for the time being with his sickly sweetness, Azerrad dived into the stacks to see if he could find a more potent book to deal with the darkness that was descending on the city. He browsed dusty tomes and ancient manuscripts, but he feared that anything worth reading may not be left for someone to stumble upon in the library, despite how fierce the guard dog was.

While her lover browsed books, Katerina set about finding some kind of weapon within the vaults that they might use should they be out in the field again, or worse, need to defend themselves here behind Citadel walls. She spoke with a quiet, fair-haired boy that Gassis often consulted to see if he might be able to point her in the right direction. The boy seemed irritated at first to have been disturbed, but as he looked upon the beauty that radiated from Katerina, he soon softened his tone. He suggested a catalogue of items that were reclaimed during one of the Order's border skirmishes with a small town that had once been venerated for their warfare but succumbed to a pack of vampires many years ago. She thanked him for the advice and browsed the catalogues manifest for something that might stand out.

Many of the items seemed fairly standard weaponry, but she did discover that this was the cache of weapons that Carstair's blood reaper pistols had come to the Citadel in, even if they were incorrectly labelled as ornate duelling pistols. Katerina picked out a few interesting items including an ornate dagger, a golden orb, and something labelled only as 'gloves' which seemed uninteresting, but the lack of description peaked her intrigue.

One by one she selected the relevant boxes from the

shelves using the references in the manifest and found a secluded desk in one of the darkened recesses of the vault to inspect the items further, opting against her and Gassis's usual workspace.

As the vampires went about their business the others set about the task of speaking to their kin. Nestor had a good idea about who he might be able to rally to their case, but in what was either a punitive measure for consorting with the others or a desire to keep the incident with Gideon under wraps, he had been assigned to watch over the attendants as they tended the stables that day. It was an easy job, but it came with next to no human contact and he was the only soldier in the stable amongst the lackeys that he felt sure were loyal to Carstair and the senior soldiers who made sure they were looked after. It seemed that he would have to wait until the lunch break to see what he could do.

The others faired a little better, having more freedom to move about the Citadel and both went to friends they had been inducted into the order with. Gassis had made her way to the dormitories as the friend she had thought of was on a rest day; Edryd headed to the vaults where he thought he might find his friend. Sure enough, when he entered the great arched doorway, he saw Elijah working at his usual station. As he made his way to talk to him, in the shadows to the rear of the hall, he could just make out the form of Katerina as she worked away at the items she had selected.

In the gloom of the stacks, Azerrad began to become frustrated that he had made little headway into developing his knowledge on the situation at hand. He banged his closed fist against the metal stack and a dull thud rang out. It was not long before the Sister appeared to see what the disturbance was. She seemed less than pleased at any aggressive sound in her library, but as Azerrad apologised sincerely, explaining his frustrations, she softened at the delicate, almost hypnotic sound of his voice and relented.

'You have been here for some time now, master vampire,' she said, speaking in a pleasant tone Azerrad had never heard come from her mouth before. 'Perhaps what you seek is not here.'

'It would seem that way,' Azerrad admitted still leaning against the metal stacks with clenched fists.

'Perhaps what you seek is too dangerous to leave lying around in these stacks for anyone to stumble on?' Agatha said quietly, the words causing Azerrad to rise from the stack and face her, curious if she knew his intentions or simply guessed the cause of his anguish.

'There are more stacks here aren't there?' Azerrad gambled, eying Agatha intently.

'What I am about to show you is the reserve of only the highest librarians, no book may leave the room, nor copies be made of their writings, do you understand?' she asked intently.

'Implicitly,' he replied, trying to hide his excitement.

'Then follow me,' she said and turned away.

Sister Agatha led Azerrad to the very back of the stacks to a darkened corner where the lanterns and candles of the library barely touched. An old oak door lay in the dusty corner, its iron hinges excessive, and the handle ornate and ancient. Though the door's surrounding was dusty, and cobweb filled, the door itself seemed untouched by such contaminants, suggesting it was used more frequently than the housing suggested. The sister drew a large brass key from inside her robes, still attached to her person somewhere by a long chain that disappeared into the robes. She slid the key into the lock and released the catch which allowed the door to swing open silently.

Inside she lit the lantern at the room's entrance and its soft orange glow filled the small room that was lined on all sides by bookshelves. The shelves were packed with books and manuscripts, many of which looked like they hadn't been looked at for years. Azerrad gazed around the room in awe at the new trove of materials and stepped into the room, the musty smell of old paper hitting him with full force.

'When you are finished, let me know and I will come and lock the room up,' Agatha said, still in hushed tones, and closed the door on Azerrad before hastily returning to her desk.

Inside the room, Azerrad let his hands skim across some of the old books, their ancient leather crisp to the touch. He settled on a section of books that seemed less dusty than the others; there were visible marks in the dust on the shelves that suggested they had been removed more recently than their counterparts. Taking several down, Azerrad began to leaf through them, lost to all time and space in the solitude of the room.

In the vault, Katerina pawed at the items she had selected. The brass dagger lay on the desk in front of her and she held a magnifying glass over it as she inspected every aspect. It was a fine blade that still held a keen edge, but she surmised that it was nothing more than a sacrificial dagger and besides its obvious lethality held no special purpose. She returned it to the box, amending the description slightly and entering a suspected place of origin, part of the mundane tasks that would need to be done anyway at some point on these things.

As she had with the dagger, she inspected the orb but also found nothing of note; it seemed to be just an expensive piece of history, though she questioned if the librarians understood its true value. The gloves, however, she did marvel at only in their lack of anything interesting at all. They were fingerless, made of leather, and bore many scratches and nicks in the leather that made it appear they had been well used in their time. She turned them over in her hands before sliding her svelte fingers into them. On their own they were far too big to comfortably be worn by her, but there were leather straps that dangled from the open leatherwork at her palms and when she wove them around her wrist the gloves fitted almost perfectly. They felt heavier than they should and given their wear were stiffer than she had imagined they would be too. She rotated her hands marvelling at them for a while before she remembered something Azerrad had told her about his first encounters with the Order; she recollected how he had endeared himself to his young companion and his friend by identifying an occulum.

She rose from the desk still clad in the gloves and went in search of the item. She found the manifest and located the occulum, taking it out of its box and returning to her desk. She released the button on its side as Azerrad had and looked down the lens, flipping between the different coloured lenses. To her disbelief, under the amethyst lens, writing seemed to glow across the knuckles of the gloves.

'Hexed gloves', she marvelled to herself trying to read the inscription, 'Argento Ferrum Vitutum' she whispered to herself, puzzling at the meaning. Desiring to know what it meant, she packed up all the items back into their respective boxes and replaced all but the box that contained the gloves. Once she was done, she logged the box out of the vault to get the words translated in the library. As she passed through the vault doors, she met with Gassis who was returning to find her.

'Found something interesting?' Gassis asked eagerly.

'Hexed gloves, but I cannot read the inscription,' came the reply. 'I'm going to get it translated at the library, come on.'

The pair turned and in doing so almost smashed

straight into Carstair who had appeared from nowhere and now stood in their way.

'Ladies,' Carstair said in a sickly tone. 'May I ask the meaning of your business?'

'I…We have been working on more items in the vault. There is an inscription on these I need translated so I am taking them to the library,' Katerina said as courteously as she could muster. Gassis just glared at the lumbering oaf.

'Excellent work, I shall have one of our top librarians look into it,' Carstair said, taking the box from Katerina. 'The inscription is on the paper in the box?' he asked reaching in and gingerly taking out a small scrap of paper between his large fingers and unfurling it to read the words that were jotted on it. 'Argento ferrum Vitutum?' he said, knowing nothing of their meaning.

'If it's all the same I would like to know what it says myself,' Katerina protested, reaching for the box.

'It is not all the same, the Order thanks you for your work though,' Carstair replied smugly and turned from the pair, box in hand.

'Dick,' Gassis whispered under her breath as the giant strode away.

'Come on, let's see if we can find out what it means anyway,' Katerina said and led Gassis by the forearm towards the library.

When they arrived at the library, they found a confused looking Edryd moping at his desk. He looked wearier now than before if that was possible but as the pair made their way towards him, his mood rose a little.

'Have you seen Azerrad?' he asked perplexed.

'No,' the pair said in unison.

'I assumed he was here,' Katerina added.

'If he is, I cannot find him. What are you doing here anyway?' Edryd asked.

'We wanted to translate a phrase… argento ferrum

vitutum,' Gassis said, and Katerina was impressed that she had remembered the phrase after only hearing it once.

'Argento...' Edryd spoke softly, 'I know that word.' He held his aching head while he tried to recall where he had heard the word before. Finally, it came to him, and he dived off into the stacks to retrieve a book. His eyes skimmed the shelves looking for the right book and his swiftness caused little dust bunnies to fly up into the air. When he found the book, he was looking for, he pulled it from the shelves and began flicking vigorously through the pages as he made his way back to the girls.

'Here,' he said, 'argento, it means silver. Ferrum is iron, it's an old dialect spoken by many of the human races here a couple of centuries ago.'

'My word, I think those gloves are hands of God,' Katerina said, confusing the librarians more.

'What does that mean?' Gassis asked.

'There were a group of knights in older times, similar to the Order, they occupied the lands to the north of my country, and they persecuted anything they found to be unnatural with a religious fervour that has since been unmatched. The legend says they had the power to render the unnatural powerless at a mere touch,' Katerina explained.

'And you think they did it using the gloves?' said Gassis making conclusions.

'Their motto was 'silver in strength, iron in will', the magic in those gloves gives the bearer the same power silver has over the unnatural without being made from it.' Katerina continued.

'Yes,' Edryd interrupted, still leafing through the book, 'it is a tricky dialogue to decipher but I think it might say 'silver strength, iron will', at least as a rough translation.'

'Great and now Carstair has them,' Gassis rued.

'Well now that mystery is solved, what about Azerrad?' Edryd asked, his mind returning to the reason for his hubris.

'I will look for him, you both go and get ready to meet at the harbour later and maybe check on Nestor,' Katerina instructed.

In the small room, Azerrad pawed at the books like a child who had uncovered a great sweet store. The information contained in these books was far more direct than the vague prophecies he and Edryd had deciphered in the past few weeks. So lost was he in the books that he had not noticed that Sister Agatha had returned to the doorway.

'I'm afraid I need to lock the room now, master vampire,' she said, breaking Azerrad's concentration.

'Please, call me Azerrad,' the vampire replied smiling, his teeth pronounced over his lower lip.

'My shift is ending I need to lock up... Azerrad,' she pressed again and Azerrad acquiesced, not wanting to lose the privilege he had been granted. Returning the books to their rightful place, he made one last check that he had left nothing out of place before extinguishing the lantern and passing the Sister so she could lock the heavy door behind him.

Azerrad looked up to the small windows on the external wall of the library that ran over the top of the stacks, he could see that darkness was already shrouding the sky and wondered how he had been lost in the room for so long.

'Thank you for your kindness today, Sister,' Azerrad said as he turned to leave. The Sister nodded in acknowledgement before donning the sour façade she sported so well.

Azerrad departed the library acutely aware that he was most likely in trouble that no one knew where he was all afternoon. He made his way to his quarters to find Katerina about to slip out of the window to make another search of the surrounding areas for him. Upon seeing him enter, a scowl crossed her face, and she scolded his stupidity, but Azerrad knew it was a charade and they were soon in each other's arms.

They watched the dusk descend before heading out to meet their friends in the cool sea air of the harbour.

Chapter 16

The sea rolled into the harbour and brought a light mist in with it that shrouded the boats moored there and gave the cool night air an ethereal feel. Azerrad and Katerina walked along the western embankment briskly; they did not wish to be seen by any of the night watchmen nor be soaked by the spray that rose up from the tumultuous sea. Dressed all in black, their long heavy coats kept much of the weather at bay and the glistening leather boots let them stomp through puddles quickly.

When they arrived at one of the old porter's cabins that sat like a solitary beacon in the mist, they pried the ramshackle door open easily for it was not locked and huddled inside. Azerrad lit a small candle and set it precariously on a rotten old shelf, the glow from which barely illuminated the tiny space and cast sinister shadows across the lover's faces.

There in the meagre glow of the candlelight, their clothes damp from mist and spray and their hair bedraggled from the wind, they patiently waited for the others to arrive.

It was not too long before Gassis appeared, her jet-black hair braided tightly back keeping it from staying across her face in the swirling sea mist. Her skin glistened as droplets of water clung to it and reflected the flickering light from the candle. She too wore a long leather coat and dark trousers and boots that had kept much of the salty spray from penetrating her clothes. The three acknowledged each other and Gassis took her place, pulling out an old barrel and huddling in next to Katerina.

Nestor was the next to arrive, he wore a tight leather jerkin over the Order's casual uniform, the symbol of the Ankh still visible where his jerkin was not closed completely. He peeled back the door and ran his fingers through his matted locks to remove the moisture from them as best he could. Sitting next to Azerrad, a stray droplet of water cascaded down his face, winking in the candlelight like a shooting star in the night sky. The others watched it trace its way across his features in silence before he brushed the nuisance away.

The four sat solemnly waiting on their final member who, when he finally appeared, looked as though he had done so by dragging himself backwards through every bush and hedgerow he could find. He had worn a casual woollen jumper that simply absorbed most of the seawater that had accosted him on his journey and still hung visibly on the weave of his jumper. His hair was nothing short than all over the place and clung to his scalp by the weight of the water it held. His trousers and shoes were muddy where he had misplaced a foot and stumbled and the thunderous look on his face suggested he was less than happy about it. But it soon dissipated as all four looking to each other and back at him fell into muted hysterics. They held their mouths to control their laughter and buried their heads in their arms at the sight of Edryd, who in turn, found amusement in his own misfortune.

'Now we've all had a good chuckle at my expense,

how about we get on with this so I can go home and change,' the young librarian said trying to move proceedings along. 'And come to think of it, where were you this afternoon?'

'All in good time, my friend,' Azerrad soothed Edryd, 'tell us how you got on, was there much support?'

'I have a good friend from before the order, Rebeka, who works in the vaults too, she can be depended on and others may rally around her,' Gassis said softly.

'I spoke to Elijah, and he too accepted what I had to say,' Edryd added in an equally hushed tone.

The vampires nodded to themselves, seemingly happy that there was a streak in the Order that still believed in what it stood for, but they both noticed that Nestor remained quiet, having said nothing since his arrival.

'Brother? What is it?' Gassis said sensing the tension at his silence.

'Did you manage to garner any support amongst the soldiers?' Katerina queried.

'I was kept away from my brothers for the most part, sent to work in the stables babysitting the attendants,' Nestor began his voice quiet yet stern. 'Over lunch, however, I did sound out some of the brothers who joined the order at the same time as me and Gideon. I told them of the manner of his demise, the underhanded nature and the reservations we held about the direction our Order is taking.'

'What did they say?' Edryd interjected impatiently, though he pressed no further as Gassis squeezed his arm to silence him.

Nestor looked up so that he caught the eyes of the others in the room one by one. In the darkness and gloom his eyes caught the glow of the candle's flame as though it burned in them not on the shelf, and the resentment he felt at that time was known to all in the room. 'They were horrified that we could do that to one of our own,' he began softly, 'they have become disillusioned with the running of the Order and Carstair's standing within it,' he continued, his voice steadily raising. 'If we move against the Order, my brothers will stand behind you.' Nestor finished, stoking the passions of all huddled in that tiny room.

'Then it is decided, if the Order continues to ignore this necromancer, we will move against them and the Order too if they stand in our way,' Azerrad spoke grimly, but his determination echoed Nestor's.

'Not without more knowledge of what we're facing. The Order may have lost its way but it is still not to be underestimated in power' Gassis said, bringing order back to the room.

Azerrad acknowledged Gassis's point and continued a little more subdued, 'I was afforded an opportunity this afternoon,' a sly grin emerging on his face that allowed his pronounced fangs to reveal themselves. 'Sister Agatha may not be the cold crone we think her to be, she showed me a secure room where all of the Order's dangerous books are kept. Only she holds the key and can grant access, save for the Grand Master.'

'A secret room?' Edryd scoffed. 'Don't you think I would have known about it? I spend all of my time in that place.'

'The room is accessed through an old oak door in the far corner of the stacks, how many times do you question something if you never see it used?' Azerrad posed at Edryd, the young librarian blushed a little in the darkness and said no more. 'That room is small, but it is filled with literature, and I found an old book that spoke of the Noctuque Grimoire. A potent spell book that holds the power to magnify spell work.'

'So, a simple unlocking spell,' Katerina said

'Could unlock a whole cities potential,' Gassis finished Katerina's thought in dismay.

'Where is this grimoire?' Nestor asked Azerrad.

'I do not know, I hope to go back to the repository and try to find a location, but chances are this necromancer already has it and is using it, which means we need to keep the books that were transported from my homeland safe within the Citadel. If their power were combined with that of the Noctuque Grimoire...'

As Azerrad's sentence trailed off into the darkness, a cold gust of wind battered against the cabin they were sheltered in. It caused the windows to rattle and the candle to flicker as it grimly held to life before it was extinguished.

'Perhaps it is time we adjourned this meeting,' Katerina said in the now almost pitch blackness of the cabin they huddled in.

The companions agreed and each made their way silently out of the cabin and into the increasingly hostile weather. Taking separate routes, they all ventured back to the Citadel, trying to stagger their arrival times. Nestor was first back as he took the most direct route not caring who saw him. He was closely followed by Edryd who longed to shower and change his clothes. It was a little time before Gassis returned and quietly made her way to her room.

Finally, sometime after the others had returned, Azerrad and Katerina made their way into the citadel. They stole in quietly and tried to dry themselves a little before they wandered the halls of the immense building. They had not made it halfway across the great hall that stood at the front of the Citadel before Carstair eyed them and made his way in their direction, a disgruntled look upon his face.

'Where have you been?' he asked wearily, something obviously playing on his mind.

'Out for a stroll,' Katerina replied, the pleasantness of her tone countering the bitterness in his.

'Shitty night for it,' he said dubious as to the answer he had received.

'Quite,' she replied and made to leave but was stopped as Carstair grabbed her arm forcefully enough to stop her in her tracks.

'We're not done here,' Carstair said his tone more neutral now. 'We've got another job to do tonight, another report of a nest of your kind has come in and we need to go and check it out,' Carstair informed the pair.

'I'm guessing this isn't optional,' Azerrad mocked.

'No, it is not, we saddle up in an hour,' came the unfriendly response.

'Is the information more accurate this time at least?' Katerina asked joining in the mockery.

'You'll see for yourself when we get there won't you?' With that, Carstair turned away from the vampires and left them to get ready. He disappeared in the direction of the stables where the rest of the party should be assembling.

When they were ready, the vampires made their way down the rear staircase that led out into the courtyard more discreetly than the usual way and amassed with the others in the stables. Once again, the two attendants from the previous outing were there, full of the joys of spring as ever. One gave the pair a dismissive look, the other not even bothering with that. There were three soldiers with them, but they all had their backs turned to the vampires. As they approached, the three turned almost simultaneously.

Azerrad was pleased, if a little surprised, to see one of them was Nestor.

'Friends,' Nestor began, drawing scornful looks from Carstair, 'This is Marius, and this fine specimen is Arjan,' he continued slapping Arjan on the back.

'Nice to make your acquaintance sir, ma'am,' the larger Arjan answered shyly.

'And yours,' Azerrad replied, looking to the other soldier but no response came.

The soldiers, attendants, and Carstair were already geared up and waiting to go, so with the arrival of the vampires they all made their way to the horses. As the soldiers turned from Azerrad and Katerina, Azerrad caught Nestor's arm and pulled him close so that only he would hear.

'Are these trustworthy?' he whispered in Nestor's ear.

'Yes,' Nestor whispered back, 'they joined with me and Gideon.'

Azerrad was weary, but the group got on their horses and trotted to the gate where the night attendant opened the cumbersome oak doors so that they may venture into the night; back into the night for some of them. As they passed under the stone arch of the door, the air seemed eerily still; no more did the wind whip around the travellers as it had when the five companions had met earlier that evening. Instead, the stillness felt almost oppressive to the party as they rode into the city which seemed to be calmer than the vampires could ever remember seeing it. The streets were silent and the few people they did come across went about their business quickly and quietly, it was as though a great depression had befallen the city and its residents were caught up in it.

Azerrad looked to the cloudless sky and saw the moon as it waxed high in the midnight sky, not yet full but that had not made an ounce of difference in this accursed city since his arrival. As the party strode on, bobbing up and down in time with the horse's gait, he felt everything about this outing was different; he felt the great calm before a storm descending.

Chapter 17

The stars twinkled like tiny diamonds laced into the black fabric of the sky overhead. As the party rode through the back streets of Uvrenmouth, the stillness of the night was offset by the rapturous wind the riders created as they rode. Belts and coattails fluttered as the riders went past but, on the streets, barely a leaf moved in the urban evening. This time the party rode for longer than they had previously, leading Azerrad to surmise that the issue was somewhere right on the town's peripheries.

As the cobbled streets and built-up areas of Uvrenmouth's heart began to morph into fields and farmland, the party began to ease their gallop. They stalled by a copse of trees that had begun to eat into the road and denoted a boundary between two pieces of land. The riders formed a circle and Carstair explained that they had received news from the watchers, of a group of unnatural beings skulking around the marshland that hemmed in the city's farms to the west. The creatures had been difficult to identify and although they believed them to be feral vampires, they could not be sure.

'Our job is to find this nest of monsters and see an

end to them,' Carstair said firmly, rousing those of the Order but eliciting little from the vampires or Nestor.

The party unsaddled and began to prepare for the hunt, attaching various weapons and talismans to their uniforms. The attendants took the reins of the horses and led them into the copse so that they were more out of sight. Once the soldiers were ready, Carstair informed them that they would head out together and split if there was no sign of their quarry.

Azerrad and Katerina looked at each other, both sensing the unusual feel to this mission. There seemed to be little intel about exactly what they were going to face nor how many hostiles there would be. Nevertheless, the group made their way into the course farmland that bordered the western edge of the city, slowly moving through vegetation that was still growing, their movements caused the plants to rustle gently as they went by and but for that sound there would have been but deathly silence in the fields.

They made their way patiently across the farmland in single file, Nestor at the head and Carstair at the tail making sure that no one misplaced a footstep. As they continued, the vampires couldn't help but feel oppressed by the lack of noise and the absence of any wind, their heightened senses finding it disturbingly unnatural. Finally, the party came to a halt as Nestor felt his foot sink slightly into the squelchy mud of the marshland at the farm's extremity, the western hills now looming over his shoulder.

Carstair signalled for the group to split up. He took Nestor and Arjan and sent Marius with the vampires. Before they went their separate ways, Carstair caught Marius by the arm and whispered in his ear. 'Watch them,' was all he said, but he gave the young lad a knowing look.

The soldiers headed south, the vampires north under

instruction to survey the hillsides and meet again at roughly the point they had started out from. The night remained still, but away from the imposing buildings and streetlights of the city, the openness of the land here was well lit by the twinkling stars and the gaze of the moon.

Carstair, Nestor, and Arjan made haste through the marshy brush towards the hillside where the sightings had been made. The hills were not of a great height, but they were riddled with caverns and mazy ridges that made them quite dangerous to traverse and perfect for a nest of monsters trying to remain hidden. When they reached the hillside, the light dimmed a little, obscured by the jutting rocks and ridges of the landmass. Shadows darted here and there as the trio progressed that made the two young soldiers feel a little unnerved. At their back, Carstair swaggered through rough hillside using the blade he had drawn to push back overgrowth and cut his way through where necessary.

The group checked crevices and scoured the brush for signs of habitation, but there was little to no sign that anything, man nor beast, had been in that area for some time. As Carstair continued his disinterested swashbuckling through the undergrowth, the soldiers kept to their task with the discipline that was expected of them.

To the north, the vampires and Marius began in much the same way, drawing swords and pushing their way through the scrubland they searched for signs of habitation. Marius let the vampires push on ahead of him as he searched with one eye on them and the other on the surrounding areas as he looked. Marius was slender and his narrow face and beady eyes made him look almost sinister, especially when only lit in the light of the moon. His movements were delicate, and his long arms and gangly legs made his movements appear arachnid in appearance. As he swept his long, keen blade through an overgrowth of grass and back, the blade caught his hawk like attention as it arced to and fro.

Pulling the blade closer to his face so he could inspect it he saw that something tainted the edge, a stain the dulled the sharpness of the weapon. The mark was clearly fluid, but thick and viscous, a deep red, almost black colour and marred the perfection of his sword. Content that the vampires were reasonably far ahead of him and occupied by their own search, he bent down to the area his blade had emerged sullied from to inspect it more closely.

Reaching a hand into the grass to part it and find the culprit that had tarnished his well-preserved weapon, he looked shocked to find nothing out of the ordinary. In a state of confusion, he pulled his sword closer to check that what he saw was not some trick of the light but sure enough, taunting him from the tip of the glinting blade was a patch of tainted metal.

Marius touched the blade cautiously to see what was infecting it, two fingers gingerly pressed the tip, smudging the gooey substance. Marius withdrew the fingers and held them up in the moonlight, the substance was sticky and a very deep red in the moonlight. As he pulled his fingers apart, a sickly string of whatever it was clung and bridged the gap between his fingers. Horrified at the substance, he wiped the red goo from his fingers as best he could in the clean marshy grass before summoning the strength to plunge his hand into the grassy outcrop.

His fingers traced down the blades of grass, their tips outstretched, and he felt a familiar substance at the grass's base. He pulled his hand out slowly, the tips of his fingers already darkened by the same substance that his blade had been. Reluctantly, he began to draw the hand closer to his face for further inspection.

'It's rancid blood,' Azerrad said in his usual hypnotic tone.

Marius flew back from his haunches landing on his rear, his arms outstretched and his already racing heart ready to fly out of his chest. He had not noticed the vampire even begin to approach, so how he had appeared inches from him he did not know. Azerrad looked down on the hapless soldier with a slight grin on his face before offering his hand out to help him up, which he reluctantly took.

Marius vigorously rubbed his hand on his trousers to remove the sticky substance, before looking to Azerrad.

'How did you know?' he asked

'I can smell it from here,' Azerrad replied, his tongue moving around his mouth as though he were cleaning something distasteful from it.

'Can you smell all blood?' Marius asked, almost sensing the ridiculousness of the question.

'When it's not inside a body, yes,' Azerrad facetiously replied. 'I can sense your heart rhythm too,' he added a little warning creeping into the words.

Marius understood that he was questioning down a path that the vampire was not all that keen to venture but his curiosity drove him on.

'Is it hard?' he asked.

'Hard?' came the confused reply.

'Being around humans, you know, being around a food source,' he explained.

Azerrad gave him a stony stare momentarily but smiled and put his arm around Marius leading him on towards where Katerina had already explored. Marius jumped slightly, not prepared for the invasion.

'I am old,' Azerrad relinquished in a quiet soothing tone, 'I have had many centuries to come to terms with who and what I am. It takes time to control the urges inside, many vampires give in to their desire to feed, and when they do, when they take a human life, it is a path that is hard to come back from.'

'Have you taken a human life?' Marius asked more sincerely this time.

'Human blood feeds our metabolism and the more we drink the hungrier it makes us, it changes us into a feral, perverted version of who we could be,' Azerrad continued, seemingly sidestepping the question. 'If we continue to drink human blood it will consume us, it will become all we can think about and no longer will we care about the things that made us human, of likes and dislikes, our desires and our dreams, all there is, is blood.' The words came out of Azerrad's mouth in a haunting melody that Marius found himself equally enraptured by and frustrated that he wasn't getting answers to his questions. Azerrad saw this in the young soldier's expression and carried on.

'Yes, I have taken human life,' the vampire conceded, 'and it was not an easy path back from it.' The sense of warning was creeping back into his voice, 'but I found someone to lead me down the path to redemption,' he said his voice returning to its usual melodic tone as he cast his gaze in Katerina's direction.

Katerina looked suitably annoyed that she seemed to be doing the brunt of the grunt work while the other two chatted.

'Come,' Azerrad said, slapping Marius on the back, a wry smile on his face, 'we've work to do,' and with that he returned to searching the landscape for a nest.

Marius hopped through the marshy ground trying to catch Azerrad, 'if that was blood, shouldn't we check the area?' he called after the vampire.

'That blood was old, but we can't be far off,' he called back over his shoulder to Marius who continued to struggle to keep up. 'The smell is getting stronger.'

Overhead, clouds had begun to encroach on the

peaceful sky and dimmed the luminescence of the stars and moon. Unimpeded by this the group ventured closer to the hillside, sure that they would find another clue as to the whereabouts of this nest. As Azerrad and Marius searched through the labyrinths of ridges and cracks in the hillside, Katerina had already scouted ahead. She came across a small inlet in the rock that was almost completely concealed by a large piece of rock that jutted out from the hillside at a sharp angle. The passage inside was pitch black, but she could smell the foul air within.

Drawing a small torch from her belt she lit the end using some flint. Once the end was suitably ablaze, she threw the light source into the opening and pressed herself against the rocky outcrop, drawing her sword as she did. Patiently she waited to see if the disturbance would identify if there were any inhabitants inside. When no such indication came, she sheathed her sword and made her way around the outcrop warily and with her pistol now drawn.

The orange glow of the torch burned strongly in the cave, and she could clearly see the mouth, but it curved to the left leaving the inner most part of the cave hidden from sight. This is where I would hole up, she thought, concealed, defensible. She edged into the cave one step at a time, vigilant of any ambush. She headed in the direction of the torch, stooping to pick it up while keeping her eyes and pistol on the darkness ahead. Lifting the torch, she began to move into the hollow of the cave, using the arm holding the torch to cover her face from the wretched stench that grew as she ventured in, her pistol arm ever vigilant.

The air was stale and oppressive, and the floor gradually became wetter and stickier as she edged in. Rounding the natural curve of the cave, she held the torch up to see and recoiled at the sight that befell her. She tossed the torch towards the back of the cave and drew her sword once more, the hollow almost completely lit by the warm glow of torchlight.

In the light, the ghoulish nature of what the cave held became clear; it was not a nest but a tomb. The walls were slick with blood, gore and viscera, the floor was equally coated and strewn with the carcasses of humans and animals alike but the worst sight of all was draped around the hollow like macabre trophies of a successful hunt; the decaying corpses of five vampires. Their bodies were twisted shapes of the humans they once were, their fangs rotten, but pronounced over their receding, cracked lips, their ears pointed and elongated, pressed against skulls where little to no hair sat any longer. Their skin bore a greyish hue that would have rendered them lifeless even before they had succumbed to their fate.

Katerina watched for any sign of life, but the cave had become a living mausoleum to the remains of this nest and after a few moments she left the cave, leaving the torch still burning within. As she emerged the still air of the night hit her like a calming wave, the stench of dead blood dissipating from her nostrils and composing her. She looked along the ridges to find Azerrad and Marius and flagged them to come down.

The pair rushed to her side, fearing she was in danger, but as they drew closer, they could see that she was not, her features and clothing bore no sign of struggle.

'What is it?' Azerrad asked lowering his pistol.

'In there,' she replied gesturing nonchalantly with her head over her shoulder. The pair strode to enter the glowing hole in the rock, but Katerina held Marius's shoulder to stall him. 'It might not be wise to see that,' she said in a low, calming voice of genuine concern.

Marius brushed off her hand defiantly and followed Azerrad into the cave. He moved hastily and found the vampire solemnly viewing the grisly scene that was laid out before him. Rushing to his side, he became acutely aware of the sticky nature of the floor, recognising it from his encounter earlier. The shock caused him to breathe deeply and upon inhaling the rancid odours of the decaying mound of vampires and bodies, he was forced to flee the cave as quickly as he had entered it, gagging as the taste of decay clung to his throat as morning dew clings valiantly in the presence of the dawn sun.

Marius burst out of the caverns entrance and proceeded to vomit uncontrollably, turning his back to Katerina as he wretched. When he felt he was finally done, he wiped his mouth with the sleeve of his coat and turned to see the look of 'I told you so' on her face. Azerrad emerged from the cave with a concerned look on his face.

'Go and get the others, Marius' he instructed to the young soldier who was about to object when the vampire took a deep breath that revealed the elongated fangs in his mouth and made him think twice.

Reluctantly, he composed himself and headed south to find the rest of the group. Azerrad withdrew the torch he had and lit it as Katerina had earlier before staking into the ground so that the others would easily find them.

'What is that in there?' he said to Katerina in a concerned tone.

'Those things look like they just burned up and died,' she replied understanding his meaning, 'it looked like their metabolism outstripped their ability to feed, have you ever seen anything like that? The fangs?'

'No,' he replied solemnly, 'something like that would take months if not years of gorging on blood to drive them to that death, if that is even possible, but there is no way they could have found a food source abundant enough to sustain that kind of relentless feasting and gone unnoticed by the Order or their watchers, or even the owners of the local livestock.'

'You think this necromancer could have summoned them? Or created them?' Katerina poised to her lover.

'Maybe, the necromantic arts are riddled with raising the dead and creating monsters, perhaps the necromancer created some unstable version of us,' he replied, 'but to what end? They killed half a dozen humans and burned up.'

'Maybe they aren't the only nest out here,' she said, her eyes darting around the gloomy hillside.

'That's a comforting thought,' Azerrad mused aloud.

Rustling of grass and undergrowth was quickly followed by the emergence of the humans, Marius leading the way followed by Nestor and Arjan and finally Carstair. The soldiers eyed the cave nervously, making it apparent that Marius had informed them of what they might find in there.

'The nest is destroyed?' Carstair asked the vampires quizzically.

'See for yourself,' Katerina offered, goading Carstair to see if he would react as well as Marius.

The soldier grunted and pushed through the younger soldiers to make his way into the cave, withdrawing a cloth from his jacket pocket and covering his nose and mouth, much to Katerina's annoyance. Azerrad followed him in and the silhouettes they formed as they went were starkly contrasting; Azerrad's agile, sculpted form offset by Carstair's powerful block-like one.

Carstair looked over the ruined forms of human, animal, and monster contemptuously, lowering the rag a little. The smell soured his throat, and his eyes watered a little at the power of the odour, but he did not wretch as his soldier had.

'Is this what becomes of you?' He asked almost pitifully.

'If we give into the hunger,' Azerrad replied honestly, 'But I've never seen anything this far gone before.'

He paused in the room as the glow from the torch flickered and flared as it began to die out at Carstair's feet. Outside, the peaceful night began to become restless again, the wind picking up and howling across the caves entrance. Finally, he decided that there was no more to be seen and replaced the rag into his jacket pocket. 'Fucking creatures' was all he said before flicking the torch with his shoe into the pile of ruined corpses, watching just long enough to ensure the ragged cloth that still hung from their bodies caught the flame and ignited.

He turned and made his way out of the cave, followed by Azerrad who stole a final glance as the fire enveloped the flesh of all that lay in that wretched resting place and his heart sank a little. Emerging from the cave, Carstair bore a look of grim fortitude, Azerrad's was just grim, and in that moment, Katerina wondered if this was not what Carstair had expected to find all along.

Chapter 18

The next morning, while much of the Order went about its daily business, it was an unusual time for those who had been out the night before. What should have been a routine mission again turned out to be nothing like they had expected, and the vampires were beginning to question what was really going on. The watchers prided themselves on the accuracy of their reports and their ability to neutralise threats as a result of this, but twice now the vampires had come up against the unexpected.

In their room high above the swarming city, the vampires sat talking of the night before. They were still dressed in the clothing they had gone out the night before, and both still bore the result of the oncoming winds that had rolled into the city as they left the outskirts, manifested in the windswept nature of their hair neither had cared to fix. Katerina sat on their bed watching Azerrad as they began to remove their weapons from their belts and holsters.

'Do you think they are holding something back?' she asked, 'or are they as clueless as we are?'

Azerrad ran his hands through his hair wearily, gazing out of the dormitory window, his silence saying all he could.

The night had wearied both of them and by the time Azerrad's gaze returned from the outside world Katerina was asleep on the bed. He smiled at her motionless form, the piercing sun glowing from her pale skin making her seem almost otherworldly in the morning haze. Azerrad took a cloth from the desk drawer and began to meticulously clean the weapons he had removed and placed on the desk.

In the library, Edryd cut a lonely figure as he sat at the desk reading over the translations, he and Azerrad had made in the previous weeks, trying to learn the language more so that he may be able to better translate the works on his own. He thought about going to see the sister and enquiring about the secret repository of books she had shown Azerrad, but he did not possess Azerrad's charm, nor did he hold high enough status within the Order's librarian guild to be demanding such privileges, and as he watched her sternly glare over the library's patriots that morning, he shelved the notion and returned to his books.

Gassis cut an equally forlorn figure in the Citadel's vaults, she sat alone at her desk mirroring Edryd at his and pawed at the amulet on the table before her, though her heart was not in her work that morning. She longed to know how the outing had fared for the vampires that night, yet without any commotion in the citadel's ranks, she doubted anything seriously bad could have befallen them.

Picking up the amulet, she marvelled at the perfectly cut amethyst crystal in its centre. Cut immaculately in an octagonal shape, it represented an enormous deal of work and effort on some craftsman's part that had simply been left in the vault to the mercy of the annals of time, a fate she feared for herself at times too. She took the small report card that the librarians of the vault were required to fill in when they had made an assessment of an object and wrote 'nothing unnatural, consign to the treasury' and took the small wooden box that housed it to the front desk to be sent to the bursar to increase the Orders considerable wealth before returning to her seat to eye her next item.

The morning came and went uneventfully and by midday the refectory was awash with members of the order clamouring to get the best and freshest food before it was all gone and only leftovers remained. Around a canteen table in the corner of the room sat the three soldiers who had accompanied the expedition the previous evening.

All three had been given light duties to commence in the afternoon on account of the late return the evening prior but none of the group looked particularly well rested. Bags hung under Nestor's eyes as they always did since Gideon's death. Unable to rest, Nestor still blamed himself for failing his friend; the red bloodshot eyes a testament to the guilt, shame, and deep sorrow he felt. Marius looked equally unrested; his eyes heavy yet he could find no peace that night. Visions of the cave still haunted his thoughts, and he could not erase the wretched smell of the desecrated place.

Arjan was the only one who looked like he may have slept for more than twenty minutes at a time; his auburn hair was neatly combed, he was the only one who wore a pressed uniform, and he leant back and joked with a few of the soldiers on the table behind them. Laughing and patting them on the back at the hilarity of their jesting. He was also the only one who had any food laid out in front of him, although he had almost devoured all of it.

Neither Marius nor Nestor could face food.

When lunch time ended and the afternoon activities began, the three of them rose from the table and silently went their separate ways to do their duties, having barely said a word to each other at the table.

With the rest of the Citadel ambling on in regularity, Carstair stirred in his bed. Seeing that the sun was already receding back towards the horizon, he knew it was mid-afternoon. As a senior soldier in the Order, he had been afforded a rest day for the excursion the previous night, but knew that although he would not be disturbed, the Grand Master would want a report of how the evening played out.

He stretched and put his hands behind his head, the ruffled hair catching between his large fingers as the interlocked behind him. Resting into the pillow he watched a flock of birds zigzag through the warm afternoon air as his eyes adjusted to being open. He marvelled at the beautiful arcs and swift manoeuvres they executed precisely in the cloudless sky.

Finally, he summoned the strength to get out of bed and gave himself a cursory wash in the basin to remove the sleep from his eyes. Refreshed from the cool water in the basin, he made his way out of his quarters to shower before returning and putting on clean clothes. He dressed in tan trousers and an off-white shirt that hung loosely on his considerable form and swung open at the collar where he had not tied the lace ties; he saw no need for formality on his rest day.

Adjusting his hair to tidy it a little in the mirror before he left, he made his way across the balcony and down to the refectory to get something to eat and a mug of coffee. The refectory was quiet, only a few members who also had rest days were relaxing in the food hall. Carstair grabbed his food and coffee and slunk quietly into a seat that left his back to the rear wall. He ate and drank and refuelled his body, then feeling refreshed he decided to go see Gallion.

Gallion's room was darker than usual, the closed drapes shed a red hue around the room as the light forced its way through the fabric. Carstair knocked and entered before being summoned and found the Grand Master hunched over another book. He sat in an emerald robe with long drooping sleeves that hung on his skeletal form unflatteringly. He held a golden magnifying glass in his spindly hand that could barely fit between his face and the pages underneath it the old man was so close to the book.

Carstair looked on sympathetically at the Grand Master's fragile form. He had come to think of Gallion as a father figure in recent years, mostly owing to the elevation in his status within the Order as Gallion's enforcer and for the wisdom he had found in his conversations with him. To see the apparent aging of his mentor pained Carstair a little but the sprightliness he showed in raising his head and lowering the glass to address Carstair's arrival made Carstair question just how decrepit he actually was.

The Grand Master sat upright in his elaborate chair; throne would have been a better word for it, but the Grand Master always asserted that he was an elected leader not a monarch here. He formed a bridge with his spiderlike fingers and rested them on his lap so that they were only just visible behind his mahogany desk.

'Carstair,' the Grand Master spoke fondly.

'Grand Master,' came the respectful reply.

'It is quite late in the afternoon; I trust I am not exhausting you with these expeditions?' Gallion said pleasantly.

'Not at all, it is my honour to serve the Order, but these last few weeks have been testing, it seems they finally caught up with me, I apologise Grand Master.'

'No need to apologise, my friend,' Gallion replied, the use of the word friend seeming out of place in the Grand Master's vocabulary to Carstair. 'Tell me of the evening's events.'

'It went as you said it would, we found the nest but it was done,' Carstair informed Gallion. 'Been that way for some time from the look of it.'

The Grand Master took the information in and broke the finger bridge he had created to run his hand over his chin. 'Yes, the watchers said it had fallen silent but only for a day or two.'

'Forgive me sir, but why were we investigating a dormant nest if the watchers knew it was that way? Shouldn't a clean-up team have gone instead?' Carstair asked a little confused.

'The report never said they'd all be dead, there was still a risk in sending untrained members in,' Gallion responded firmly, not liking his judgement to be questioned.

'Well, it's clean now, I torched the place before we left,' Carstair replied, brushing off the Grand Masters tone.

'Yes, and the watchers had to put it out before it spread to the hillside and caused a wildfire,' Gallion added, causing Carstair to blush a little at his impudence. 'The watchers have found several of these nests in the past few weeks on the peripheries of the city, I was concerned that the vampires are right and that our enemy has indeed made the city into a beacon that is drawing the monsters to our door, but these vampires in the nests are as feral as we have encountered in our time and they seem to be burning themselves up, what do you think of it Carstair?' he added moving the conversation on.

'Those things we found had gorged themselves on the fat of the land, there were animals and humans torn apart in there,' Carstair recollected, 'but that was the strangest part, the victims were torn apart like the vampires couldn't get to the blood quick enough. If they were wolves I would understand, but vampires usually drain the victim and they don't waste blood, but the nest was slick with it.'

'What do you know of vampire lore?' Gallion asked sincerely, not trying to mock Carstair's assessment.

'What we are told when we train here, I admit I am not as learned on these matters as you sir,'

''There is much I know and much I am yet to learn, but in here,' Gallion began, patting the book on his desk, 'in here I am learning more than I ever thought possible.'

'Sir?' Carstair asked nervously.

'As far as we know, vampires are turned by another, their curse transferred through bite and blood. The subject must be bitten by the vampire then drink of his blood for the curse to take hold, correct?'

'That is my understanding of it,' Carstair answered, 'that is why we never leave victims alive, in case they have been turned.'

'Quite so,' Gallion said smiling at his protégé, 'but werewolves can be turned through bite alone or made by being cursed under the blood moon on its biannual cycle.' Gallion looked up to see that Carstair was following. 'What if vampires can be created through a similar curse?'

'Is that possible?' Carstair asked in disbelief.

'The book talks of three cursed creatures, werewolves, vampires and revenants. One cursed by the light of the moon, a slave to its call, able to change its shape; another cursed by blood, to be bound to it and ruled by it, to forever hunger for its taste but in each taste lose themselves; and one cursed by man to walk the earth, a penitent that cannot die for it is already dead,' Gallion said reading from his notes. 'We know that werewolves can be made through a curse and this revenant it says is manmade, so why not vampires too?'

'You think someone is creating vampires by cursing some poor souls?' Carstair asked his ashen face drained of all vigour.

'Possibly, I speculate that without a sire to teach them they are just ravenous beasts, do you have a better explanation?' Gallion asked, but didn't wait for a reply, 'if what I suspect is right then this necromancer we seek is in the city somewhere, and if I have come to this conclusion the vampires may be onto it also. Sister Agatha gave Azerrad access to the hidden repository to do some extracurricular work.'

'I will have words with the good Sister,' Carstair threatened.

'No need, they are our allies after all,' Gallion said calmly, but the emphasis on the word allies made Carstair question his meaning. 'One of our watchers think they have located a site this enemy may have used, though he will no doubt be long gone, I want you to take the vampires to search it and look for evidence of these nefarious acts, perhaps this will show the vampires we take the threat seriously.'

'Very well, I will inform them and head out at dusk, where is this site?'

'Not too far into the city, the old chemist building that has fallen into disrepair,' Gallion answered.

'I will see to it,' Carstair said nodding as he turned to leave the room.

The Grand Master did not stop but called out before he opened the door, 'let the vampires go in first. If the necromancer is still in that place, we cannot risk our own.'

Carstair again nodded as he left the room and closed the door gently behind him. He paused outside the Grand Master's sanctum, trying to take in all that had just been disclosed to him. It angered him slightly that the Grand Master thought he and his men couldn't handle some dark spell master and wanted him to let the vampires lead on his.

His head hurt again as he tried to decode whether Gallion felt genuine concern for his men or if it was something else entirely. He sighed heavily as he thought of another night out in the city skulking around, and another night spent in their company. He rolled his eyes and departed, heading for the great hall to find a menial to send word to the vampires.

Night-time fell too soon for Carstair's liking. He had changed into more suitable clothing and was waiting in the grand hall where he had sent word for the vampires to meet him. Exactly at the time he told them to meet, they appeared from the hallway that led to their room. Both were clad similarly to the night before, but they wore heavier coats as they had been informed there would be no horses needed this evening.

The pair made their way across the hall towards Carstair, who rose from his seat and also donned a large, heavy overcoat which concealed his pistols and dagger. He drew the belt of the coat tight around his waist and it strained as he locked it in place.

'Is this it?' Katerina asked defiantly, 'we're your work dogs and we have to come running at your summons?'

Carstair hid his disdain for the tone Katerina had used, 'Yes.'

Katerina scowled at this reply, but Carstair was already making his way through the great hall and out into the stormy night.

Where the previous evening had been eerily still, this one was tumultuous. The wind howled as it blew lashing torrents of rain at the buildings and the three humans that huddled under the external gate waiting for the vampires. Azerrad was disheartened to see that the only other soldier in attendance was not Nestor but felt better to recognise Marius whom Nestor had advocated support of. They were accompanied by a lone attendant who carried a large leather hold all that bristled with weapons and other equipment.

'Your note said we were checking out an empty building that may have been used by the necromancer,' Azerrad said pointing towards the arsenal the attendant held.

'That's right,' Carstair replied, 'never hurts to be prepared.' He pulled his collar up to the horrific weather and ventured into the streets, the rest of the party following suit. Overhead the rain lashed down and a flash of lightning forked across the sky, briefly illuminating the group. As they made their way through the winding cobbled streets of the city like rats evading the storm, they encountered little of the city's inhabitants in the poor weather and a familiar sense of foreboding crossed over Azerrad as the party carried on.

Chapter 19

Thunder boomed and lightning continued to fork overhead as the small group proceeded on foot in the torrential rain. The group kept up a casual jog, splashing in the puddles that were quickly forming on the uneven street, trying their best to reach their goal as quickly as they could. By the time Carstair stopped them on the corner of Bridge Street, which directly overlooked the old pharmacy, the group were soaked from head to toe, their hair clinging to the sides of their head or unflatteringly across their foreheads.

'That's it,' Carstair informed them quietly.

'How sure are you its unoccupied?' Azerrad asked, not trusting the Order's intelligence after the previous two missions.

'Sure enough. But let's scout it out anyway,' Carstair suggested sounding unsure now.

The group split into two—Azerrad and Katerina went to the left, the humans to the right—to look out for any sign of inhabitants or other issues. When they were content that there were none that they could see from the outside, the smaller groups met up and made their way to the front door.

Carstair tried the handle and found that although it

was stiff, it depressed and the latch came undone, freeing the door from its resting place. It swung open slowly on its rusted hinges that groaned as they were made to work for the first time in a long time. Azerrad got the feeling that if this had been used as a hideout by the necromancer, then they were not using the front door to gain access.

'After you,' Carstair said to Katerina, feigning chivalry, but following orders.

Katerina was unaware of this but was not put off either and drew her sword before using its shining blade to push the door open more and slowly, cautiously entered the shop front. Azerrad was quick to follow but Marius and the attendant needed a little goading from Carstair to follow them in. As Carstair entered he checked the street for any sign of life, but the biblical downpour had ensured their presence went unnoticed.

The air inside was dusty and the more they moved the more dust entered the air. It was dark as most of the windows were boarded up and what little moonlight could break through was dampened by the downpour. The attendant pulled a handful of candles out of his bag, lit them one by one, and distributed them around the group. In the dull glow of the candlelight, the tall shop shelves were more visible and more imposing than they had seemed in the darkness.

The five of them rooted around, rummaging through drawers and moving debris around with their weapons or their feet. It was a fruitless task, however, as the shop was essentially ransacked of anything worthwhile, first by the departing chemists and them by the ravages of time. The wood was unloved and beginning to rot away in places, glasses lay smashed on the floor, their remnants scattered around first by vermin or other small animals and now by the clumsy rummaging of the group, though they tried their best not to make too much noise as they went about their task.

When they were happy there was nothing to be gained from the shop front, they turned to the back room. The cavernous, black hole that loomed behind a ruined pole that limply hung from the doorway at the back, barely able to keep the ragged curtain that hung listlessly from it attached, beckoned. Katerina used her blade to tear at the curtain, causing it to detach from the pole and fall lifelessly to the floor, before striking the pole with the hilt of her sword to cause it to break and fall in a clatter to ground in the curtains wake.

With the walkway clear, she bent to the floor tore a rag from the curtain, wrapped it around a broken part of the pole and lit it using her candle. Eventually the curtain caught ablaze, and Katerina tossed it through the doorway. Its glowing flame lit the room in a warm glow that illuminated almost every corner and from the shop front they could see that room appeared to be empty. Nevertheless, Katerina edged her way through the doorway slowly, taking caution before quickly moving to the far side of the room and spinning to make sure there was nothing lying in wait for them.

The speed she moved surprised all bar Azerrad; her form made it look like she shifted into a shadow and back to corporeal form in a blink. Azerrad followed her in an equally quick fashion to support if there was something waiting before Carstair strode through bullishly, almost in defiance of the caution the vampires had shown. They searched the old stock cupboards and drawers but found little of note, save for the torn page of a manuscript that Carstair snatched up from the ground before declaring that he couldn't read the writing.

Azerrad took a look and informed him it was the same language of the books that were transported here, although the torn piece was too fragmented to decipher any meaningful phrases from it. The fact it was in a language not native to Uvrenmouth at least suggested that perhaps someone had been here suspiciously. Carstair shoved the torn fragment into his coat pocket and carried on with the search.

The rest of the search found nothing and Katerina and Azerrad couldn't help but notice that the dust patterns on the floor and surfaces suggested that whoever had been here either had not been there for a very long time or had disturbed very little. Azerrad held his hand to his mouth as he mulled over the situation. He had expected more than just a slip of paper.

On the cusp of leaving, Marius lost his footing on the floor, seemingly catching it on an old tatty rug that spanned much of the floor under the debris of more broken glasses and rotten wood. Carstair caught the boy by the arm before he hit the ground full force, but his clumsiness had disturbed the lay of the rug and exposed what looked like a broken board. Azerrad knelt and pulled at the rug, revealing a series of broken and damaged boards that looked out of place in the relatively unscathed floor.

He ran his hand over the rough wood and where there was a fracture in one of the boards, slid his fingers into the gap prying the board up with unnatural ease. Underneath there was some sort of hollow; he could see that in the dim light, but as Katerina picked up the torch and held it over the boards, it was clear that they were in fact concealing a tunnel. Azerrad pulled at the next board and the next, prising them from their counterparts and laying them to the side as the extent of the hole below was revealed.

The hole was easily four feet across and dropped some seven or eight foot down. It fed into a tunnel that looked like it had been carved out by hand. In the glow of the torch Katerina held, the five members of the group who stood around the hole looked at each other unsure of what to do.

'After you,' Carstair again directed at the vampires.

The lovers looked at each other, knowing this would only end with them in the hole one way or another, and silently decided that it was better on their own terms. They found an old stack of shelves and with the help of Marius and the attendant lowered it into the hole to serve as a makeshift ladder.

'I would've just jumped in,' Carstair observed childishly.

'It's a way out not in,' Azerrad pointed out.

Carstair simply gave a grunt and gestured again for the vampires to enter the tunnel. Katerina again flung the torch into the pit and followed it down in a flash, collecting the torch and holding it aloft so that the others could easily make their way down. The air in the tunnel was stale and warm, almost oppressive as they tried to breathe in the confinement of the mud walls.

As water continued to drip from their coats and persons, the floor become slippery quickly. Azerrad checked that the shelving stack was secure in its place before Katerina headed out in front. The tunnel was tall enough that even the large frame of Carstair could fit into it easily so none of them had to crouch, but they had to make their way in single file in order to be comfortable. Azerrad followed Katerina and behind him Marius, then Carstair and finally the lowly attendant brought up the rear, still lugging the bag of weapons and tools Carstair had insisted on bringing.

Katerina pressed on into the tunnel, the others following carefully behind her. They had all drawn weapons of some kind; Katerina led with her blade, Azerrad and Marius also had blades, while Carstair and the attendant had pistols drawn. The air stifled their breath and the stench of the cave the night before came flooding back to Marius who was forced to control a heave.

The moisture present in the tunnel from their breath, the rainwater on their clothes, and the natural dampness of the earth was causing the air to become humid and uncomfortable for the group and the humans had begun to wipe sweat from their brows in the damp rankness of the tunnel.

Ahead of Katerina, it was clear that the tunnel was about to arc to the left, but it seemed as though it was going to go on forever, unrelenting. The torch's glow was only just enough to penetrate the near darkness a few feet in front of Katerina, further than that the abyss swallowed the light without remorse. Nearing the bend in the tunnel, Katerina was already several steps ahead of the rest of the party and as she pressed on it became more and more difficult for the others to steadily keep their footing in the mud which was quickly churning beneath their feet.

The air in the tunnel was still and there were few noises save for the squelch of mud beneath the group's boots and the odd movement of drier mud from the walls as an arm or weapon or bag dislodged a little as it brushed past. Time even seemed to have stalled in this world of semi-darkness and stifling air.

Ahead, Azerrad could see Katerina had made it to the bend in the tunnel that was about to take her out of sight and with it much of the light as the torch moved with her. He looked back at the humans, unsure whether he should keep a slower pace to match theirs or speed up to match Katerina's. As she disappeared around the bend, the rest were left with the small candles the attendant had given them earlier. The group lost sight of her silhouette and only the glowing walls gave a clue that there was even someone else down here.

Katerina found the air even more stifling as she made her way into the bend, tugging at her collar a little to see if she could catch more breath. The air was pitch black and she held the torch high, above her eye line to try to see further forward. That is when she heard it and stopped dead in her tracks. Ahead, though she could see nothing, there were clearly the sounds of something writhing in the dark. Clawing, scratching at the mud, muffled shrieks and inhuman noises followed that she was all too familiar with. Gradually the clawing drew closer, and a low hissing sound and the gargle of someone with fluid stuck in their throat became audible.

She kept the torch aloft, straining to see in the gloom, but it was no good. Step by step she edged further forward to meet the oncoming sound. Her eyes were wide and in the darkness the reflection of the torch light echoed in them, burning like a beacon through her gaze. For what had seemed like a lifetime she slowly edged further into the abyss, holding her ground. In reality, it had been only moments, and gradually the darkness began to move.

Ahead, the shadows wriggled and writhed as though held in place by a clear film, then she saw an arm manifest in the torches light before disappearing again. Then another, clawed and pallid, covered in cuts and dark veins. More and more limbs appeared and moved as the teeming mass became a swarm of feral vampires clamouring at each other to get forward, the only thing that gave her a moment to decide what to do.

She threw the torch at the impeding horde of ghoulish monsters which struck the ground and caused them to briefly pause, pained by the glow of the fire. But it was less than a second before they swarmed over it, extinguishing the flame, their demonic forms spurred on by the promise of fresh blood.

The rest of the group paused in the tunnel when the hissing, scratching sound echoed out from ahead. Then watched the scene play out in the light of her torch as it carried around the bend in the tunnel. They saw the light move higher, then push further away from them before dying in the near distance, shadows moving maliciously on the tunnel's walls. They held up their candles to try to see more in their meagre light and were startled as Katerina burst around the corner facing them, her eyes wide and bulging, dread and fear etched across her face, which transmitted to Azerrad's gut as he witnessed the horror she felt.

'Run!' she said in a hopeless, sorrowful voice, tears welling in her eyes as she looked upon her lover.

Frozen in fear, the soldiers looked on in horror as a mass of deformed arms grabbed at Katerina from behind. She held her arms wide, blocking their advance, but the sheer strength of the mutated forms pulled her back, enveloping her in grasping, clawing hands and biting jaws. Her porcelain skin glowed in the candlelight as red gouges and wounds appeared across it. Blood spurted from wounds in her cheeks and neck, her clothes were torn to ribbons that fluttered in the frenzy, for no wind caused them to flutter.

'No!' Azerrad bellowed as he lunged forward, arm outreached to grasp for his love.

The blood curdling cry of the vampire was too much to take, and the attendant dropped the bag he was carrying and fled back the way they had come, slipping in his terror, his fingertips grasping at the walls, mud accumulating under the fingernails of his desperate efforts. Reaching the makeshift ladder, he looked back but all he saw was darkness as he made his climb to freedom and ran for the safety of the streets.

Carstair was caught in two minds; he was outraged at the cowardice the attendant had shown in jettisoning their weapons and fleeing. But neither did he intend to die like a dog in this tunnel alongside the vermin that inhabited it. He grabbed Marius by the chest, gripping his jacket and feeling the metal Ankh he wore at his neck, pushing him backwards and forcing him to turn. This broke the transfixion that had entered him and as his senses flooded back, he turned to follow the attendant out of the hole.

Carstair stooped to get the cache of weapons and hauled them over his shoulder with one arm before looking back to see what was happening. The candles lay strewn on the floor and barely clung to life, causing the scene to play out in a series of flickering stills. More and more hands ripped at Katerina's exposed flesh, blood now gushing from her open wounds and her eyes looked blank. She struggled to no avail as her fingertips struggled at her belt, a final gift to make sure her love made it out with his life. With great struggle and more blood pouring from her mouth, she was able to release the belt from her waist causing her weapons to drop in the mud.

It was only seconds, but Azerrad felt time stop as he watched the teeming mass drag Katerina into the darkness. He had tried to pull her back to him, but the teaming mess of ravenous vampires would not let their prize go. Tears streamed down his face from eyes as red as glowing embers in the darkness. His lips had formed into a snarl that demonstrated his elongated fangs to their fullest and his chest heaved with anger, pain and sorrow. The vampires were receding now, carrying the limp form of Katerina with them as they went.

'Go,' he spat, not knowing if any of the others were even still behind him, so incensed at the atrocity he had been forced to endure. He drew his curved dagger from his belt and paced to the belt Katerina had discarded, withdrawing a matching blade from it. Rising up, the final candle flickered and as it died, Carstair caught a glimpse of the vampires' face, his bloodshot eyes full of hate, his fangs lethal and drawn, his brow furrowed so tightly he almost lost his human resemblance, and in the dark, Carstair turned and ran.

Azerrad ran the other way into the darkness, into the unknown, into the mass of vampires that taken everything from him. Furiously he sped, his feet never faltering in the churned mud, his senses spiked as adrenaline coursed through his blood. He could smell them. He could smell the old stale blood that adorned the nest's walls, he could smell the fresh blood they had made the error of spilling that night, and he could smell her. He fragrance lingered in the air, for centuries he had known that smell, it had comforted him as he struggled with his new life, loved him and been loved by him and in less than an instant they had taken that away.

The blades he wielded began to bite into flesh as he forced his way into vampire nest. The feral creatures huddled together, sucking the remnants of blood from their fingers all too distracted to put up a fight. Each swing of Azerrad's blades never missed. They punctured arms and legs, chests, and faces, causing blood-curdling screams to come from his victims. The mass of bodies was forced to release their grip on Katerina's body in a vain attempt to fend off the ferocious attack and lifelessly she slumped to the floor of the tunnel. Azerrad did not care that the fiends had released his beloved and neither did he care for the art of warfare in that moment. He wanted to take everything from them. He wanted to feel each wretched creature suffer and die by his blades. The vampires hissed and screamed as the blades went about their work cleaving limbs and punching craterous holes in their flesh.

They tried to fight back but as their claws and teeth punctured wounds in Azerrad's flesh, they never slowed him down, merely fuelling the hate-filled fire inside of him as he felt how Katerina felt. Fury caused him to drop the daggers to the floor and they fell with a wet thud in the mud bath that had developed. He lashed out with his fists, finding more pleasure in feeling bones break and flesh tear in his hands. Though he could not see it, he could feel the blood and gore that coated him, he tasted the tainted blood as it ran down his face and onto his lips and as the battle ebbed and flowed, eventually even the feral vampires began to fear their assailant as they were pushed further back into the tunnel and the darkness they had emerged from.

Some tried to run but he caught vampire after vampire, tearing at their flesh and biting at their necks, feasting on the blood and though it gave him no pleasure, the power their blood gave him rushed through is veins and drove him on. Body after body fell until finally, he could see no more movement in the darkness. The only sound he could hear was the animalistic breathing of his own chest and the gentle sound of blood dripping from him and forming pools around his feet.

He reached into a pocket and withdrew a pack of large matches. One by one he lit them and they burned fiercely but quickly and in the flashes of light he saw the carnage he had wrought. He could not tell how many he had slaughtered in his rage; the pieces of bodies were too numerous to count. His hands were crimson, as was his face and neck, his long dark hair dripped with blood and pieces of gore hung in it like grisly trophies. He made his way backwards, discarding each spent match as he went and lighting anew one until he dropped to his knees at the resting place of his lover.

Tears streamed and cut clean lines through the blood as they cascaded down his cheeks. He looked upon the ruined form of Katerina, her wide eyes lifeless, her flesh crisscrossed in wounds and peppered with deep teeth punctures. He let the last match die and hung his head in shame at the carnage he had wrought, holding Katerina close as the cries of grief came. In his despair, he had become no better than the monsters he had killed and thought how it would have broken Katerina's heart to see him like this.

But they had broken his heart and they deserved the fate they got. As the blood he drank coursed through him, he found himself conflicted and worst of all, he could already feel the hunger for more.

In the torrential rain, the attendant had fled back to the sanctuary of the Citadel. Carstair had instructed Marius to catch the attendant and make sure they entered unnoticed and to await his return without alerting others. In the down pour, bag slung over his shoulder and rain gushing from his saturated hair and clothes, he watched the chemist shop front from a distance, alone in the dismal night. For over an hour he waited, statuesque in the miserable weather before departing for the citadel. There had been no sign of the vampire and from what he saw, he was sure that Azerrad had met the same fate as Katerina.

Chapter 20

In the dark of the tunnel filled with death, Azerrad's heart heaved with sadness. The emotion seeming the only thing tethering his humanity to his body as every other inch of him ached to feed. Blood and gore filled his nostrils, but it was not the sweet scent of human blood, it was the bitter tang of the tainted blood he had spilled that night and still coursed through him. Tears still fell from his eyes, but he no longer felt he was weeping them. He couldn't bear to let Katerina go. Knowing the moment, he left this tomb he had created, he would be forced to face the reality of walking this earth without his soulmate forever more.

Finally, he found the strength to raise himself from the ground after hours of sitting and grieving at the side of ruined form of his lover. In the darkness, his hands had passed across her pale flesh, remembering it as it once was, though it was now a wreckage of bite marks and claw wounds. He had saved her from being torn apart, but he had not been able to save her life. He knew he couldn't take Katerina with him, but the thought of leaving her was too much to bear. He leaned forward, gently kissing her forehead one last time, savouring the remnants of her sweet scent before he gingerly placed her head back to the ground and pulled himself up.

Clawing himself from that wretched hole, he entered the back of the chemist's shop. The room was still dark, and, in the haze, he made out the features of the room they had searched hours ago. Fumbling around splinters of glass pierced his hands and caused small trickles of blood to emerge from his skin and blend into the blood of the vampires that already saturated him. Shaking off the dizziness he felt, he stood up tall and brushed into the shop front. The light was a little brighter here and the sun was stirring in the east. He could hear the rain still pounding on the panes of glass, a steady torrent streaming down each window.

He moved towards the door, leaning into it with his shoulder and smearing blood across its frame as he did so before emerging from it battered and bruised. The external wounds he knew would heal, but in the pouring rain he stopped in a vain effort to let their cleansing waters wash away his internal wounds. As the rain beat down upon him, a red puddle began to form at his feet as the night's exploits washed from his skin and clothes.

As his senses returned to him, he slowly spun around, surveying the area to see if there were any signs of life. It was still early in the morning and though the sun was on the cusp of rising, it had not yet really breached the horizon and in the murky weather the city lay sleeping. He realised that it was not wise to return to the Order while he still fought the hunger for blood, but he had to get out of the streets before the humans started rousing. Quietly he made his way to the old, abandoned house where he had stored his things all those months ago. Melting into the shadows, he swiftly disappeared to find refuge in the dusty, emptiness of the derelict house.

In one of the citadel's meeting rooms, Carstair and Marius sat at the oak table that took up much of the space of the room. Through the window they could see the sun rising and spraying its rays as the rain began to ease into a fine mist. In the room, a log fire burned warmly in the hearth, helping to stave off the chill they both felt as they had returned soaked to the bone. At their feet lay towels that had been brought for them to dry themselves with and on the walls the lanterns glowed a deep orange illuminating the room.

Marius itched in his chair, nervous about what was about to happen and sick from what he had witnessed that night. The things Nestor had told him resonated in his head as he thought about meeting the Grand Master face to face for the first time since his induction into the Order. Carstair, however, was comfortable enough save for the way his clothes irritated him with their dampness. He had sat here on numerous occasions for no end of different agendas and held the ear of the Grand Master so had little to feel anxious about.

'Let me do most of the talking,' Carstair said firmly but quietly to Marius, sensing the boy's nerves. 'He'll only want to know the events of the evening.'

'What's he like?' Marius asked gingerly.

'Old,' Carstair replied with a touch of sadness, 'but he carries a great deal of power in the way he talks,'

Their conversation was brought to an abrupt close as two soldiers in uniform entered the room, acknowledging Carstair with a nod before taking up ceremonial positions at the far end of the room flanking the biggest and most ostentatious chair at the table. The curtain that covered the doorway was held open by the soldier who had stood guard at its entrance while they waited, and a tall, lithe figure passed through with an ease that contradicted the aged look of his body and face.

His robes flowed as he strode across the room, seemingly hovering around the skeletal form that bore them. The Grand Master's skin was paler than usual, something to do with the fact that Carstair had not seen him in natural light for many months now, he thought. It was wrinkled at the hands and face, which were the only really visible pieces of skin to the two men that sat at the table, but the way the Grand Masters hands grasped his cane and the glint in his watchful eyes suggested to Marius that he was not as frail as his demeanour and appearance gave off.

He gave the cane to one of the attending soldiers who withdrew the regal chair so that the Grand Master could sit at the table's head. Once he was sat, a soldier entered bearing a tray of breakfast pastries and a decanter of liquor that sloshed around as it was transported. The soldier placed the refreshments on the table between Marius and Carstair before giving a gentle nod to the Grand Master who returned the subtle nod, allowing the soldier to depart.

'Eat, drink,' the Grand Master said in a pleasant tone that set Marius a little more at ease. 'You must be tired from your exploits.'

Marius greedily dived into the pastries, selecting the largest one he could find and proceeded to demolish it in record time. Carstair opted only for a glass of the brown liquor that accompanied the breakfast. He poured himself a small glass, necked the contents and then poured a larger glass and relaxed back into his chair.

'So, tell me what happened tonight,' Gallion asked, directing his words at Marius.

'Another fuck up,' Carstair began trying to deflect the Grand Master's attention.

'Marius has a tongue, does he not?' the Grand Master asked, halting Carstair's intrusion.

Marius looked up from the pastries nervously,

gulping down the mouthful he held, his eyes watering slightly as the huge partially chewed pastry made its way agonisingly slowly down his throat.

'Like Carstair said,' he spluttered as the last few crumbs escaped his lips, 'things went… south.'

'South?' the Grand Master enquired.

'There was little sign that place had been used for anything less than maybe a homeless shelter,' Carstair said again, drawing a glare from Gallion that told him to shut up or be silenced before he turned his attention back to Marius.

'Carstair found a little scrap of paper that suggested maybe someone had been there reciting spells, but it was fairly inconclusive,' Marius managed to get out.

'And the others, what happened to them?' Gallion again asked Marius.

'Dead,' Marius said but his voice sounded worried for his own safety, not sad at the revelation. 'Katerina was taken by the things in the tunnels we found under the Chemist, Azerrad followed her but there were too many, he couldn't have survived.'

'They are both dead?' Gallion asked in a quizzical manner, 'you are sure, you saw them die?'

'No,' Marius admitted shamefully, 'I ran.'

'Thank you, Marius,' the Grand Master said earnestly, 'you may leave.'

Marius did not need to be told twice, and even though he felt perhaps he shouldn't have left Carstair alone, he wanted to be as far away from the Grand Master and his questions as he could. He thanked the Grand Master for the food and left without looking at Carstair.

Passing into the hallway, he found a solider waiting to escort him away who he did not recognise. He was older than Marius by a fair few years and his grey beard suggested he had long since ceased his martial duties. He gave Marius a friendly smile before offering his arm in the direction Marius should go, though he knew how to get to his room without assistance.

The pair made their way to the staircase that led towards the dormitories and the soldier paused, letting Marius continue on his own from there. As he ascended the stairs, he looked back and could see two librarians being escorted across the great hall by another ceremonial soldier, but he thought nothing of it and retired to his quarters to process the night's events.

'Are they?' Gallion asked Carstair.

He shrugged in response before offering an explanation, his ego clearly bruised by the telling off he had received for trying to protect the boy, 'The girl was taken, she could not have survived, she was punctured by too many wounds,' he finally admitted, 'but Azerrad, that damned fool went into two, maybe three dozen of those wretched things. If he survived, he didn't surface for over an hour,'

'Could he have?' was all the Grand Master replied, not shocked or appalled by the information he was receiving.

'Maybe, but I'm almost certain he couldn't have fought off that many creatures with a single blade. It looked like a suicide mission to me,' Carstair said honestly, a pang of guilt passing over him at the memory of leaving the vampire to fight alone.

'Then it seems that the vampires are no longer our problem,' Gallion mused, 'send in the others,' he called to the guard at the door.

Once again, the curtain was held back to allow entrance to the meeting room and the two librarians Marius had witnessed being led across the Great Hall entered, a puzzled look upon their faces that turned to dread as they saw the occupants of the room. They took the seats offered to them either side of the table and sat, Edryd wriggling as he found the chair to be unusually damp.

'Please, eat if you wish,' Gallion offered as he had earlier to the young soldier that sat in Edryd's chair.

Edryd looked at the breakfast pastries eagerly, eyeing up which one to take before being subtly kicked in the shin under the table by Gassis, making him think twice before declining the offer.

When his offer was not taken, Gallion began. 'I am Grand Master Gallion,' he said proudly, 'you have been called here because of your roles aiding the vampires Azerrad and Katerina.' Gassis and Edryd stared at each other across the table nervously, unsure where this conversation was heading. 'You have both worked closely with the vampires have you not?' Gallion asked the pair.

'Yes,' Gassis said, not wishing to add any more, but sensing that it was expected from the annoyed look both Gallion and Carstair were firing at her, so she relented, 'I worked with Katerina in the vaults, we have been identifying some of the relics in the repositories there. Edryd was working with Azerrad deciphering some of the old texts in the library.'

'You have become quite close then?' Gallion pressed

'Yes,' Edryd blurted out almost defiantly.

'Why?' Gassis asked sensing something amiss.

'It pains me to tell you this, but they died last night,' the revelation hit the librarians like a ton of bricks, unable to understand or even accept that this was even possible; Edryd filled with sorrow, Gassis with rage.

'That cannot be true,' she finally said, 'how?'

'We went out to check a possible site of necromancy last night, instead we found a nest of vampires in tunnels underneath the site. They killed Katerina and Azerrad perished trying to avenge her,' Carstair informed the grief-stricken pair.

'How could they die, but you live?' she spat, tears

beginning to well in her eyes now.

'Azerrad drove them back into the tunnels so we could escape,' Carstair said but Gassis was not listening to the response.

'It is unfortunate that they should have perished like this,' Gallion interjected, 'but it is the case and there is little we can do about it now.'

Once more Gassis felt fury rise in her stomach at the indifference the Grand Master was showing to their friends.

'Little to be done now Carstair and his cowards have escaped,' she accused, firing daggers with her eyes in his direction.

'Edryd you are to continue your study on the old texts using Azerrad's interpretations. It is my hope that what you are doing will help me in deciphering the texts I am working over,' Gallion said ignoring Gassis's choler. Receiving a nod from the downbeat librarian, he turned to the animated form of the furious Gassis. She stared hard at the Grand Master, but he was not about to the shirked by a librarian and stared back equally hard. He paused as he decided her fate.

'You will return to the vaults to whatever is needed by the sister, do you understand?' he said offering a lifeline.

She rose from the seat angrily, sending it skidding back as she did and departed the room as the tears began to fall. Edryd looked to the Grand Master, unsure how to proceed. The Grand Master waved him away and he scuttled off after Gassis whose rage had taken her well down the hallway before he emerged chasing after her.

'Insolent bitch,' Carstair said holding his forehead in his hands. 'At least the timid one had the good grace to wait to be dismissed.'

'Quite,' the Grand Master spoke almost chuckling to himself. 'They could be dangerous, worse they may not even realise it themselves. Put a man on them to keep an eye on their comings and goings,' his tone changing to a more serious one. 'We could be on the cusp of a great evil here if there were as many vampires in that tunnel as you said. If the necromancer finds a way to control the monsters, we will need the entire force of the Order to fall in line.'

'Do you think that's their plan?' Carstair asked surprised at the turn the conversation had taken.

'I believe so. With the number of sightings, there should be more of these creatures breaching the city. It would appear something or someone already has some control over their movement, they merely lack the power for it to be of use at this stage,' Gallion posed.

Carstair thought silently for a second and guessed that the Grand Master was right, though he never voiced his opinion. He raised his head from his hand and looked at the Gallion who sat rather relaxed in the chair, his own spindly hand clawing intently at his chin while he thought.

'I think we are done here,' Gallion finally decided, 'don't forget to have them followed,' he reminded Carstair who had already risen, weary and cold from the night before.

'I have just the man,' Carstair said thinking of the attendant who had accompanied them last night, 'I owe him a visit anyway.'

'Good,' Gallion replied to Carstair's back.

'One last thing,' Carstair spoke over his shoulder in a hushed tone, 'what of the nest?'

'Burn it.'

Chapter 21

The days that followed the events surrounding Katerina's death were strange in the citadel. It seemed as though the whole place was on edge and despite trying to return to some sort of normality, those who had been close to the vampires found it difficult. Aside from the sense of being under constant suspicion, they found it hard to go back the mundane routine of their work having been caught up in the fantastical events of the previous months.

Nestor found himself less and less an active soldier in the order and more a babysitter for whatever tasks required supervision in the citadel; Arjan the same, though he was content to see out his tasks in relative comfort. Marius was seen less and less by his comrades, finding himself given more rewarding tasks to do.

Down in the vault, Gassis quietly succumbed to the will of the vault's Sister, returning to the cataloguing of what could only be described as the least pressing collection of artefacts in the history of the Order. She sat in sadness, slowly removing books on ancient art and piss poor portraits and landscapes that accompanied them. Why the librarians needed to catalogue artwork of this nature was beyond her comprehension, but she understood that she was being punished and tested by the Order, most likely at Gallion's behest, but possibly by order of Carstair in retaliation to her scathing comments. Either way, she hated being suppressed by lesser men.

In the library, Edryd fared the best out of the group of companions; he was the only one who had begun to understand the translations Azerrad had started with him and so long as he surrendered his work every night, life returned more or less to normal for the young lad. But he no longer looked forward to his work, lost in grief for his lost friend. He sat at his usual desk pouring over the work and drawing the same scorn he used to from the older librarians as he sought to make a name for himself in the annals of the scholastic branch of the Order. The only change seemed to be in the thawing of the frosty attitude Sister Agatha gave to him. If anything, he thought that maybe she pitied him now but the general warmer feeling he felt from her was welcomed.

Even though things had returned to normality for most in the Order, things could never be the same for those few faithful companions of the vampires. As such, the feeling of resentment towards their own people began to fester within them.

It was the third night since the incident that Carstair brought a small group of attendants to the chemist shop to set fire to the tunnel and eradicate any evidence of what had been lurking in the damned darkness underneath the abandoned building. He had entered gingerly at first, making sure that nothing lingered in the ruined shop front, he had had it watched for the three days to be sure, but he felt that one can never be too cautious when dealing with monsters. When he decided it was clear they moved in quickly with canisters of oil.

Inside the building there was an eerie silence that unnerved the group of men as they prepared to purge the memory of the place, as though some unnatural element was enclosing the backroom and shielding it from noise. At the mouth to the tunnel the bookcase still stood proudly and so Carstair took it upon himself to venture into the dark with the oil canisters. He descended into the abyss carrying two canisters, one under each arm, and silently edged into the pit. The entrance was dimly lit by the torches the attendants held up above, but the light quickly faded as it was swallowed by the dark.

Carstair had as strong constitution and it took a lot to scare him, but he crept along the tunnel in darkness, not wishing to see the aftermath of the battle and hoping that whatever had survived was long gone. Pressing on, he found himself stumbling as his feet struggled to pick their way slowly and quietly through the mass of disgorged bodies. It felt like a lifetime for him to reach a point where he no longer felt the horrific touch of a mutilated cadaver or a decapitated limb, but finally when the floor seemed clearer and the overpowering stench of rotting flesh was just a tad more bearable, he decided he had ventured far enough and began the arduous process of relieving the canisters of their payload.

Making the same slow and purposeful route backwards through the carnage and gruesome smell, he let the oil the canisters contained slowly pour out, the scent of the viscous liquid masking some of the rot that filled each breath. Making his way back, he wondered if at any time the flesh that had molested his feet belonged to Katerina or Azerrad, but in that pit of abomination he could not tell. Once he could see the dim glow of his escape in glances back over his shoulder, he shook the canisters to make sure they were empty before stepping several feet back. He discarded the canisters back in the direction he had come from and drew a book of matches from his pocket.

He lit the book and paused briefly, the glow of the

matches lighting up his face in the darkness, to reveal the stern demeanour and sallow skin of his face. He thought if he were religious then this would be the time to utter some words of praise to whatever deity would listen, but he was not, yet peculiarly he noticed that his other hand had subconsciously made its way to the Ankh that hung from his neck and was grasping it tighter than he ever remembered doing.

He tossed the matches into the dark before they burned up, the glow arcing as he did so, before the whole tunnel was illuminated by the cleansing fire as it set oil alight. Into the darkness the light fought and drove the dark away, revealing in glimpses the red stains and deep claw marks that adorned the walls. Carstair felt regret at the manner of the vampire's demise, despite his distaste for working with them it was a horrid way to go and deep down he was relieved that most of the fighting had occurred around the bend in the tunnel where he could no longer see.

He gave a last cursory glance down the tunnel, but all was silent save for the roaring crackle of the fire that now began to rage in front of him. The smell of burning flesh began to rise so he turned and left via the bookcase, which he kicked back into the tunnel as he escaped to make sure that no one would go back down there. He ordered the attendants to gather their things and instructed one to remain and ensure the fire did not find its way into the shop, though he felt he had left a sufficient gap to avoid this happening.

The attendants nodded their acknowledgement of Carstair's instructions and packed up their things, with one of them finding a comfortable spot to keep watch. As the left their comrade to his vigil, they left the shopfront in single file with Carstair bringing up the rear. In the dying haze of the torches that were extinguished as they left the building, he looked around the room, analysing the footprints that were left on the floor. Amid the new, wet prints that his party had left he could see there were older prints visible amongst them. He wondered if they had been left by them a few nights ago and began wondering if the red hue in their appearance was merely being cast by the dying light.

As the last torch went out, it broke his concentration, and he thought nothing more of it before moving out into the street with the attendants. The city was still, and a gentle, warm wind blew through its streets. In the distance, the light of taverns could be seen but their cacophonous sound did not carry into the streets that surrounded the chemist.

Carstair and the group trudged quietly in the opposite direction to the light, which was a little further out of their way, but they wanted to avoid being seen by too many that evening as they always did. Lost in thought, their pace was relatively slow until they were stopped dead in their tracks by the sound of a woman's scream that carried through the streets to them. Carstair looked around to see if anyone else heard and were making their way, but as the streets remained still, he sighed deeply and after telling the attendants to get back to the citadel, he drew a pistol from inside his coat and sped off in the direction the noise had come from.

He ran as quickly as his tired body would let him, but there had been only the one scream and without further clues as to where it was, he found it difficult to locate the source. He burst into alleyways and streets gun ready but found mainly emptiness and a few straggling drunks who could not tell him their names let alone if they heard the scream.

Finally, some distance from where they group had been, Carstair saw the shape of a human leaning forlornly against the walls of building, partially obscured by bins and almost consumed by shadows. He made his way towards the crumpled form purposefully, his eyes darting around the alley way looking for any sign of danger. Out of the corner of his eyes he swore he saw the shadows around the form move substantially, but by the time he had turned to look they were still. He couldn't tell if the shadows had lifted from the form somewhat, but he dismissed it as a trick of the light as he advanced on the body.

When he was close enough, he could see that the crumpled form that leant against the building was that of a young woman; beautiful and well dressed. He got closer and grasped her wrist to see if she was okay, but her skin was already cool to the touch, and he found no sign of life. He looked sadly at the figure in front of him – stolen of life, she could have been no more than mid-twenties and would see no more.

Carstair gently nudged her head to one side and saw what he had dreaded. Two puncture marks in the glistening skin betraying her attacker's identity. Carstair sat and thought for a while, trying to work out the best course of action. He couldn't leave her to be found as she had clearly been attacked by a vampire, but how would he get her to the citadel unnoticed? Despite his reservations he had no choice but to get her off the streets. Holstering his pistol, he stooped down and scooped her up in his strong arms.

He tried to make it look as though she had simply fainted or had too much to drink before discreetly sneaking out of the alleyway. He made it home with little issue; those who saw him took no heed of the lifeless body, as he had hoped, but all the way he couldn't help but feel the shadows were moving unnaturally in his peripheries as he went.

When he made it back the Citadel, he entered via the side gate as the attendants would have done earlier and quietly made his way to the mortuary where the Order's dead were incinerated or embalmed if they warranted such status. The room was all stone walls and unlike the rest of the Citadel, no tapestries of paintings hung there. There were several lanterns that lit the room, but they could not remove the cold lifelessness of the bare stone walls or the harsh flagstones of the floor.

He laid the body he had carried from the streets onto a stone table that was more reminiscent of an alter than a table and looked on in sadness until he was disturbed by the mortician's orderly who appeared from a small lit room at the far end of the cold building, having heard Carstair enter.

'I need this looked at when your master comes in,' Carstair said, gasping a little as he tried to catch his breath.

'Yes sir,' the orderly replied respectfully as he came over to see.

He drew a cover from a set of shelves in the room and draped it over the dead girl's feet, bringing it up over her head, pausing as he looked at her wounded neck.

'Nothing to worry about,' Carstair said sensing the boy was looking at the bite, 'it'll all be dealt with.'

'Sorry sir,' he replied, 'it's not that I am afraid, but this isn't the first one to come in like this,' he explained.

'What do you mean?' Carstair asked confused, he had not heard of any other incidents like this.

'Two nights ago, a watch brought in a young man with a bite mark like that,' the orderly said pointing to the young girl's neck.

'What watch?' Carstair asked rather impatiently.

'I'm not sure sir,' the orderly replied, 'I am not too familiar with the different watches, it was a senior soldier who brought him in though, dark skinned with a grey beard.'

'Keystone,' Carstair mumbled to himself, 'the old

fool never said anything to me, what was the verdict?'

The orderly ran to a filing cabinet that stood next to the shelves that he had drawn a towel from and flicked through one of the drawers hurriedly before returning with a small brown paper file in his hands. He handed the file to Carstair to read for himself. Carstair flicked the file open, there were only two pieces of paper in there and the information was easy to locate: cause of death – exsanguination via the neck vein.

'When did you say this cadaver came in?' Carstair pressed.

'Two nights ago.'

'You're sure?'

'Yes, definitely sir,' the orderly seemed sure of his information and Carstair ran his hands through his shaggy hair as he thought of the implications.

Handing the file back to the orderly, Carstair began putting things together and feared the worst. The Grand Master was bound to know about this, yet Keystone and Gallion had said nothing to him about it. He told the orderly to get the mortician to inform him if there was anything other than the obvious out of the ordinary about the girl and left in a fluster.

In the warm night air, Carstair thought about how to proceed. Did he confront the Grand Master? Did he confront Keystone? Or did he bide his time? He thought better than to get into anyone's faces, angry as he was, so instead he headed to the refectory to get an ale and mull things over.

The refectory was empty as it was the middle of the night and Carstair enjoyed the silence as he sat with his flagon of ale in front him. The days since the tunnel had been strange and more and more, he felt there were things going on in the Order that even he was not aware of.

His quiet reflection was interrupted as a soldier

entered the refectory and made his way casually over to where Carstair was sat. Pulling out one of the rudimentary wooden chairs that were littered around the room, he sat and looked around the room without really acknowledging the lumbering giant in the chair next to him.

'Marius,' Carstair said wearily, already tired of interactions for the evening.

'Carstair,' he replied, the familiarity irking the senior soldier a little. 'I saw you sneaking in roadkill earlier,' he slyly added.

'If it's something you need to know about, you will,' Carstair spat back already tired of the conversation before it started. 'What do you want Marius?'

'Thought I would give you an update on Nestor,' he said trying to spark some interest but when it did not come, he continued, 'seems our friend still harbours some ill feelings towards the Order after everything that has happened, might be rousing others to his cause, better to keep an eye on him.'

'Then that's what you'll do Marius,' Carstair said firmly.

Marius sat looking disgruntled at Carstair as he realised, he'd been hoisted by his own petard. Sulkily he rose from the seat, sliding it under the table with his foot and retreated from the refectory bested. Carstair drained the last of his ale through a smile before leaving behind the young soldier.

When Carstair left the refectory there was barely a sole around. The gate keeper and the few sentries were all that adorned the great hall at this hour. As he moved into the hall, he could see a significant difference in the lighting; the hall being dim compared to the glaring lantern glow of the refectory.

He could see a few of the lanterns had gone out along the corridors that branched off to other rooms and the dormitory stairs which caused great shadows to be cast around much of the far side of the Great Hall. He watched the shadows as they swayed, feeling uneasy as he did so. He began to walk over to one of the sentries but stopped and spun as he felt he was under the gaze of another. The shadows billowed and he saw shapes cast in their dance, but as quick as they appeared, they were gone, lasting only long enough to send a shiver down his spine.

He closed his eyes tightly to shake the sleep from them and continued over to one of the sentries, who saluted the senior soldier when he stopped.

'Sort out the lanterns, soldier,' Carstair said abruptly, 'it's not like you're rushed off your feet,'

'Sir?' the soldier said sounding greatly confused at the order.

'The lanterns man,' he replied starting to get irate in his tired state.

'Sir, they're all lit,' the sentry said calmly and respectfully.

Carstair spun around with a confused look painted on his face. To his surprise, he found that the hall was now properly lit, and all the lanterns of the Great Hall were alight.

'But–' he began in his confused state.

'Sometimes the wind can blow through and temporarily make them seem like they are out,' the sentry offered to try to ease Carstair, but he did not want soothing and it only made him angrier.

'Then check the fucking windows,' he said before storming off, unsure of what had just happened. Was it a trick of the wind that in his tired state he confused for something more sinister?

As he walked away the sentry looked to the other sentry who was staring awkwardly at him and both just shrugged their shoulders until one made his way around the hall checking for open doors and windows in case Carstair was watching.

He was not. The last few days had caught up with him and he had quickly retired to bed. When he pushed the old oak door of his room open, he was met with a cool chill and could see the curtains fluttering in the early morning breeze. Strange he thought, it was unusual for him to leave windows open when he was out of the citadel. Stretching out, he pulled the windows shut and locked the latch in place before he stripped into his night clothes and fell upon his bed making the sound of a tree crashing to the ground in the process. That night he slept a restless sleep.

Chapter 22

If the days following the tunnel incident had seemed to flash by in haze, then the weeks that followed that did so at an ever-increasing speed. The autopsy of the girl Carstair had found showed up nothing unusual other than a death by exsanguination, just like the young man that had come in days prior. In the weeks after, another three bodies turned up on the mortician's altar-like tables, all dead, drained of blood by neck wounds. All the victims had one thing in common: they were young, virile humans. But other than that, there were no links and no leads that Carstair and the Order could follow.

Carstair was not even sure if these were the only victims or simply only the ones that they found as the bodies became more sporadic and located some distance apart. The Watchers had failed to identify any suspect, the only thing in the reports that worried Carstair was the continued mention of shadows that moved without light nor reason. As Carstair looked down on the last victim to come into the Order's mortuary, he played with that mop of hair that now needed washing and cutting as thoughts of the watcher's reports played on his mind.

He too felt that he was being followed by a

mysterious shadow of late. Something that moved in the corner of your eye, but you could never get a fix on when you turned to look, and it was beginning to take a noticeable toll on him. He had not slept well since the night he brought the girl back to the citadel. His eyes were greying and the stubble that clung to his face made him look unkempt.

'That's number five,' the greying mortician said over Carstair's shoulder. The mortician had identified himself to Carstair as Santiago and although he was much older than Carstair, his beautiful olive skin tone and well-cut hair—even though it was grey—made him seem on a par in age to the rough form of Carstair.

'They seem to be slowing down though,' Carstair noted in reply.

'Aye, that they do,' Santiago agreed. 'You've been down here a lot lately,' he added.

'This turn of events is concerning me,' Carstair admitted.

'Quite,' the old man chuckled and Carstair turned to see what had caused his mirth, 'after all, isn't it your job to stop this happening?'

The quip cut at Carstair, but he could see the old man had not said it with any malice. Nevertheless, he was right, this was his job, to protect the citizens of Uvrenmouth from the creatures in the dark. But here they were piling up and they had no idea who the assailant was or where to find them. Carstair once again rubbed his eyes and pinched his nose in a futile effort to banish the tiredness he felt and see through the haze that had fallen across him of late. It was no good, he would have to confront the Grand Master.

The sun burned high in the Autumnal sky over the city and its warming beams flooded into the refectory through the many windows on the one side of the room. Gassis, Edryd, Nestor, and Arjan sat around one of the aging wooden tables eating their lunch, but the high spirits that once filled their group had been long banished. It had been five weeks since they were told of their comrades' fall in battle and things in the order seemed to be changing.

Nestor particularly but also Arjan and some of the other soldiers who had lent a sympathetic ear to Nestor in the past were beginning to be alienated from the core of the soldiery. They were being overlooked for any mission outside of the Citadel and increasingly given menial tasks that were more befitting the novitiates than their rank. The librarians were also being given increasingly menial work to carry out in the library and vaults if they were known to be on friendly terms with Gassis and Edryd, with only the latter carrying out anything meaningful due to his work with Azerrad.

The Order seemed to be fractured and it appeared that it was trying to remove those friendly with the vampires like a cancer cut from the body, but they were made of sterner stuff than to be routed out of their home. Regardless, something had to be done.

'We can't just sit on the side-lines while they push us further away,' Gassis finally said, breaking the silence the four had sat in for some time.

'What do you want to do? Rise up? We are few but they are many Gassis,' Nestor countered, resigned to the futility of their efforts.

'We lost our most powerful allies, Gas,' Edryd chipped in forlornly.

'So we rally more people to our cause,' Gassis pleaded, ignoring their doubts. 'There has to be more who believe in the ideals that we signed on for.'

'Maybe the librarians are more idealistic, but the soldiers are trained to follow command, they will not turn in sufficient numbers without good cause,' Nestor said, with Arjan nodding his agreement.

'So we give them good cause,' she continued, 'we tell them of the necromancer, of the writings we uncovered, and that the Order is doing little to move against this evil, surely the soldiers cannot stand such a trespass?'

The soldiers dipped their heads for they felt that it was a plan that they could never execute. Though they could not fault Gassis for her determination, they simply could not see a way to draw enough support. Edryd could see in their demeanour that they did not think it was possible and tried to reason with Gassis.

'Our best chance of support is from the librarians Gassis, but they are not soldiers, they cannot be asked to fight,' he said trying to soothe the issue.

'We cannot sit and do nothing,' she replied, determined as ever.

'We will see what we can do,' Nestor said finally relenting, 'but do not hold your breath, I do not see this going in our favour.'

'Good,' Gassis said, a slight smile creeping in her face as she realised, she had won. 'Edryd and I shall do the same.'

The four returned to their silence, realising that the precipice they stood on may be a treacherous one that they would not be able to traverse. The coming weeks would be pivotal if they were to be able to do anything to return the Order to its intended purpose.

As the sun set on another strange day over the Citadel of the Order, Carstair made the familiar climb to the Grand Master's chambers. It had been a couple of weeks since he had last spoken to Gallion and he was a little apprehensive about it now he was finally returning. The corridor was dimly lit, with only a single lantern burning and the gloom left Carstair with a pit in his stomach. Of late he had demanded that wherever he was be well lit as the shadows cast by even the most mundane thing caused him unease now.

The Grand Master's room was silent as it often was; Gallion would normally be found pouring over the books that had come from Jatrador these days. He rapped gently at the oak door and waited until he was summoned inside. Sure enough, sat at his impressive desk in his throne-like chair and dress robes the gaunt figure of the Grand Master arched over a dusty old book. Several others lay open on the desk and one to his right lay open next to a quill and ink, Carstair could see that the Grand Master had been recording something down on the open pages.

The Grand Master did not look up from his work, he knew who it was at his door and knew that Carstair would eventually take a seat and pour a glass of liquor from the decanter on the small table that sat next to his usual chair. Carstair did just as was expected of him. In the green upholstered seat that Carstair always choose, he rolled the brown liquid back and forth in the crystal glass, watching as it sloshed about like a tiny raging sea caught in his hand. He was unsure how to proceed and thought it better to let the Grand Master take the lead, so patiently he formed a mini tempest in his palms, his eyes transfixed on the liquid storm.

'You look terrible,' Gallion said without actually looking up at Carstair, 'you have not come by here in recent weeks.' The statement was meant as a question and Carstair realised this so finally broke his silence.

'There has been a lot going on,' he muttered, 'strange shit that I don't understand.'

'Don't you normally come to me when there is something you don't understand?' Gallion asked, picking up the quill and forming another line of notes in the open pages of the book to his right. The long arching strokes of his spindly fingers forming immaculate letters on the canvas before them.

'You haven't exactly been forthcoming of late,' Carstair said, the words sounded accusing, but he hoped the Grand Master would not take them that way.

'If I have been guarded it has been for the good of the Order, my old friend,' he replied in a gentler tone. 'You have known everything you have needed to, I assure you of that.'

'Have I?' Carstair asked unsure whether to believe Gallion's words, 'seems like every time I have been out lately something unexpected has happened.'

'I am not a psychic, Carstair,' the Grand Master said, keeping his tone constant and giving away no indication of anger at the line of questioning. 'Things happen in the moment. We can only prepare based on the advice we are given.'

'You've seen the bodies mounting up in the mortuary, have you?' Carstair asked already knowing the response.

'I am aware,' Gallion confirmed.

'Keystone inform you?' Carstair asked, this time meaning to accuse the Grand Master.

'Is that why you have been sulking? Because another senior soldier here carried out a task and never told you?' Gallion asked, never wavering in tone, but his words made Carstair feel like a little boy being scolded by a parent.

Unsure how to react, he merely grunted at the reply and downed the liquor in his glass before topping it up.

'I have told you before that I consider you the most loyal of the soldiers here, but you are not the only soldier here,' Gallion explained and Carstair felt more and more childish. 'My plans for the Order are advancing and I will need you more than ever in the coming weeks.'

'For what?' Carstair asked confused about what plans Gallion was talking about.

'When the time is right I will reveal all, do not worry about that. But for now, I need you to trust me,' Gallion said, finally looking up from the books to gauge Carstair's reaction.

Looking into the tired, bloodshot eyes of his loyal servant the Grand Master felt a little sorry for him, but he needed to know where his loyalty lay. Carstair nodded in agreement that he trusted the Grand Master and his plans, even if he was unsure deep down. Perhaps once he knew the plans, he could be more sure.

'Tell me, 'The Grand Master continued, 'what have you made of these recent attacks?'

'They are the work of a vampire,' Carstair replied, 'all of them.'

'Yes, that much is obvious,' Gallion quickly added, 'same one?' he asked.

'Probably,' Carstair agreed.

'Do you think it is him?' Gallion asked and Carstair knew immediately who the Grand Master was referencing. The thought had been a constant plague on Carstair's mind since the first time he saw the girl in that cobbled alleyway.

'Yes,' Carstair said truthfully, and it felt like a small weight had been lifted from him.

'But you were sure he perished in that accursed tunnel,' Gallion said again letting the statement act as a question.

'I never saw him leave but I never saw him die either, perhaps the events changed him, or perhaps he was always what I expected,' Carstair revealed. 'What monster would know the city well enough to avoid detection for so long from our watcher's?'

'Indeed,' Gallion softly bridged his hands across his

chest as he thought. 'This thought has crossed my mind also.'

'It is not just a thought Grand Master, I feel as though I am being haunted by him.'

'Haunted?'

'Yes, my sleep is rife with images of monsters and monstrous acts, the very shadows of the rooms I pass seem to form into shapes and disappear when seen, I feel like he is... around me.' Carstair was unsure how to put into words the strange feeling of surveillance he felt, but he had to tell someone before he lost his mind.

'Tricks of the mind are powerful things sometimes. Perhaps you should seek the council of the physicians on the matter,' Gallion's suggestion was received as an order by the loyal Carstair and he rolled his eyes but nodded in agreement.

Outside the wind howled and caused the window to rattle gently in its frame. From somewhere a draft simultaneously swept through the room and caused the fire burning in the hearth to roar into life from its gentle flames and made the lantern light flicker around the room. Carstair watched the shadows throw themselves around the walls in the lantern's flickers and nervously drained his glass again as the familiar strange feeling came over him.

Gallion watched as Carstair did so and rose from his seat, his robes flowing down from his shoulders and almost touching the floor, billowing around his ankles in the draft. He slid the chair back under the desk and turned to make his way over to the window. He did so far quicker than Carstair would have thought possible from the old man's decrepit form, but he was more concerned with the shadow show that was enacting on the walls.

Gallion peered out of the great, arching windows in front him into the gloominess of the autumn night. There were few clouds obscuring the sky and the stars shone brightly, winking back at the city as it buzzed into life. The darkness of the streets beaten away by the bright orange glow inside the city's taverns and restaurants and in the unusually warm evening breeze, the Grand Master could see the citizens swarm about without care. The city folk looked like ants to the Grand Master from so high and he felt a degree or resentment pass over him as he thought of how easy they found life not knowing of the struggles his Order went through to keep things that way for them.

Carstair sat quietly as the lanterns regained their composure and watched the fire as it crackled and spat little embers onto the expensive and intricate rug in front of it. He poured himself another glass of liquor as he inspected the rug, finding little black singe marks throughout. It seemed a shame that such a beautiful thing had been so recklessly used by the Grand Master and began to fear that it might be a metaphor for how the Grand Master was using him also, but he was not the kind to think in metaphors thankfully.

Eventually Gallion turned away from the window and made his way to the fireplace where the fire was slowly ebbing away. He rummaged through the pile of logs that lay at the fireside until he found one that suitably pleased him and tossed it on the fire before reaching for one of the black metal pokers that hung by the wood pile. Using the poker, he stoked the fire into life and his pallid flesh was lit in an unearthly orange glow, the flames reflecting in the blackness of his eyes.

'Perhaps it is time I revealed to you my plans for the Order,' Gallion said turning now to look at Carstair with what looked like concern.

Pleased to know he might finally be able to get a grip on things that were happening, Carstair nodded and began to cheer up a little, visible from the gentle smile that passed his lips.

'I will send for you tomorrow and all will be revealed, but for now see the physician and get some rest,' Gallion promised.

Carstair wanted to protest and Gallion could sense the words were about to come out of his mouth so he raised a bony finger to stop them.

'Tomorrow,' he said and Carstair knew that it signalled the end of the meeting.

He downed his third drink and rose from his emerald chair, leaving a slight depression where his large frame had sat, and made his way from the Grand Master's chambers as Gallion returned to provoke the fire once more. As he carefully shut the door, he could have sworn that the Grand Master was talking into the flames, but he was in no position comment on another's sanity while his hung by a thread. He entered the dimly lit corridor and decided that getting something to help him rest might be a good idea after all and made his way to the physicians' offices.

Chapter 23

That night, Carstair drank the tonic that the physicians had prescribed as he sat on the edge of his bed looking out into the darkened sky. He thought it strange that although all was black, he could not see the twinkling of any stars that night. That was the last thing that he remembered as he sank into a deep and dreamless sleep.

When the sun rose on his still form it was still many hours before he finally stirred. The tonic had done its job and he felt more refreshed than he had in a long time following the deep sleep. He sat up in the bed and ran his hands over his face to wake himself up before deciding to shower and get something to eat. As he stood, he realised he had no idea what time of day it was and looking out of the window he could see the sun was reaching its apex.

Once he had washed and dressed, he headed to the refectory for a light breakfast that was really more like lunch and some strong coffee. He sat contentedly as the soldiers and librarians came and went, realising that he had not felt this good in a long time. He watched the lunchtime come and go and aside from a few deathly stares from the bane of his existence, Gassis, the time passed quietly and without note.

Once he had finished refuelling, he decided to make use of his time until he was summoned by heading down to the mortuary and do some investigating of his own. He had not heard of any new bodies being found or brought to the Citadel but felt it would be best to go and get the information first-hand for himself.

He made his way across the courtyard and found himself taking his time to enjoy the cool breeze on his face as it rustled through the hair that overhung it. He knocked firmly on the door and entered, not waiting for a recognition of his knock. The air inside was equally as cool as the courtyard, mainly owing to the stone walls and lack of warming adornments thereof. It was still fairly dark in the room as it had no windows and as such no natural light ever entered. The lanterns of the wall were lit, however, and two six-foot candelabras that held several burning candles were present, no doubt a way of moving the light source for the mortician.

Carstair scanned the room but found no signs of life. The stone tables were empty and wet, which led Carstair to believe that the orderly must have been washing them sometime recently and must still be around somewhere. The air smelled almost sickly sweet of flowers, an old trick to hide the smell of death of and decay, but Carstair was used to that, not the floral scent that assaulted his nostrils.

Straightening his waistcoat, he began to look for the mortician or his orderly. He found them crammed into the back office where the orderly had appeared from the first night Carstair had come here. The orderly jumped up with a start at the imposing sight of the senior officer, but the mortician, Santiago, simply remained seated, smiling at the doorway.

'Master Carstair, your visits are becoming increasingly frequent, I hope we are not under some sort of surveillance,' the old man joked and began laughing at himself.

Carstair smiled a little awkwardly at the insinuation before diving straight into the crux of his visit. 'No, no, you mistake my purpose, I am not here officially,' he explained.

'Then pull up a stool and get some coffee,' Santiago said, the smile still beaming on his face, 'Klein, get Carstair a cup,' he instructed.

The young orderly did as he was instructed, returning with a mug so that Carstair could help himself to the pot of coffee. He then drained his own mug and took his leave to let the senior members talk. He returned to his mop and bucket a little dissatisfied at losing the chance to savour his drink and break.

'So, what brings you back?' Santiago asked, sipping at his coffee.

'Have any more bodies come in lately?' Carstair asked, 'like the others, I mean,' he added for clarification.

'Like the exsanguinated souls?' the old man asked sadly.

'Yes, I brought the girl here on the 5th of September and your orderly informed me that the guy was brought in on the 3rd,' he said as though ordering the events in his mind.

'You are quite right, then the third body came to me on the 12th but had probably died closer to the 10th,' Santiago added.

'Then the 17th and 28th according to the reports, right?' Carstair asked.

'Yes,' came the reply, 'but I am a little confused at what you are getting at. They all died the same way, same wounds, the positioning of them was almost identical too.'

'The point is that the attacks appear to have been

slowing down, and it is the 15th of October now, that's almost three weeks without a corpse being found,' Carstair said explaining his train of thought.

'Thant's a good thing though, right?' Santiago said, this time needing clarification.

'On the face of things, yes.'

'But?'

'I haven't seen any reports that there have been any vampire kills since the last body wound up on your slab, which means that either whatever was doing this just stopped or we are no longer finding the victims,' Carstair outlined his fears and he saw the demeanour of the mortician change a little at the events that could be unfolding.

'Dear God,' Santiago was genuinely a little shaken by the thought, 'do you think there could be more out there?'

'I don't know,' Carstair said honestly and grimly. 'Thank you, Santiago, you have been much help,' he added before quickly shaking the old man's hand and leaving the small room they had sat in, his coffee nearly untouched on the side by the pot. Carstair breezed out of the mortuary quicker than the orderly could make a comment, leaving only a slamming door in his wake.

Santiago slumped in his chair in thought as Klein appeared at the door. Noticing Carstair's untouched coffee, he retook his seat on the stool in the corner and decided to help himself before enquiring what was wrong with his mentor.

Nestor watched with intrigue as Carstair left the mortuary and stormed across the courtyard quickly before disappearing into one of the doors that led into Citadel's corridors. He puzzled at the scene that had briefly unfolded; Carstair did not look as though he was angry as he stormed across the courtyard, but troubled. He checked on the attendants he was supervising in the stables were hard at work and would not notice his absence before sneaking off to find Marius and Arjan to discuss what he had seen.

Inside the Citadel, Carstair made his way to the gate keeper like a bullet, refusing to be impeded by the bustling crowds in the great hall. When he reached the small room where the gate keeper resided, he rapped the door impatiently. When it opened, he did not wait to exchange pleasantries.

'Where are the Watcher records?'

'I have the ones that have come in from this week here,' the gate keeper said stretching out an arm and indicating a pile of papers stacked on the desk in the small cabin.

'And the others?' Carstair asked as though he had obviously meant more than this week.

The gate keeper looked at him a little flustered by the intrusion and urgency Carstair seemed to be pressing him with, 'They will have gone to the library for archiving if they had no relevant information, or to...' the gate keeper paused looking at Carstair.

'Or?'

'Or you, sir. Or whichever senior soldier is on duty if they have information that needs acting on,' the gate keeper explained and Carstair realised that he looked a little foolish asking questions that he knew the answers to.

'Gimme that pile there,' Carstair said gesturing at the pile of reports.

The gate keeper could see that Carstair meant business and did not try to protest, instead reaching quickly to grasp the pile of papers and handing them over to the disgruntled Carstair.

He took them and turned without thanking the bewildered gate keeper who was just glad to shut the door and return to his quiet afternoon shift.

Carstair strode, papers in tow, towards the library as he prepared to sift through them, a task he was not relishing. Entering the library, he saw Edryd deep in study over the books he and Azerrad had been translating. He made his was quickly to the front desk to speak to the Sister and find out who had been tasked with archiving the reports.

Sister Agatha informed him that it was a new recruit to the librarians called Asmund who had been given the task as a noviciate to the librarians. Carstair thanked her insincerely and found the boy Asmund, taking the desk next to him. He placed the papers on the desk and turned to speak to the startled boy.

'Asmund, right?' Carstair began, 'I am Carstair, I am one of the senior officers here.'

'I know,' Asmund said sheepishly.

'Good,' Carstair replied, 'I need you to do something for me. You are archiving reports that our watcher network bring back to us, I need you to find every report as far back as the 3rd of last month, do you understand?'

The young lad nodded his understanding before looking at the work in front of him; it was an imposing prospect. As Asmund set to his task retrieving the relevant binders of reports and removing all the ones from the 3rd onwards, Carstair sat and began reading through the new ones he had received from the gate house moments ago.

As time pressed on, Carstair had unearthed zero mention of anything vampire related in the reports. The watchers had seen no dubious behaviour, no attempted infiltration of the city by a suspected vampire, nor any kills that were attributed to vampires. When he had finished with the new ones, he began on the reports Asmund was pulling out and made his way through those too. Only once he was disturbed as many of the librarians finished their day's work and left, including

Edryd who, having already clocked Carstair, made his way past without making eye contact and met a group of other librarians including Gassis.

'I didn't think he could read,' Gassis quipped to the group loud enough that Carstair could hear but he was too preoccupied to do anything about it and the group moved on.

The sun had set an age ago and Asmund had left Carstair to his work having pulled all of the reports he had requested out of the relevant binders. There were few people left in the library, save for the night Sister who had taken over from Sister Agatha and a few of the older librarians who used the evenings to read for pleasure or their own research. He had read every report from that day back to the day the first victim had been found and he found no mention of anything out of the ordinary.

He tossed the final report on the scattered pile in front of him in disgust at his failure to uncover anything. He leant back in his chair, stretching his arms out before letting them rest behind his head, his hands interlocking to take the weight of his head as he leant back. He sighed audibly which drew scorn from the elder librarians whom he ignored. He was about to clean up the pile so that it would be a bit neater when Asmund returned in the morning, but he was interrupted by a panting soldier who also drew the scorn of the library's patrons. Carstair hushed him and directed him out of sight of to talk.

'The Grand Master has sent word, he cannot meet with you this evening,' the soldier said, 'I've been looking for you, I didn't expect to find you... here, sir.'

Carstair frowned at the instigation, 'I know how to read,' he blurted out more for his own peace of mind. The soldier stared, a little taken back by the outburst.

Carstair dismissed the soldier curtly, annoyed at Gallion's delay. Leaving the library, he found the great hall had quietened down, though there was still a buzz of noise coming from the refectory as the soldiers and librarians that had finished their duties went to get their evening meal. Carstair was pleasantly surprised at how normal everything seemed this evening and despite his disappointment at the Grand Masters avoidance, he thought he could do some more digging into the past few weeks to make better use of his time.

The gate keeper was even less enthusiastic than earlier to see Carstair making his way in his direction again, not least because his shift was moments from ending. Carstair could see the look of reluctance in the gate keeper's face, but he couldn't care less how a soldier with such a comfortable position felt at his intrusion.

'I need to know something else,' Carstair said.

'What can I do for you?' the gate keeper replied, feigning sincerity.

'I would like to know if any of the watches have returned with anything,' Carstair explained.

'Anything?' the gate keeper moaned, 'that doesn't narrow it down does it.'

'Well, I don't mean a fucking trinket, do I?' Carstair barked, annoyed at the gate keeper's attitude, 'something more along the size of a human,' he added with a frown.

The gate keeper rustled through a few pieces of paper in a pigeonhole at his back and emerged with two notes, handing them to Carstair without saying anything, before his eyes lit up to see his relief coming on shift and granting him freedom from the cubicle that Carstair had made quite uncomfortable to be in today.

Carstair read the notes quickly and saw the look on the gate keeper's face. He raised the notes in the air to gesture he was taking them with him and headed through the huge front doors of the Citadel as the two gate keepers exchanged roles.

The night was breezy, and the dark was already creeping in, making the pathway to the stables dark and shadowy. He browsed over the notes again, squinting in the poor light but it was barely legible in the gloom, so he stuffed the notes into his pocket and strode into the stables.

The stable was quiet, the horses gently brayed as they ate their supper and the single night guard stirred from his semi-sleep-like state, spilling the half-drunk mug of coffee that was precariously resting on his gut and kicking the stool his feet were resting on flying across the stable floor. He got to his feet, straightened his top, wiping the coffee away as best he could.

'Have you been the attendant on every night this week?' Carstair asked, deciding against pointing out the attendant's lax attitude to guarding in the night.

'Aye sir,' the attendant confirmed.

'So, you were here when the watch brought back a 'six-foot item wrapped in liniment' three nights ago?' he said reading from the note he had drawn from his pocket.

The attendant wriggled on the spot, uncomfortable with line of questioning he was being presented with. Carstair could see from the way he squirmed and the way his eyes could not hold Carstair's gaze that he had been and for some reason was either unwilling to divulge that information or was under instruction not to.

'Your dancing has given away the answer,' Carstair said sarcastically, 'now tell me what you know.'

'They brought something in, all wrapped up in great bandages,' the attendant relinquished.

'Go on,' Carstair urged.

'It folded like you would expect a person to when handled, but there was no blood that I could see and they never took it to the mortuary, they told me to forget what I'd seen.'

'Who did?'

'They were riders, head to toe in black, their faces were hooded, I couldn't make out who they were from their voices, but they knew the Citadel well enough,' the attendant blurted out.

'Knew it well? How do you know?' Carstair asked.

'They took whatever they brought in through that door on the far side of the courtyard and I ain't ever seen anyone go through there, so they must've known where they were heading.'

Carstair sent the attendant back to his seat to keep vigil on the horses but warned him about doing the job he had been assigned to do. He then turned his collar up to the breeze and headed over to the door that the attendant had pointed to. When he got there, he realised that he didn't know the door. It was old, much older than any of the other doors of the Citadel and Carstair thought that when they had replaced the old rotting doors, they must have missed this one. It was oak, but the wood was a faded brown that almost looked grey in the moonlight. The hinges that had once been black, wrought iron, now held an orange tinge of rust all over them and the bolts and handle looked in equally dilapidated a manner.

He placed a hand on the door, running his fingers over the ancient wood, before looking around to see if he was being watched. He could see the attendant's fire winking to him from the other side of the courtyard, but despite the uneasy feeling he felt, he appeared to be alone. He eyed all around the doorway trying to figure out where in the Citadel it could lead to but the closest thing he could figure were the cells under the Citadel, but not only did he know there was no external entrance to them, they were still a little way away by his estimation.

He tugged at the handle and gentle pushed himself against the wood, but it did not budge one bit and he stared at the strange keyhole that lay under the handle he was holding. The keyhole was in the centre of a great brass bat and looked newer than any of the other metalwork held on the door. He tried a few of the usual keys that he kept on the keychain resting in his pocket, but nothing seemed to do the trick.

Annoyed at his failings, he headed back into the Citadel and returned with a crowbar. He wielded the blunt instrument with ease, wedging it into the door and after several agonising minutes as he tried to keep the noise he was making to a minimum, he finally dislodged the door from its resting place, which then flung open and Carstair was hit with a familiar scent.

Before him he could see a flight of stairs that descended more or less straight down from the open door and the air was stale and filled with the sickly scent of blood. He went to the stables and found a torch which he lit and returned to the busted door and made his way into the darkness. The stairs were narrow with walls either side and even though he held the torch out in front of him, he could not see far ahead as the flames struggled to penetrate the gloomy haze that filled the space.

Steadily he made his way down, the stairs were precariously wet and slimy and all Carstair hoped was that it was moss and algae that were making them so. Finally, he reached the bottom and found himself in a small room barely able to contain him. The walls were made from un-rendered concrete and the flagstone floor was damp with small puddles everywhere. In front of him stood another door, though this one looked more rotten from the damp than the one upstairs he had prised open.

He tried the door's latch and found that the cool metal was not locked in anyway and released the door with relative ease. The door squeaked open as the damp wood complained at being moved and Carstair ventured through, torch held out in front of him. Ahead of him he could see was a corridor and on either side, he thought he could see the glint of metal bars. Curious, he thought, it seemed like another cell block, but he had not known it was here, nor had he ever heard it spoken of.

He found that there were older torches hanging in hooks that were attached to the walls. As he passed them, he lit one then another and slowly the darkness began to lift, and the corridor was bathed in an orange glow. Now he could see that he was right, the sides of the corridor were indeed lined with metal barred cells of some sort.

'Fuck me, what the hell is holed up in here?' he whispered out loud to the gloom.

For the first time in a long time Carstair felt genuinely scared to proceed along the corridor. The air was rank, and shadows cast by the flickering torches made him nervous. But he summoned all the courage he could and moved in front of the first set of bars, holding the torch high so that he could better see. The cell appeared empty at first and a sigh of relief passed over him, but as he continued to stare into the abyss, he saw the unmistakable signs of something moving, albeit slowly.

As he continued to stare into the cell his face was almost pressed against the cold bars as he strained to view what it held. Slowly, the thing inside made its laborious way into the light of Carstair's torch. When it did become clear what he was looking at Carstair felt sick to his stomach. He reeled backwards at the decaying form of the vampire in the cell, stumbling back into another cell behind him. As his back pressed against the bars an arm shot out from the cell and tried to claw at his chest. Carstair jumped and swatted at the mangled arm with his torch, realising that as he did so there was a dying werewolf in the cage, barely able to make any noise.

He made an effort to get into the middle of the corridor as far away from either side as possible to regain his composure. His heart was pounding hard in his chest, almost unbearably so and he realised he needed to light more torches. He made his way to the next two and lit them both allowing him to see into the next set of cells. The one he was looking into was empty as far he could tell and stunk to high heaven, but as he turned around, he was sent sprawling backwards again as a far sprightlier vampire lunged at him through the bars of the cell.

He looked at the creature as it struggled to get near to him, the mutated face biting and drooling as the pallid arms flayed wildly. The damn thing must be starving, he thought with disgust and waved the torch in its direction to try to drive it back somewhat. The torch had the desired effect as the creature bayed away from the burning flames.

There were only two more cells left and Carstair dreaded what he might find in them but carried on anyway. He lit the remaining two torches, the corridor was now quite well lit, and in the cells that were left he made another grisly discovery. There were not vampires or werewolves in these cages, but the rotting corpses of humans, reanimated to life without humanity nor dignity. Upon seeing Carstair the decaying forms made their way to the bars and sluggishly reached through trying to grasp the soldiers clothing.

Carstair had seen enough of this pit of horrors and drew one of the pistols from his jacket and cocked the pin before aiming it in the direction of the revenants in the cell before him. He took aim but paused at the realisation that was dawning on him. One of the poor bastards in there that had been left to rot was the ruined face of Gideon. His eyes seemed human, but his skin was rotting, almost melting away from his skull and the low groans that escaped his mouth were anything but human. As a wave of remorse crashed over Carstair he heard movement in the corridor and swung to see what it was, his pistol aimed and ready to fire.

In the corridor before him were two soldiers of the Order and a tall thin person completely hooded and draped in black robes. As Carstair held the gun out, his arm beginning to tremble as he heard a familiar voice.

'No need to point that at me, old friend,' the Grand Master said, lowering his hood to reveal himself. 'Perhaps we should have that talk after all.'

Chapter 24

The Grand Master's room was unusually dark. The only source of light came from the fire in the hearth that burned with its usual lustre, but none of the lanterns or candles—that seemed to be permanently lit to aid Gallion as he poured over texts— were alight. The sole source of illumination gave the room an unearthly feel and the whole scene was made even creepier by the billowing curtains that rustled in the breeze that entered through the open window. Outside of which, all was black.

Carstair was still shaken by the events of the evening and was downing the usual brown liquor that the Grand Master kept in his chambers at a rate of knots. His hands were gently trembling, and he had yet to process the things he had witnessed in the secret dungeons. He couldn't help thinking about what else the Grand Master could be covering up. After what seemed to him like an entire age of man, he heard some noises coming from doorway to his back.

Carstair turned around to see the Grand Master in the same black robe he had been wearing in the corridor of horrors, with the hood pulled over his head again. In the darkness he was barely visible and the whole charade of the evening gave Carstair the chills. The Grand Master passed across the room swiftly and took a seat at the large desk he was often found at and flipped through a book that lay open until he found the page he was looking for.

Carstair dragged his favourite green chair over to the fireplace and sat down apprehensively. He knew it was ridiculous, but in the dim light of the Grand Master's chambers, he found himself more comfortable in the glow of the fire. He tried to look at Gallion as best he could but found the aura the Grand Master gave off made it difficult for him to keep his eyes trained on him.

'Do you know what this is?' Gallion asked patting the book in front of him with reverence.

'There are more pressing questions to answer than talking about a damned book' Carstair said more hostilely than he had anticipated but he was highly strung and wanted more than anything to know what was going on in the Citadel.

'Do you know what this is?' Gallion repeated himself again touching the old pages of the ancient book that sat in front of him, ignoring his protests.

'A book,' was all Carstair would offer, tired already of the Grand Master's games.

'Literally, yes,' the Grand Master said, though he was not losing patience, 'then let me ask you, do you know what this book represents?'

'It came from the collection that arrived from Jatrador, one of the books we were warned about,' Carstair replied curtly.

'That it is,' Gallion spoke smoothly, a wry smile passing his lips. 'This book represents victory for the Order, Carstair, it is this organisation's reckoning and through it I will lead us into a new era.'

The words fell from Gallion's mouth so smoothly it was as though he had practiced them a thousand times over, but Carstair knew the Grand Master's true power lay in his oratory. Carstair remained seated but his hands began to grip the arm of the chair tighter as the Grand Master spoke.

'I have been working hard to translate the books, and while the young librarian has been an unwitting accomplice in this matter, I have managed to unlock many of the wonders of the collection and this book, the book the vampire sought to conceal all that time ago is the key to unlocking the power the books hold,' Gallion continued, his eyes barely moving from the pages of the old tome, drawn to them it seemed by some other power. 'We have been taught to fight the things in this world we do not understand, first we banished them to the night, then we spent our nights persecuting them to the brink of extinction, when all this time we could have controlled them.' The Grand Master's words became more animated as he spoke, his voice rising in a crescendo.

Carstair remained rooted to the chair, his mentor was beginning to sound like a madman and the horrors he had witnessed in the dungeons only served to perpetuate that image, but the power of his words kept him silent and still, the knuckles of his hands whitening as they gripped the chair's arms.

'It was I alone who began harnessing the power of these books. I awoke the city,' Gallion's voice had returned to its usual tone as he revealed the truth triumphantly, 'I turned our city into a beacon for the unnatural to wield the power held within the pages of this book.'

Finally, Carstair found the strength to rise from his seat, 'You're the necromancer,' he almost whispered as the grim reality of the situation flooded his senses.

'Necromancer, saviour, deliverer, it is not important what name you have for me,' Gallion said in a determined tone. 'I will make the city remember why they fear the dark, and I will make the city remember who it is that protects them from the monsters that stalk it.'

Gallion's tone had begun to take on a sinister, threatening edge and Carstair's mind was swimming with the information that was overloading it.

'What you're talking about goes against everything the Order is supposed to stand for,' Carstair replied almost pleading for the Grand Master to see sense.

'The Order is the only thing between Uvrenmouth and the darkness, why shouldn't we remind the people what that means? This was once a powerful place and look what it has become. Filled with drunkards, vermin. And they look down on us?' Gallion spat, his words increasing in their venom.

Carstair turned away from the fire to look at his mentor who remained seated at his desk, his spindly fingers tracing lines over the open book.

'What you're talking about is madness,' Carstair cried, 'what you've got holed up beneath the Citadel is madness.'

'No, it is deliverance,' Gallion shot back rising from his chair to meet Carstair's imposing form, though his skeleton-like appearance was no match.

'Deliverance?' Carstair questioned but he was cut off before he could say anymore.

'If you do not stand with us, then you stand in our way,' Gallion continued, his voice getting more forceful.

Outside the door, Carstair heard the faint noise of armoured soldiers moving along the corridor and settling at Gallion's door, no doubt the ones who had escorted him from the dungeon up here in case things did not go the way Gallion wanted.

'What of all the people who may die as a result of this? Those who have already lose their lives to the monsters you bring here?' Carstair asked, trying to reason with the humane side of Gallion.

'There are always casualties in war,' was the reply.

'So that is what this is... War,' Carstair said regretfully.

'You are a soldier are you not? This is what you were bred for,' Gallion said trying to stoke the fires in Carstair. 'Besides, it will be a quick war if I control the creatures that we are fighting.'

'If?'

'Yes, regretfully I never got to test the full potential of my new-found knowledge on the monsters we kept as pets. I knew that they would need to give in to their animalistic tendencies for me to control them, they harboured far too much humanity before,' Gallion revealed and Carstair knew that the Grand Master had crossed a line he was not going to return from.

'You set the whole thing up?' Carstair said a tear welling in his eye.

'You couldn't know my friend, not then.'

'I led people to their deaths,' he replied ruefully.

'A necessary evil,' Gallion said softening his tone, 'the city has been kept safe by the blood of our people for centuries, this is the way it has always been, but what fanfare do we receive? What thanks is there in a population that barely even remember monsters are real?'

Fear and anger welled inside Carstair to hear his mentor talk like this but deep down he also knew that what Gallion was saying was in part the truth. They had become almost social exiles to the people of the city, scurrying around in the dark, but that was for the good of the populace.

'By making them remember what it is our people protect them from, perhaps they will honour our fallen heroes, this is our chance to write ourselves into the annals of history Carstair,' the Grand Master began pressing home his sell. 'My predecessors did a huge dishonour to our Order by allowing the world to forget who we are and what we stand for.'

'There are better ways to do it than raising the dead,' Carstair said in a raised tone.

'Do not act holier than thou, you have as much blood on your hands as I do, or have you forgotten the civilians you have 'silenced' to protect the city from the things in the dark?' Gallion's next gambit bit at Carstair's conscience and momentarily drained him of his fight. 'What you did was for the greater good of the city and that is exactly what I am doing now.'

Carstair began to waver, he thought of the young girl he had shot and buried in a shallow grave on the outskirts of the town the night he met Azerrad. He thought of the woman he had abandoned and left to die in the warehouse. They could have been saved if he had helped them, but he had felt no pity for them then. Then he thought of Gideon, the ruined face of his reanimated corpse fresh in his memories.

'Sometimes the line between good and evil is blurred and difficult to traverse, do not blame yourself for making the hard decisions,' Gallion said gently, absolving Carstair of the responsibilities of his actions.

'What I did, I did to protect the Order. How can this be in our best interests?' Carstair asked, 'I did not even know what was happening.' His voice broke as he realised how far from the Order he felt in that moment, how disconnected from his brothers and his home.

'There are few who do,' the Grand Master replied, 'I have a handful of soldiers enlisted to do what needed to be done, but I could not tell you until the time was right.'

'Would you have told me if I had not found your chamber of horrors?' Carstair spat furiously but Gallion did not reply. His silence was damning.

Carstair's face began to become pink as he raged

inside himself. He didn't know what to do, he felt utterly betrayed, deeply hurt that the Grand Master, the person he looked to as a father, didn't trust him. In his anger he drew the small silver dagger from within his waistcoat. He did not usually go before the Grand Master armed, but he had come straight from the dungeons. Gallion watched in sadness at Carstair's actions and called for the guards who had been at his door.

The soldiers charged through the door at Gallion's behest to see the lumbering form of Carstair lunge in the Grand Master's direction at a speed that belied his figure. The Grand Master recoiled from the desk in a measure of self-preservation and then both he and the guards watched in confusion.

Instead of attacking the Grand Master, Carstair fell to one knee, drawing the blade across his palm so that crimson blood spilled into the closed fist that he had formed. He grasped the Ankh that hung from his neck and streams of blood began to run down it as he grasped the silver form.

'The Order is my life and I swear my life to the Order's will,' he said kneeling before the Grand Master. Even though he meant the words he was saying he could not hide their defeated tone.

Gallion smiled a wide sickening smile. Sensing that any danger had passed the Grand Master floated ethereally towards the kneeling soldier, the billowing robes making him seem more like a phantom than a man. He placed a spidery hand on Carstair's shoulder and whispered in his ear.

'I knew you would not abandon me, my friend,' the words flowed smoothly and sincerely but they still made Carstair feel uneasy.

'He is one of us,' the Grand Master announced to the room so that the soldiers would back off. They obliged and as they returned to stand guard in a quieter manner than they had entered the room, Carstair realised that their skin was pale and sickly looking, their eyes a piercing blue and their movements unnaturally quick. He also did not recognise a single one of them.

Carstair looked alarmingly to Gallion but before he could speak the Grand Master intercepted his thoughts.

'They are under my command.'

Outside, the rain lashed against the Grand Master's windows and the wind howled down the fireplace causing the fire to rage back at it like a stormy sea. Forks of lightning cascaded across the dark backdrop outside the window. The Grand Master turned to look out of the window and Carstair began to wonder if he had conjured the weather for the dramatic effect.

'I will be making an announcement to the whole Order tomorrow in the great hall,' Gallion said without turning to look at Carstair. 'Messages will be sent out tonight.'

Carstair rose and replaced the dagger in its sheath. His hand stung where he had made the incision and his mind hurt too. For good or bad he had given himself to the Order and the Grand Master. He would not, could no betray his vows or his loyalty to Gideon. If he said this was the right path, Carstair knew he had to have faith, even if he couldn't see the path for himself.

'Go and get some rest Carstair,' the Grand Master ordered. 'It has been a tough few weeks and things are going to get tougher.'

The finality of the Grand Master's words made Carstair feel drained, and he took the advice and turned to leave.

'It is a new dawn, and I am glad to be facing it with you,' the Grand Master said though neither were facing each other. 'It would have been a hard decision to have you killed.'

Carstair felt a chill run down his spine at Gallion's

implied threat and he passed through the door quickly, slamming it shut and resting his back against it, wondering if he could have ended up like the poor damned souls in the dungeons beneath them. His chest was heaving and his mind aching as he understood that for him and probably the Order, things had irrevocably changed forever.

Chapter 25

Those of the Order who were not on night shifts sat in the dorms, some reading, others pursuing more artistic outlets, and some watching the dreary weather pass through the night. All of the Order not working, had been told they were not to leave the citadel that night. For some, like many of the librarians, this had meant little change to their regular routines, but for many of the soldiers they had felt quite put out by not being able to frequent the taverns of the city that evening.

The city was quieter than normal as the evening raged on. The weather had made an impact on that, but there was a noticeable absence of any members of the Order in the taverns of the city or even many of the streets that led that way. Those who had braved the weather that evening conversed with their peers or the landlords of the bars and questioned the Order's absence that night. Some speculated a disaster, others tightening of the rules, and some suggested that it had to do with the unusual deaths of the past weeks. Whatever the case, most townsfolk seemed more at ease without the presence of the Order's soldiers in their taverns.

In her room Gassis sat and read from a book detailing

some of the history of the city's founding when it was merely a town. Engrossed in the details of the horrors that the settlers found and the how valiantly the knights of the Order were portrayed, she did not notice the small piece of paper slide under her door. The weather crashed at her window finally distracting her from the pages of the book and carefully replacing her bookmark she closed the book and rested it on the table turning to peer out of the window.

Rain lashed against the panes and ran quickly down to sill. She could see and, more importantly, hear the gutters as they overflowed and sent torrents of rainwater crashing over their sides and into the ground far below. The wind howled through the storm, and she watched lights in the city dance as they flickered and saw the scurrying of the night guards as they tried their best to stay as dry as possible. She did not envy them at this moment in time.

The storm showed no sign of abating and even though the weather was terrible, Gassis felt hot and flustered. She made her way to the small china bowl that sat on the dresser in her room and splashed the cold, clean water on her face to try to refresh herself. As she sat back on the bed, patting her face with the small cloth she had grabbed from the dresser side, her eye was drawn to the piece of paper that sat just behind her door.

From the bed she could see that it was written on an official piece of paper as the Order's seal was visible. Curious at how long it had been there and what it contained she approached the door and knelt to retrieve the note. Flipping it over she could see the whole seal of the Order and puzzled at the words that it contained:

You are requested to attend the Grand Hall tomorrow at nine in the morning. Head straight there and not to your workplace.

The Grand Master will be addressing the Order.

There was no signature or indication of who sent the note, but up and down the Citadel all the members of the Order received one. A pit began to form in Gassis's stomach. She had no proof, nor any real inclination, but she felt that this was the moment the last few months had been preluding to. If there was something rotten at the core of the Order, it was about to be exposed, she could almost taste it she was that sure.

She glanced back out of the window and was met by the unrelenting rain, the sky dark, almost pitch black which suggested it was well into the night. The old folk tales would call this sort of time the witching hour. Apt, she thought, as she re-read the note a final time before deciding that she needed to speak to her friends, she needed their council. She quickly threw an old shawl over her casual clothes and gently opened the door, not wanting to disturb anyone who may still be on the landing and alerting them to her presence. Even though she was pretty sure she hadn't broken any rules, she felt like a prisoner in the dorm and felt any passing guard would try to send her back to her quarters.

The corridor was quiet, only the faint hum of the refectory carried along the air up to the landing where her dorm was found. She pulled the shawl tightly around her shoulders and hastily sped off to find Nestor and Edryd. Edryd's dorm was close to Gassis's; in general, the different sections of the order were housed as such, so most of the librarians habited in close proximity.

She gently rapped at Edryd's door but received no answer. Inside the young librarian was asleep at his desk, a small pool of drool forming in the open book that he lay resting on. Though Gassis could not tell, the small note that had been passed under Edryd's door too lay unnoticed. Gassis rapped the door once more a little louder, she turned to see if the increased noise had alerted anyone to her arrival, but it appeared not, though the noise of two people ascending the stairs from the refectory sounded like they were getting closer.

She could make out the sound of an older man and woman, making it unlikely that they were guards, and again she had to remind herself she was not doing anything wrong, at least not at this moment. Even so, she pleaded within her mind that Edryd would open the door. As the sound of the pair grew louder, she leant against Edryd's door with her back deciding her next move when all of a sudden she was propelled back as the young librarian opened the door and Gassis came tumbling into his room.

The pair looked at each other a little confused and Edryd blushed at having made Gassis fall into his room in such a manner. She kicked the door shut behind from the floor as the two people from the stairs passed Edryd's door, causing them to start at the bang. Edryd helped Gassis to her feet despite her protests before finally breaking the silence by laughing riotously at her expense.

'It's not funny you fool,' she said half-heartedly as she too started to redden. 'You could have killed me,' she added softly punching him in the arm.

'You knocked my door,' he pointed out between fits of giggles. 'What's the matter anyway?' he asked realising there must be a reason for the call.

'Did you get a note too?' Gassis blurted out, 'about tomorrow?'

'Uh, I guess,' he answered, confusing Gassis.

'You guess?' She said, 'Either you did or you didn't.'

'Well, this was on the floor when I answered the door,' he replied producing a similar note to the one that Gassis had received, 'but I don't know if it is about tomorrow, I haven't read it yet.'

Gassis frowned, 'read it.'

Edryd read the note and flipped it over but found no more information. 'Yes,' he said, 'it is about tomorrow.'

Gassis all but held her face in her hand at his seeming ignorance. 'It's happening Edryd, something is going to go down tomorrow, all the weird shit that's been going on, Azerrad and Katerina's deaths, Gideon's, they've all been leading to this moment where the Grand Master is going to reveal whatever rotten thing has been eating away at our Order.'

Edryd was taken back at the seriousness of what Gassis was suggesting, 'You really think that something that bad could be going on under our noses?' he questioned

'C'mon Edryd, you know what we've found, what Azerrad and you uncovered already. Do their deaths seem normal to you?' Gassis said, still filled with rage over her friends' deaths, 'we talked of what was to come, I think that moment is upon us.'

'You think that the Grand Master is going to tell us all that evil lurks within our own walls? That we can't keep ourselves safe, let alone the population out there?' Edryd asked feeling the insinuation a little ridiculous.

'No, he's not going to come out and say that,' Gassis replied a little annoyed at the facetious way in which Edryd framed the question, 'but he is going to say something and if that something makes us question his motives, even the motives of the order, then we will need to be ready to act, for better or worse. We are already outcasts, what do you think they will do with us if the Order gets behind his plans?'

'What do you suggest?' he asked imploringly.

'We have to fight for what we believe is right, we have to fight for the Order, we have to fight for our friends,' she countered defiantly.

'How can we fight against the whole Order?' Edryd

asked feeling almost ashamed at his defeatism.

'Maybe we can't,' Gassis admitted, 'but that doesn't mean we shouldn't.' she didn't mean it to but the words came out like a shot and made Edryd feel a little ashamed. 'I am going to speak with Nestor tonight, but we have to be ready to make a stand Edryd,' Gassis said eyeing the worried young librarian, 'all of us.'

With that, she turned and left Edryd's room, the sweet smell of her perfume hanging in the air as she did. Edryd enjoyed the smell momentarily and slumped on his bed to think about what had transpired that night. He wanted to help, lord knows he did, but without Azerrad and Katerina, there was no resisting the Order. They would be kicked out or worse killed if they tried to go against them. After all, he had taken his vows just like the soldiers had.

Wrapping the shawl around her again and slipping away into the darker recesses of the corridor, Gassis made her way across to the stairs that led to where Nestor's room was located. Quietly she went about her business, passing a few off-duty soldiers as she did who gave her curious glances but were otherwise uninterested. When she came to Nestor's door, she found it slightly ajar so knocked and let herself in calling Nestor's name gently.

'Come in Gassis,' he said matching her tone, though she was already practically in the room by then.

She could see the note on Nestor's desk and the young soldier sat at it brooding.

'The door was open,' Gassis explained her intrusion away.

'When I saw the note, I knew you would come,' Nestor said, his tone grim.

'What do you make of it?' she asked.

'I do not know but my gut tells me that it isn't going to be good,' he said, 'it seems that perhaps you were right, perhaps our worst fears are true and some evil manifests itself within our walls,' he continued shaking his head mournfully.

'I agree, we have to be ready tomorrow, we must make a stand,' Gassis said firmly testing Nestor's resolve.

'You know I will,' Nestor said, 'but what can we do realistically?'

'If things go badly tomorrow and we have to stand against the Order, maybe enough of our brothers and sisters will see sense and join us.' Gassis replied, though she doubted even her own words.

'More likely we'll be cast out or killed,' Nestor admitted, 'but I want justice for Gideon, and many of my brothers feel the same.' His voice sounded brave as soon as Gideon's name passed his lips.

'Speak to them, share our fears with them and make sure that if we give the signal, they are ready to act.' Gassis spoke determinedly knowing Nestor was as loyal a friend as there could be. She knew deep down he wouldn't let her down.

'What of the librarians?' Nestor asked, his words growing more and more sorrowful again.

'Edryd is afraid, many of them will be, they are not warriors like you,' she admitted.

'They are true of heart though?'

'They want the order to stand for what it should,' she assured him.

'Looks like tomorrow is going to be a rough day,' Nestor said anticipating Gassis's departure.

'I'm sure of it,' was all she said as she turned to leave.

That night, the two of them worked hard canvassing their friends within each camp. There were plenty of librarians who worked with Gassis who felt that their work was undervalued but few who would openly support a rebellion or whatever it was Gassis was suggesting. Undeterred, she spent the better part of the evening working away at them before finally retiring to bed sometime in the early hours of the morning.

Nestor was true to his word and also spent the evening going about his brethren garnering support as and when he could. He spoke to Marius and Arjan first to see if they would share the burden of visiting dorms, which they gladly accepted and agreed to help. Later that evening Arjan returned to see Nestor and spoke of his evening, but Nestor was disappointed that Marius had not done the same.

It was the early hours of the morning when they too managed to get some rest, though it would not be for too long if they wanted to be ready for the grand spectacle that the morning was set to offer. From their beds, many of them sat and watched sheets of rain slowly recede into drizzle and dry up as the light of the morning seemed to banish the rain clouds of the previous evening.

Having barely slept through the night, those loyal members of the Order who had spent their night scuttling around the Citadel reluctantly rose with the rest of their brothers to see what the morning would bring, though none of them felt it was going to be anything particularly good.

Chapter 26

A blaring autumnal sun rose over Uvrenmouth that morning and the air was unusually warm and still. It seemed as though the very air around the city stood still momentarily as the city awoke and began to teem with life. Merchants and workers wiped sweat from their brow as the made their way about the city or heaved cases and crates of wares to sell. The citadel's refectory was jammed with members of the Order desperately clamouring to get breakfast before they had to get ready for the Grand Masters speech.

Though it had not been stated in the notes that had been passed around the citadel earlier that night it was well known that any formal engagement by the Grand Master or any of the more senior officials would require those in attendance to be wearing their formal robes if they were a librarian or full uniform if they were a soldier. For the librarians, the robes were fairly light and not too cumbersome but for the soldiers the restrictive nature of their full dress uniform combined with the stifling air meant it was going to be uncomfortable for them in the crammed hall.

In her room, Gassis had no appetite for food and so prepared herself ready to receive the Grand Master's words, though she had no stomach for that either. She tugged at the form-fitting tunic of her formal robes here and there to try to get a bit more room, but it was futile and, in the warmth, it was starting to make her perspire. She dabbed the sweat from her brow and cheeks carefully and began to tame her hair. In the rooms around the citadel so did most of the Order's members.

The great hall looked unlike it ever had, certainly in recent memory. To the one side a stage had been erected at the foot of the stairs that led to the Grandmaster's rooms. It was fairly plain in appearance as there was no need for it to be ostentatious, but it was imposing, nonetheless. In a hall of standing adults, it would allow those on the stage to tower over the crowd and be seen and heard by the entire hall. The guards that were overseeing its erection had commented that anyone on that stage would command the room with ease; something the Grand Master could have done from a pit.

Any unnecessary furnishings such as chairs, desks, and statues had been relocated for the time being and with the hall almost empty at this point, the room look vast, and every footstep echoed around the hollow chamber. Those who had worked through the night had been dismissed to wash and change and those who took their place clanked as the metal clasps and buckles of their formal uniform clanged against other adornments. Guards took up posts at the gate and regular intervals around the perimeter of the hall as the rest of the Citadel entered in small groups taking up spaces closest to the stage and filling backwards.

Every now and then a group would congregate further from the already bustling masses as though they may be called on to participate if they stood too close, but by the time the whole Citadel was in attendance there would not be an iota of space left to fill anyway. One by one in separate groups Edryd, Gassis, Nestor,

Arjan, and Marius entered the hall amongst several other members chatting and pointing to the stage.

Gassis still wriggled uncomfortably against her formal attire, but when she saw how warm and heavy the soldiers' uniform looked, she began to feel a little more grateful for her robes. The groups of friends placed themselves at different positions within the crowd, subconsciously feeling as though if something did happen it would be far harder to round them up if they were spread throughout the hall.

More and more librarians and soldiers piled in and to one side, Gassis could see that many of the watchers were also in attendance, though they remained hooded and cloaked and almost segregated to the rear of the hall. It seemed that whatever this gathering was for it was something of great importance. It was unusual for so many watchers to abandon their posts to gather at the Citadel. The noise of the crowd was rising as more and more people filled the hall and the din was almost deafening. Edryd hopped nervously from foot to foot as he waited for something to start, Nestor stood stoically and patiently still, Marius never took his eyes from the stage where currently a lone soldier stood guard at the stairs entrance.

As nine o'clock approached the room was sweltering and noisy. The crowd was a sea of royal blues and silver metals. Ankhs could be seen adorning the robes of every member apart from the watchers. The crowd began to grow restless when finally, some movement from the direction of the stage could be seen. From the stairwell, Carstair emerged with three other senior soldiers. They looked immaculate in their formal dress. Indeed, Gassis had to admit that she had never seen Carstair look so well presented.

At his hip hung a great sword in a lavish scabbard that almost touched his boots, which was impressive given his height. His reaper pistols hung at his hips too, ornate and polished so that the gleam looked like eyes winking back at the crowd. His polished silver ankh hung at his neck as did all the other officers and as they stepped out onto the stage Carstair and another officer split to the left of the pulpit on the stage, the other two remained on the right flanking the area that was no doubt going to be taken up by the Grand Master.

As the four entered the stage the crowd began to quiet, and an air of anticipation swept across the crowd as the heat continued to stream in through the high arching windows of the great hall. Finally, the suspense was broken and the curtains that semi hid the Grand Master's stairwell stirred and hinted that they were about to reveal the final entrant to the stage. Sure enough, in a regal blue gown that bore the order's ankh symbol in exquisite silver stitching down the front and billowed around his form as he moved, the Grand Master entered the stage and took up his place in front of the pulpit in the centre.

He looked as old as many of them had ever seen him, but the way he moved was sprightly and he no longer bore the cane that was familiar to those who saw him passing around the Citadel on rare occasion. The crowd silenced at the spectacle and the senior officers looked on with approval at the respect that was shown to their Grand Master. Each took an at ease pose flanking their leader as he looked out over the crowd in preparation to speak.

Gallion cast his eyes across the diverse members of the Order and smiled as his spindly fingers grasped the side of the pulpit. The whole hall silently awaited his words, but he remained silent for a time as he took in the sea of followers before him. Carstair spent the whole time scanning the audience for any trouble or anyone not paying enough attention.

Finally, he broke his silence and addressed the congregation before him, 'Servants of the Order, friends, thank you for gathering here to hear my address.' He spoke clearly and his enrapturing voice gripped many of those in attendance immediately.

'The work we perform in the Citadel is of vital importance to the security, prosperity, and longevity of the city of Uvrenmouth and our gratitude goes out to each member for their efforts,' Gallion smiled and paused allowing a ripple of noise to pass over the crowd as they humbly accepted the praise of their leader.

'It is this work that leads us, however, into the dark and mystical world that plagues our city, and many of our members have fallen foul of that dark world. We have had to bury brothers and sisters, and it is by our fallen blood that the city is made safe,' Gallion continued to speak fluently, keeping any hint of emotion from the words he spoke as he riled up the crowd before him.

The crowd in turn cheered at the mention of their fallen brethren and nodded their approval at their sacrifice. The senior soldiers behind Gallion mirrored the crowd's nods; most in the Citadel knew someone who had lost their life for the Order, and it was an easy way for the Grand Master to stir emotion.

'We are the unspoken heroes of the city and for an age we have been the defenders of mankind, beacons of light in a sea of darkness,' Gallion's voice began to emphasise words like heroes and light to illicit greater response from the crowd before him, manipulating them into rapturous applause, so that he could drive the hammer home.

'But let me ask you this, brave soldiers and learned librarians of the Order,' Gallion asked, his words changing the tone of the address and causing the applauding crowd to pause and take note, 'to what

applause are our efforts and sacrifices made? Does the
city thank us for what we do? Are our fallen
remembered outside of these walls? Are you lauded in
the street or shunned and avoided as though you carried
a plague?' Gallion's questions rained down on the
absorbed crowd and slowly smiling faces turned to
frowns and looks of confusion as the members of the
Order were made to search themselves for answers to
questions they had never thought to ask.

Gallion let the questions hang in the air for dramatic
effect as he continued his sickening smile, while his mad
eyes scoured the agitated crowd. Gassis stared on
nervously from the back of the crowd, the Grand
Master's words were heading in a direction she knew
there would be no coming back from and though much
of the crowd was absorbed in his rhetoric and
counselling themselves, she remained stoic and looked
for her allies within the crowd.

She could see Edryd still nervously fidgeting and
looking around the crowd himself, but he was a few
rows in front of Gassis and did not look backwards.
Glancing sidelong she could see Nestor quietly
whispering to Arjan and demonstrating something with
his hands, but the two looked equally concerned at the
manner of the Grand Master's address. Finally, she
found Marius, but was met unnervingly by his own eyes
staring back grimly at her, before looking away sharply
as their eyes met. It unnerved her and she returned her
gaze to the stage where she found that Carstair too
seemed to be now staring directly at her. She lowered
her gaze a little trying to fade into the crowd more, but
he remained fixed on her position.

She risked another glance in Nestor's direction and
found him looking back at her, his hand firmly clasped
around the ceremonial sword that hung at his waist and
bearing a reassuring look on his face. Her eyes widened

to hint that something was wrong and she wrenched her neck towards the stage, taking care not to meet Carstair's gaze. Nestor looked in the direction she was alluding to, finding the stern face of Carstair looking at where Gassis stood before slowly turning to make eye contact with Nestor. Carstair's glare felt like it carried a fury and hatred that Nestor could almost feel, but he did not cower from the gaze, meeting it and holding with determination until the Grand Master resumed his speech and drew Carstair's eyes away from him.

'So tell me, brave and noble members of the Order, is this a just fate for the protection and salvation of the great city of Uvrenmouth?' the crowd jeered as Gallion pulled their strings like the benevolent puppet master he was. 'What if I told you I could change all that? Return our Order to the proud symbol it once was, one that the people not only thanked but revered as we should be?' The crowd cheered wildly.

'There is a new dawn on the horizon, a dawn where this city will know us for the protectors we are,' Gallion proclaimed with belief and fervour, 'a new dawn where we will be the masters of mankind.'

The crowd looked on eagerly as he continued to become more animated and Gassis and Nestor eyed one another sensing that the time was nearing that they would need to make their voices heard. Both began whispering to those beside them who nodded their understanding and passed the word on to others, a chain reaction sparking in the midst of the raucous rally.

'Put your trust in me and I will lead us into a new era. I will shepherd you into my new dawn,' Gallion had the crowd in the palm of his hand, his features twisting in maniacal glee, 'we tried to work with the monsters, but I see now we should have been controlling them, and I alone possess the power to do just that.'

The hall applauded more, as did the senior soldiers

on the stage, coaxing the crowd by mirroring their applause. All apart from Carstair who was watching the little sequence of events in the back of the hall nervously. His eyes darting from Gassis to Nestor around the crowd and then to Marius. Gassis saw that Carstair was not entranced in the Grand Master's speech as the others were and knew the time was almost upon them. Carstair continued to scan the crowd, always to Gassis and Nestor then back to Marius.

'We will wage a war on the monsters and bring them under our control,' Gallion spat, 'a war that will spill onto the streets of the city and the city will know what it is that haunts the dark, and more importantly who it is that protects them from the horror.'

At the Grand Master's use of the word war, Gassis, Nestor, and those faithful to the Order's ideals knew that there was no going back. Soldiers began to grip sword hilts and look for a way forward, but the crowd was dense. Carstair shot a glance at Marius whose hand left the hilt of his sword and instead grasped his Ankh, his tense arm crossing his chest before he slipped backwards out of the crowd.

Carstair threw a knowing look at one of the soldiers near the stage that set off a chain reaction as soldiers made their way to the back of the crowd and then began to surge into it, apprehending Gassis, Nestor, Edryd, and around a dozen other members before they could make it more than three feet forward.

'Our time is now' Gallion roared into the cheering crowd, who barely noticed the bodies that were being dragged out of the crowd by Carstair's soldiers.

The Grand Master retreated from the stage watching the baying crowd in pleasure, and in the back the wriggling forms of the loyal friends were disappearing quickly.

'Brother, do you not see how folly this all is?' Nestor

cried as he fought against the strength of the soldier who was dragging him off with his friends.

His assailant remained silent as they descended the steps that led to the interrogation cells, and as the flickering torchlight caught the soldier's face, Nestor could see that he bore a resemblance to a soldier he knew, but the flesh was pale, almost translucent. As he struggled his skin brushed the flesh of the soldier which sent a chill down Nestor's spine; the cold clamminess of his skin shaking Nestor to his core and causing him to fight against his captor whose strength was overpowering.

He couldn't see any sign of the others, but he could hear the faint noise of scuffles and feet being forced against their will. When they reached the bottom of the stairs Nestor made a break for it, releasing himself from the soldier's tight grip and running as fast as his trembling legs would carry him, but he only made it a fraction of the way down the hall before the soldier grasped him with unnatural speed, pinning him to the wall as he kicked open a door to a cell.

The soldier threw Nestor unceremoniously into the dark, damp cell and slammed the door behind him. Nestor heard the bolt slide into place sealing his fate as it was locked in place and as Nestor hung his head in defeat in the grim darkness of his cage, he heard the soldier mutter through the door, 'We are brothers no more.'

Gassis, Arjan, Edryd, and two other soldiers suffered the same fate as Nestor, occupying the five adjacent cells to Nestor. One by one the tell-tale thud of a cell door and the ominous clink of the bolt latching the door shut could be heard until all the cells were full and the hall silent and dark.

In the hall, the crowd was disbursing, seemingly overjoyed at the revelation that they were to become heroes of the city. Even though many of the librarians shared a weary outlook at this prospect, the soldiers were in buoyant mood as they returned to their work or headed to the refectory for refreshments. Few if any seemed to pick up on the troubling words Gallion had chosen at times during his speech. Gallion spoke to the senior soldiers out of earshot of the disbursing crowd.

'That went well, things are changing for the better and I will need my loyal officers for this,' Gallion's words were directed at the senior soldiers, but Carstair was the only one he did not look at to make sure that they responded affirmatively. Once he was content that they understood he dismissed the three soldiers and placed a cold spidery hand on Carstair's shoulder informing him that he should stay.

'Our plan is advancing as anticipated my friend,' Gallion said smiling, 'did I see some more volunteers for my programme being escorted away?'

Carstair hesitated before answering, unsure if he wanted to commit the apprehended to such a fate, no matter the pain in his ass they had been. 'Yes,' he finally relented, 'we received intel of unrest and a possible attempt to disrupt your address, they have been dealt with accordingly.'

'Excellent,' the Grand Master said in a sinister way as he clasped his hands together, 'let them stew a while, I will deal with them then.'

Carstair hated the bluntness with which the Grand Master said the words, but he nodded and turned to leave the stage. The great hall was nearly empty now and as the Order returned to work, some cleared away the hall, sweeping up and returning the ornaments that had been removed. Gallion departed beyond the curtained veil to his chambers, Carstair thought he would get a beer somewhere away from the Citadel, and down in the dungeons of the Citadel, Nestor sat with his head hung low in despair, Gassis paced furiously but impotently, and Edryd softly wept in the dark.

Chapter 27

A third day passed in the rank, airless cell as Gassis sat with her back rested upon the cold, damp rock of the Citadel's exterior. She only surmised that three days had passed because she had received three portions of bread and water and three candles that burned for about an hour with which to eat by. She had not seen anyone until she had been wrested from the great hall, not even the food givers who passed the plate of bread and jug of water through a hatch in the door.

The only sign of life that she got were the silhouettes that formed in the hatch, lit by the torches that blazed in the corridor the cell sat on. She assumed that her co-conspirators were down here in the other cells but again had no means to know for sure nor communicate with them. Her days were instead consumed with regret at losing their most powerful allies and guilt that they were unable to do anything in their absence.

She wondered what kind of horrors she might find once she was released, if she was released. They must let us out eventually, she thought, they hadn't actually done anything wrong when they were taken. The unusually strong, cold and foul-smelling soldiers had seen to that, nullifying them before they even got started. She sat and played out almost every eventuality she could think of in her head and was only broken from the trance when the shutter slid open and a stream of light flooded into the cell piercing the darkness as it always did. She raced to the door, demanding to be told what was happening, but the stoic guards ignored her pleas and shoved the little tray with food, water, and a candle through the hole into her chest before slamming the hatch, not caring if any of it spilled.

She slumped onto the floor holding the tray, her stinking clothes a little damp now from the water that splashed onto her, but she did not care, this mental torture was rendering her more insane by the day.

To the left of her cell, Edryd scampered to the hatch and greedily pulled the tray into the gloom to eat. He was starving and thirsty, his back ached and his eyes were sore from the grief of his own predicament. He guessed the others were close by and suffering at least as badly as he was, but it was no comfort for him. He had kept himself sane reciting some of the language that he and Azerrad had been translating in the months prior to this unjust incarceration, but as time drew on even that began to send him crazier as he could only repeat the same few phrases.

He lit his candle and placed it carefully near the tray so that he could see what he was eating and drinking. Though it looked unappetising for the fourth day in a row, it did not look like it had been tampered with at least. He demolished the bread like a starving rat and gulped down the water in equal speed, then sat in regret at having so quickly finished his only repast for another day. In the low glow of the candle that could barely lift the gloom he studied the cell he had been forced to call home.

Nestor limped over to the pitiful excuse for a meal

and felt glad Gideon was someplace better and not embroiled in the shit he had found himself in. He wondered if it was day or night outside. He had spent so long in the gloom that he could no longer work out if they were fed in the morning or the evening, not that it mattered he supposed. He reached for the tray and drew it closer to his body. He too lit the candle just as Edryd had done and rested it on the metal tray to eat.

In her cell, Gassis had lit her candle in preparation to eat what hadn't fallen to the ground when she noticed that her meal was not the only thing to have been passed into her cell. On the ground near the door she saw a small scrap of paper lying face down in the damp. It must have been put there between her last meal and this one as she would have seen it otherwise. She stooped down to pluck the paper from the ground praying it was not just a scrap that had fallen in from the soldiers delivering her meals.

In his cell, while he was studying its every fibre, Edryd too found a small scrap of paper on the floor near the door that he had not noticed there before, bending to retrieve it held it close to the candlelight so that he could read its message.

Sure enough, in Nestor's cell a small scrap of paper with writing on it had been found and was being read.

Gassis turned the note over in her hand, pulling the candlelight close to read the words upon the note. In a beautiful and archaic script she read the words aloud softly to herself, 'Courage is its own reward.' She looked the paper up and down for any other hints but could see nothing and though she was buoyed to have received communication it hardly amounted to a rescue attempt.

In his cell, Edryd read the note that was written in the same beautiful script as Gassis's, it simply said 'Patience is an uncommon virtue, especially in times of strife'.

Edryd's heart leapt as he read the words that Azerrad had spoken to him so long ago in the library, when the two of them struggled so hard to find any clue as to what was happening in the city. He paced to the door and listened for any sign that his friend had returned from the dead, but he could hear nothing and saw only the barest sliver of light glowing at the doors base, but he knew in his hear that his salvation lay somewhere out there.

In his cell, Nestor stood still, his face red with rage, tears streaming down his flushed cheeks, though it was not visible in the dim light. The note he had received in that fine script was crumpled in his hand that was clenched in fists of anger. In that moment of pure rage, he knew that he would get out of this cell and end this madness once and for all, of that he had become certain.

While the prisoners had been forced to guess at the time of day, Carstair sat in his room, knowing full well that night had descended early that evening as autumn began to evolve into winter. The wind that blew so warm only a few days ago now carried with it a bitter chill and Carstair was forced to pull the windows shut to stop the curtains flapping uncontrollably in the icy breeze.

He lay on his bed watching the clouds in the night pass by on the wind and every now and then he saw the little black blur of a bat hunting for its evening meal. Carstair's dinner lay half eaten on the desk, he had not felt all that hungry in recent days as the Grand Master continued to inform him that the time was upon them. He lay his head on the pillow to try to get some sleep but every time he closed his eyes he was met with the same haunting visions. He saw the ruined faces of the poor creatures in the dungeons below the Citadel and thought about how their ranks were about to swell with more of the Order's members. Other times he saw the accusation etched on the faces of those he had silenced for the greater good of the Order, to protect the city, to keep its citizens safe or whatever other bullshit he had told himself to diminish his responsibility in what was no more than cold blooded murder. The worst of his nightmarish dreams, however, came in the form of the vampires he had left to die then roasted in the tunnels beneath the city. Their anger, their wrath, their desire for vengeance plagued his sleep and he tossed and turned in a cold sweat as the spectres of his past haunted him in his slumber.

He started bolt upright at the loud bang that disturbed his already troubled sleep. He glanced around the room to see what the hell made that almighty racket and as his eyes came into focus, he could see that his window was wide open. Damn it, he thought to himself, the latch must have broken, and the window swung open.

He forced himself out of bed and felt a strange sensation. Chills ran down his spine as the bed sheet fell from his frame, but he could feel no intrusion of the wind despite the open window. He shuddered at the feeling before examining the window to find that there was no broken latch. He puzzled at it for second, sure he had secured the window before he fell asleep.

Outside the night was at its darkest, clouds covered the stars and only the smallest morsel of the moon peeked past their dense cover. He rubbed his eyes to remove the sleep though he could see he had not been asleep for that long. He shut the window once more making doubly sure that he had latched it in place properly before heading to the small cupboard in the desk and rummaging around to find a glass and a bottle of liquor. He pulled out the glass and set it on the desk and sighed as he looked at it. The glass was old and chipped and held a permanent cloudiness that no amount of washing could remove, but it held the brown liquor and even though it was a mile away from the fancy glasses found in Gallion's chambers it did the trick.

He downed the first measure he poured for himself before topping the glass back up and sitting in the chair that sat at his desk. He rolled the brown liquid around the cloudy glass as its predecessor left a warm sensation in his throat. Having brought himself back into check, he felt better and looked around the room for something to take his mind from the evening's intrusion and faces in his dreams. That was when he noticed the small fragment of paper pinned into the frame of his mirror by the door.

Curious, he sipped from the second measure of liquor and carried it with him as he rose from his chair and ventured over to see what the paper was. As he neared the paper, he could see that there was something written on it but until he got right in front of it, he could not make out the words, such was the fancy script it was written in. He stared in disbelief at the small piece of paper as its words were made manifest to him.

Even the good falter when the dead rise.

Carstair dropped the glass from his hand, and it shattered around his feet. He tore the note from its pin, raced back to the window and flung it open. He pushed his head out of the window and scanned the surrounding area from the ground up, but he saw nothing out of place. His heart pounding and his mind racing he slumped into the chair at the desk and read the note again and again though there was no doubt in his mind whom it was from.

Wide eyed and spaced out he looked at the floor of his room where he could see the ruination of the glass he had dropped, its fragments scattered across the floor which was awash with the brown liquid it had once held and small droplets of red blood where the glass had cut his foot. Carstair remained in that seat until the first rays of the dawn made their way into the room.

The next day passed unremarkably for those in their cells in the heart of the Citadel, as it did for Carstair and the rest of the Order. The enthusiasm had passed on the previous day's rally as the Order settled back into its usual routine, but none had forgotten the promise of glory either, and as Carstair made his way around the Citadel that day he overheard snippets of conversations questioning what the future held or the desperate clamour for recognition. He marvelled at how easily the Grand Master had found it to bend the Order to his will and knew that he was the person he had to see about the note he had been left.

'Pinned to the mirror?' the Grand Master clarified, 'best be having words with our sentries then.'

Carstair had found the Grand Master buried in his books as usual and even though he seated himself in his favourite green leather chair, he did not help himself to liquor on this occasion.

'It's him,' Carstair replied with grim assurance.

'How can, you be sure?' Gallion questioned again.

'Who else? He could have killed me in my sleep if he'd wanted but this is about more than that,' Carstair spoke the paranoid words and their realisation shook him.

'You have a high opinion of your worth Carstair,' the Grand Master put to him bluntly.

'I led them to their demise, I wouldn't expect

anything else,' he replied as a matter of fact.

'This presents a problem then Carstair, I will have to move my plans forward, I won't have that wretch interfering now,' the Grand Master's usual unshakable façade slipped briefly, and the words came out with venom.

'Plans?' Carstair asked.

'The war my friend, I am going to start the war that will begin our ascent,' his usual demeanour returning.

Carstair did not reply but he knew that difficult times lay ahead.

'Set your best men on the Citadel's watches tonight Carstair and ready yourself. Do you feel that wind? The storm is coming.' Gallion returned to his book, scribbling notes in the pad that lay next to the book every now and then.

Carstair rose from his seat and took a look around the room, remembering it in fondness for he had a terrible foreboding that it would not be the same again. He quietly left the room and headed back to his own quarters where he would spend the day meticulously sharpening his weapons and cleaning them. When he was satisfied with his armoury, he realised that the room had darkened considerably and upon peering out of his window he found that night was already encroaching on the city.

He sighed and heaved himself from the chair he had sat in long enough to have left a sizeable imprint in and began to arm himself. Around his waist he strapped his holsters, placing his reaper pistols proudly in them after admiring them for a time. Under the pistols he wrenched a heavy belt that held an array of pouches and clips and into one pouch he poured a handful of silver bullets with an intricate filigree etched into each one. He clipped his short sword to the belt too, leaving his bigger blade hanging in place as it made manoeuvring around the building more difficult.

He pulled a short jacket over the top of his tunic and leather waistcoat that hid the pistols from view as he usually liked to do and pulled on his heavy boots, strapping them tightly and buckling them at the top. When he was satisfied, he made to leave, pausing to glance in the mirror. The face staring back at him worried Carstair, it seemed older than he remembered; the dark rings at his eyes and stubble adding years in mere days. He too caught sight of the pin that had held the note left for him and he shuddered to think of it.

Carstair slipped out of his room and made his way into the realm of the Citadel to ensure that the guards were alert, and the sentries were doubled. Once he was satisfied with that, he sat for a time and watched as darkness enveloped the city, ushered in by a cold harsh wind that whistled through the windows of the great hall.

Chapter 28

In the city of Uvrenmouth the cold dark night that fell did not dampen the resident's hearts as they flooded the cities taverns drinking and revelling as the night passed by. In the Citadel, watches moved around the place in more frequent fashion than usual and the place had a greater buzz about it than a usual night.

Down in the dungeons the friends sat in their cells wondering if the notes had simply been a cruel device of mental torture to make their stay worse. They had received their meals for the evening but none of them had lit the candle, instead eating in darkness so they could put their candle to better use later on if the chance came.

Time ebbed away and with it so did the heart of the captives until out of the darkness an unfamiliar sound echoed through Edryd's cell. He leapt to his feet, straining his ears to the darkness, he was sure that in his saddened state he had heard the door to his cage knock gently. In any other time, such a rap would have borne no connotations, but in that pit, it was the only noise that he had heard in days apart from when their meals were brought to them.

He felt around the floor for the candle and hurriedly

lit it, its glow fighting back the dark a little. He aimed it towards the door and silently crept across the cold stone floor, searching for any more correspondence until he was pressed against the door and in the hazy glow of the candle, he pressed his ear to the wood and listened to the dark.

For moments he heard nothing, but as time crept on, he heard the sound of someone or something moving. He marvelled at how well soundproofed the cells in this part of the Citadel were but from his post he could hear something happening. Maybe this was it he thought, either they were coming to carry out their fate or maybe, just maybe, they were about to find their salvation from this hell.

Moments passed that seemed to Edryd like days but in his nervousness, he heard the sound of a lock being released and a latch unhinging. He cowered from the door momentarily, unsure of what fate lay on the other side. Slowly the door creaked open, and a small stream of light flooded the cell. Edryd's eyes burned at the influx of light and he struggled to see as his eyes fought to adjust to the new light.

No one appeared at the door and as he squinted to try to ease the struggle he was undergoing, he edged himself towards the doorway. Slowly he inched forward, the longer he remained alone the more he became emboldened as he guessed that if they were being taken to their doom it would have happened by now.

Emerging from the darkness of the cell into the light he could see that corridor was filled with bodies, but they were little more than silhouettes to his still adjusting eyes. One of the silhouettes approached him and he strained to see more clearly, as the stranger came face to face with him his heart leapt as he recognised who it was, though it was not whom he was expecting. The form that appeared was the imposing figure of Sister

Agatha.

Sister Agatha smiled at Edryd, and he returned the smile through a look of puzzlement and thankfulness. As his eyes returned, he could see Gassis, Nestor, Arjan, and two other soldiers rubbing their eyes and embracing at their release. The sister was accompanied by two younger female librarians that Edryd recognised by sight but not name.

'Quickly now, the guards might have been caught off guard, but more will come' the sister whispered, though her tone was as harsh as normal, 'we don't have much time.'

'How can this be?' Gassis asked confused by the manner of their liberation.

'We have a mutual friend Gassis, and I too wish for a return to the ideals of the Order, not this bastardisation Gallion is proposing,' Agatha answered venomously, 'but we do not possess the means to stop him.' She emphasised the word we as she spoke.

'Then who?' Nestor chimed in.

'You know who,' Agatha replied as a slight smile momentarily passed her lips. 'But come,' she insisted, 'he needs your help.'

The group quickly abandoned their captivity, racing up the stairs as quickly as possible to avoid detection simultaneously trying to avoid the knocked out guards. Near the top, one of the librarians dropped the torch she was carrying and stamped out the light ensuring that as they emerged, they would not be given away so easily. Stealthily they crept in the shadows of the Citadel's corridors aiming for the sanctuary of the library where they could regroup. Darkness had enveloped the city completely and the sisters had already extinguished any torches that led to the library, so their travel was unnoticed.

Reaching the doors of the library they were greeted

by a fair number of other librarians that seemingly felt the same as the sister. Many of them were younger members of the Order's librarian wing, but there were older patrons too. As the refugees entered their eyes darted around the crowd looking for the familiar face, they were so desperate to see, but he was not there.

Gassis spun to face Agatha and made to ask the question, but Agatha intercepted the thought and cut her off before she had chance to form any words.

'Patience,' she said in a calming tone, 'he will need your courage soon enough.'

The sister shepherded the group in and closed the doors to the library behind her. She instructed one of the librarians to disappear and when the young lad returned, he had the soldier's weapons with him. Nestor, Arjan, and the others armed themselves and in the dim light of the library, they waited.

Carstair stomped across the great hall agitated. He felt that something was coming but as of, yet nothing had materialised, and it irritated him immensely. Halfway across the polished floor he stopped and looked up at the corridor that ran across the balcony, not because something caught his eye but rather because nothing did. The corridor was in darkness, no torches glowed, and no movement could be seen, unnerving him further.

He motioned to one of the guards of the hall who marched quickly to meet Carstair, saluting as he reached him.

'What's going on up there?' he asked gesturing to the darkness.

'Sir, I have no idea,' the guard protested.

'Go and see to it,' Carstair ordered, 'sweep the area while you're there too.'

The guard saluted again and rushed off in that direction. Carstair watched him for a minute before deciding to pay the prisoners a visit. If he's contacted me maybe he's contacted them, he thought to himself, and stomped off in the direction of the staircase that led into the depths of the Citadel. He found that the entrance to the dungeons was also in darkness, and he began to become wary, his suspicions confirmed as he trod on the torch that had been left at the top of the stairs.

Bending down he grasped the torch and lit it before descending the narrow stone steps into the Citadel's cells. He reached the bottom and in the light of the corridor he could see that every door lay open, and the guards lay unconscious on the flagstone floor.

'Shit!' he cried out and tossed the torch to the ground, bounding over to one of the guards who lay on the floor. He lifted his head and roused him.

'What happened?' he cried in the poor man's face as he struggled to come round.

'Wh- what?' he finally got out.

'What happened here?' Carstair repeated agitated to find out, 'Who did this?'

'Agatha,' the guard said as he slipped back unconscious.

'That stupid bitch,' Carstair spoke, releasing his grip on the soldier allowing him to slink back onto the floor.

Enraged, Carstair flew up the stairs like a madman and burst into the great hall to everyone's surprise. Seeing that the senior soldier was in distress, several guards came running over to Carstair to help. He brushed them off and began issuing orders. He sent one to inform Gallion of the breach and another to get Marius and a group of soldiers, the final two he sent to library to apprehend Agatha.

'I'll be up there now I have to go get something,' was all he said before speeding off again in the direction of his quarters.

Gallion quickly dismissed the guard after he had

informed him of the breach, smiling as he did so and bolting the door behind him. So certain was he in his plans, nothing worried him now, not even his most trusted librarian joining the rebellion.

The guards who had been sent to apprehend Sister Agatha approached the library but found a gang of librarians congregated outside its doors. They looked at each other, drew their swords, and began to advance cautiously on the group.

'We are here for the sister, this doesn't have to get nasty,' one of the soldiers exclaimed.

'It might be a little too late for that,' came the reply from someone in the crowd, and as the words were spoken, Nestor, Arjan, and the others emerged from the crowd brandishing weapons of their own. The four soldiers formed a line in front of the librarians an awaited the guards' next move.

'More will come,' the guard said pitifully, 'just hand her over.'

Nestor spat at the guards who lowered their swords and waited for the arrival of reinforcements.

It was not long before Marius appeared with the soldier that had summoned him and five others all with swords drawn.

Marius stepped forward and began the negotiation.

'We outnumber you brothers, give her up or we take her, you know it must be,' he said to the four soldiers forming the protective line.

Nestor winced at Marius's use of the word brother, 'You have no right calling us that traitor,' he spat back at him. His face reddened with anger and as Marius opened his mouth to speak, he could hold back the rage no more and lunged forward to attack. As he did so, a small, crumpled piece of paper fell from his hand and his brothers followed suit.

Form the crowd of librarians, Gassis and Edryd could

see the writing on the paper and recognised the familiar script.

Marius killed Gideon

The pair clashed and their swords rang with force as they met. The other soldiers also met as brother fought brother. Swords cried out as blows were parried, but Nestor's rage would not abate. He rained blow after blow at the defending Marius whose arms tired and weakened at the sustained attack. Nestor swung a high arcing blow that crashed into Marius's defensive stance causing him to fall to one knee. Still reeling, Nestor slashed at his chest and Marius had to lean back to avoid the blow, allowing Nestor to drive his foot into his chest sending him sprawling on the floor.

Marius's face was aghast with horror at the brutal attack that Nestor led and began to beg for mercy, but Nestor had none for the coward who had murdered Gideon for the pain was still fresh in his heart. He kicked Marius's sword from his hand, pinning the arm down with his foot. Marius struggled but Nestor's stance was too well grounded.

'The only mercy I offer, is a quick death,' Nestor said in a cold, unfeeling manner.

With tears falling from his eyes, he drove his blade into Marius's heart and watched as the wound pumped crimson blood onto the royal blue of Marius uniform and slowly pooled in his mouth. Breathing heavily as the toil of the fight began to tell, he wiped away the tears and looked up at the ongoing melee.

His friends were holding their own, but they were outnumbered and losing. Arjan already carried several flesh wounds to his arms, but he was resolute and gave no ground. Nestor dove back into the fray to aid him but just as it seemed they may have the upper hand, Carstair appeared in the corridor flanked by two more soldiers and Nestor and Arjan's hearts sank as they parried off blows.

The four soldiers backed off towards the crowd of librarians to give some breathing space between them and Citadel's soldiers who did not press on with Carstair's arrival. Carstair cut a menacing form in the corridor, he had dispensed of his jacket and the pistols that hung at his waist glinted in the glow of the torch light. In his gloved hands he held his sword and he bore a look of unfettered fury on his face.

As he reached his other soldiers, he looked down at Marius's corpse as it lay bleeding into the carpet of the corridor.

'Where is he?' Carstair spat angrily.

'He?' Nestor replied confused.

'You know who the fuck I mean,' Carstair reiterated.

'He means me,' a familiar voice spoke, though no one could see from where it came. Carstair spun at the voice and out of the shadows of the corridor Azerrad appeared. He was dressed all in black from his boots to the hooded jacket he wore, but as he let the hood fall from his head to reveal his face, there was no mistaking those piercing blue eyes.

They bore a hole into Carstair's sole as he stared at him, but the burly soldier did not back down. He clenched his fists showing Azerrad that he had the Hands of God on as they glowed a faint blue momentarily. The entire scene was mixture of sweat and emotion as the friends were reunited with their ally only to be separated by their possible doom.

With Carstair and Azerrad eyeballing each other and everyone else on tenterhooks as to what to do, it seemed like no one would break the stand-off. Finally, Carstair threw his head in a gesture to the soldiers under his command to retrieve the sister while he himself began to run headlong at the vampire whose beguiling form was only broken by the curved blade that protruded from his silhouette.

Carstair ran and swung his short sword as hard as he could at head height, but the swift vampire easily ducked the clumsy attack and in a swirling blur of coat tails and glinting blade he slashed across the brute's thigh causing a painful but superficial wound. Carstair winced but held in any cries of anguish; he was not here to inflate the creature's ego. Turning around he lunged at Azerrad again, this time head on, but the wily vampire leapt back parrying the blade before delivering a blow to the back of Carstair's head with the pommel of his sword. A wry smirk emerging on Azerrad's lips that revealed the pointed fangs he possessed.

Carstair again refused to acknowledge the blow and turned to face his tormentor once more to see him dragging the tip of the sword in a circular motion on the carpet before him. He could tell the vampire was faster, more agile even than he had expected, but still Carstair closed the gap and slashed across Azerrad's torso, the vampire ducked again but Carstair had put little energy into the slash and was ready for the evasive move, his glove covered hand delivering a horrific blow to the side of the vampires head that landed with a sickening crack and sent Azerrad sprawling into the wall which partially gave in under the force, plaster and brick dust raining on Azerrad's crumpled form. Looking at the glove with admiration, he tossed his sword to one side, deciding that they were much more effective.

The other soldiers fought their own battles, Nestor felling one soldier, though he took no pleasure in this kill. One of their own, an older soldier named Gartell, fell too, cut down under the weight of attacks. Behind them the crowd of librarians looked on nervously, many of them holding their Ankhs in silent prayer, Sister Agatha amongst them. Gassis and Edryd watched the fray. Gassis had her arms outstretched, doing her best to keep the librarians and Edryd back as Edryd grasped his Ankh so hard his knuckles turned white.

Carstair gripped Azerrad by the back of his coat and raised him from the floor, the dazed vampire slashed out with his sword and the tip caught the brute in stomach but did not fully hit home. The pang of warm pain annoyed Carstair though who batted away the sword and upon dropping Azerrad to the ground, proceeded to raise him again by his throat this time. The vampire struggled but in the vice like grip of the hands of God he could not overthrow his captor.

Carstair pummelled the vampire in the face, laughing as he rained blow after blow on him until the gloves and Azerrad's face ran red with blood. He dropped Azerrad finally who coughed a globule of blood as he crashed into the ground. Reaching to his waist he pulled one of his blood reaper pistols from its holster and checked it was loaded.

Watching on aghast, Edryd did something he never thought he would have had the courage to do. Sensing his friend's life in mortal danger, he pushed past Gassis and hurled himself headlong through the raging battle ducking flailing arms and stray weapons miraculously before crashing clumsily into Carstair's legs, sending him sprawling, the pistol falling from his hands in the process. Seeing her vulnerable friend enter the fray, Gassis picked up the sword of a fallen soldier and joined Nestor and Arjan to even the score, parrying blows as best she could.

Carstair rose from the floor and looked at the cowering form of Edryd, the young librarian rose to his feet and tried to run but Carstair grasped his robe and yanked him backwards, a look of pity briefly passing his face as he delivered blow after blow to the boy's face that split his lip, burst his nose, and blackened his eyes, a jet of blood exploding from his face.

'Stupid boy,' he said solemnly as he delivered a final, fierce blow to Edryd's ribs, breaking them with ease as he released him from his grip. The librarian cried out in pain as tears and blood streamed down his ruined face and he crumpled to the floor. Carstair turned back to find Azerrad had dragged himself further down the corridor out of his reach so reached to his waist to remove the second pistol form his holster, but as his fingers felt around, he found the gun was missing. He spun in horror to find the barely conscious form of Edryd trying to lift the gun up towards him. Shaking his head Carstair snatched the gun from Edryd's fingers, the boy slumping to the ground as he did so.

Carstair again turned to bear down on the wounded vampire, he cocked the pistol and balled a gloved fist letting the blood flow into his pistol as Katerina had all that time ago, and with all his malice, he drew a line on the sprawling vampire and fired three shots into his chest.

Azerrad lay prone on the floor of the corridor, blood gently seeping from the wounds.

A sense of calm passed across Carstair as he looked at the dead form of his adversary. But that calm was short lived, it was instead broken by the hysterical laughter intermingled with the gurgling sound of blood that was being emitted from Edryd's throat. Carstair turned furiously to look at the laughing form of Edryd. Unsure why he was laughing or if lunacy was just the last step of Edryd's death he knelt to look the boy in the eyes.

'What's so funny?' he asked but Edryd could not respond. Carstair gripped Edryd's collar and as he shook him, the librarians hand rolled open and six silver bullets fell from his hand. Six silver bullets beautifully engraved with filigree and ready to receive the bearer's blood.

Carstair took a moment to process it but by the time he realised what had happened the sinister form of Azerrad was looming over them. In an instant, the vampire had swept his blade down on the arm that held Edryd, severing the hand at the wrist and causing Carstair to reel in pain and shock. He tried to strike out at Azerrad with his remaining hand still clad in one of the hands of God but Azerrad skewered it with the tip of his blade driving down into the floor and pinning Carstair where he was forced to lay.

An unholy shriek ripped from Carstair as Azerrad picked up the pistol he had dropped to the floor to interrogate Edryd and cocked it. Looking down at the pitiful form of Carstair.

'They won't work on me, but I bet they will on you,' was all the vampire said before placing a bullet between Carstair's eyes.

Seeing the defeated form of their leader and the snarling fangs of the blood-soaked vampire, the remaining soldiers quickly threw down their weapons, begging for mercy. Nestor looked at their wretched forms and raised his sword to put them out of their misery, but Gassis interjected and stopped him delivering the blow.

'Enough of our people's blood has been spilled,' she said.

Nestor relented and lowered his sword.

Outside thunder rolled in and forks of lightning flashed across the sky, before torrential rain and hail began to bombard the city. The noise disturbed the respite being found in the corridor, causing many of the librarians to jump.

'Where is Gallion?' Azerrad wheezed as his body tried to fix the damage that had been inflicted on it.

'You need time to heal Azerrad,' Sister Agatha protested, emerging from the crowd of librarians.

'There is no time Sister,' he replied, but his feet faltered, and he had to stop himself from falling.

As she prepared to put her foot down the group were disturbed by the gurgling noise that came from Edryd as he tried to speak.

'Rest brother,' Azerrad said as he knelt beside his fallen friend. His injuries were severe and his face hardly recognisable from the beating he had endured.

Edryd waved his hand beckoning Azerrad to come closer, which he obliged.

'Use me to heal,' he slurred into Azerrad's ear.

'No Edryd, I cannot,' Azerrad pleaded.

'My blood can heal you, let me do this final thing for the Order, for my friends,' he sputtered, tears falling from his eyes as blood came from his mouth.

Gassis broke down at the sight of her broken friend giving his last breath to their cause. She knelt at his side, squeezed his shoulder and placed the lightest kiss on his cheek before she rose and ushered the other librarians away. Nestor smiled at the librarian's bravery and followed the others.

'Edryd,' Azerrad whispered, resting his head against his friends as his eyes became blurred with tears. Edryd smiled once more, and his breaths became almost undetectable as Azerrad bent to his neck and sank his fangs deep into his throat. Azzerad's eyes went wide at the taste of fresh blood, and he felt the pain from his wounds wane.

He pulled away from Edryd's neck, feeling the fresh blood course through his veins, breathing life into his limbs again. His wounds began to heal, and his breathing started to return to normal. He looked once more at Edryd, sadness like he had only known once before filled the vampire and reminded him of his humanity as the blood did its best to make him forget. With tears falling and sadness overflowing he knelt once more to say a silent thank you to his friend before rising and leaving his fallen brother to join the others.

'Where is Gallion?' he asked again more vehemently than before.

'I will show you,' Sister Agatha replied stepping over the ruined corpse of Marius.

Chapter 29

In his barricaded office, Gallion stood behind an improvised alter of books and boxes on top of his cluttered desk. He was dressed in the black robes he had been wearing when he visited the dungeons the night Carstair learned the truth. The hood was pulled over his head and only the barest sliver of his nose protruded far enough to see anything in the darkness.

His door was guarded by two of his soldiers, their pale clammy skin a stark contrast to the black uniform they bore. Both looked similar in features and height, their blue eyes shining though the room remained quite dim. They had swords at their waist and stood almost ceremoniously protecting the entrance to the Grand Master's lair.

At his alter, the Grand Master had books and scribbles laid out before him with candles stacked on candles around him. In the desk he had carved great glyphs and as he chanted words from the scriptures, they would glow an unearthly variation of blue, green, yellow, and purple. As each glyph lit like a beacon in the dim light of the room, lightning would flash across the obsidian sky, causing the candle flames to burn higher and brighter momentarily illuminating the twisted features of the Grand Master's face.

In the town, many people had made their way out into the torrential rain to marvel at the lightning that crossed sky and comment on the unusual nature of the weather that had rolled in that evening. Groups huddled in doorways and under awnings as the splashes of rain became a deafening din on the rain-soaked streets. Thunder rumbled and they would jump, and now and then one of the elder citizens on the street would remark that something terrible was on the horizon.

The Grand Master continued to read from the scribbles in front of him, never faltering on the words he had been practicing for so long now. The more he read the harder the rain fell, the louder the thunder rumbled, and the more frequent lightning descended upon the city. He paused at every chance he got to look out into the night that hung over the city of Uvrenmouth and smiled gruesomely as lightning struck the ground and buildings and small fires began to break out across the city. It was finally starting.

Agatha held a torch out in front of her as they made the short trip down to the great hall. Azerrad was hot on her tail and Nestor and Arjan followed suit. Gassis had remained to mourn the passing of Edryd and organise the librarians to regain civility in the Citadel.

As they entered the great hall, they found several of the Citadel's soldiers staring at them in disbelief, but none dared delay the furious form of Agatha as she marched towards the Grand Master's staircase, never mind the fact that the three figures following were soaked in blood and one was the supposedly dead vampire. As they watched in confusion more soldiers arrived, but they were met by many of the librarians who had descended behind the small entourage who suppressed their curiosity and explained the gravity of the situation.

As each disappeared behind the curtain of the Grand Master's staircase, Arjan halted, turning to keep guard on the great hall his imposing arms folded across his blood strewn chest. The stern look on his face would have been enough to keep all but the most determined soldiers at bay. As the librarians worked their way around the soldiers that were piling back into the great hall, the vampire and his allies made the climb to the Grand Master's room.

Agatha held the torch aloft as they rounded the corner to the door that led into his chamber, the hall was dimly lit and none of them could see very far. Agatha paused at the old wooden door and informed the vampire and Nestor that she could go no further, they both understood and prepared for the assault on the Grand Master's chamber. Nestor ran his blade across the bottom of his robes to remove the blood and gore as best he could. Azerrad reached into his tunic and pulled out one of the pistols that Carstair had carried that he had retrieved from the debris in the corridor where their battle had taken place. He checked it was loaded and when the two were ready, Agatha dropped the torch on the ground so that its light would still illuminate the door and made her way back down the staircase they had come from.

Emerging into the great hall, she found Gassis stood on a makeshift podium made from boxes, she was telling the Order of the events that had transpired and of the Grand Master's deception. As she stood there orating to the crowd that had amassed, Agatha smiled and watched as every member hung on her every word.

The Grand Master was still methodically reciting words from the books in front of him when the door began to shake and creak under the hammer blows it was being dealt from the other side. He turned his head unnaturally quickly and scowled in the doors direction as the two guards did their best to brace the door from the inside. Pressed by the assault from Azerrad and Nestor, the Grand Master began to read the words aloud quicker, though his translations began to stumble a little in his haste.

In the streets of the city, the marvel of the onlookers quickly turned to dread and fear as the first of several blood curdling cries echoed through the damp and dingy streets. Terrified, the citizens that were out in the storm quickly looked for safety as the attack seemed to come from nowhere.

Feral humanoid creatures scampered around the streets and across the rooftops, vicious claws swiping at anything unlucky enough to be in their way. As the onlookers bundled into the taverns and bars to get off the streets, they were besieged by the living dead, risen from their graves, dozens of reanimated corpses stalked the outskirts of the city and in-between the shambling bodies and deadly claws the wolf-like forms of other monstrosities raced up and down the streets, tussling with the feral creatures for prey.

As patrons used what they could to barricade themselves into the buildings they sought refuge in they were forced to witness the recently slain in the streets, their friends and neighbours, reanimate and join the mass besieging them.

Gallion laughed as he watched the fires begin to spread in the city and saw the teeming creatures he had risen or drawn here swarm over buildings and down streets. Behind him the door to his chamber shook in its frame, dust and splinters raining on the guards who braced it holding their attackers at bay. From the outside, Azerrad and Nestor were relentlessly pounding on the door with boots and hacking at it with their swords. Sweat poured from Nestor's brow but Azerrad looked unfazed by the exertion save for the fact he was caked in drying blood now.

The door looked ruined form their side but looked unblemished from the inside. Undeterred, they continued their attack until they were exhausted. Almost at the edge of failure they were saved by the hulking form of Arjan who appeared at the top of the stairs carrying a great sledgehammer. In his monstrous hands the hammer looked smaller than it should, and he wielded it with ridiculous ease, swinging it around his head and landing a blow in the centre of the door. The impact made a great thud and splintered the wood around it even causing it to splinter on the inside.

In the streets, the weather continued its unrelenting downpour, and the creatures made their way further into the city, causing homes and shops to come under attack. The people were fleeing wherever they could with those close enough making a break for the most defensible place in the city – the Citadel.

In his chamber, Gallion's chants got faster and more animated, he was relishing the havoc he was bringing down on the city until finally he finished his work, culminating with a giant lightning strike that crashed into the main gates of the Citadel, tearing through stone and wood and rendering the Citadel's main defence useless.

Arjan swung the hammer once more, striking the same part of the door with incredible accuracy, the head of the hammer finally breaching the doors sturdy defence. He pulled at the hammer to dislodge the head, a hole in the door now visible. Through the hole the warriors could see the candle-lit chamber and the old man who stood at his makeshift altar. Sensing they were about to break through, Azerrad and Nestor readied themselves, swords and pistols in hand as Arjan swung the hammer a third and final time, its impact tearing the door asunder as two halves split to reveal their quarry and sent the guards bracing it flying off their feet backwards.

The vampire and the soldier stormed the breach traversing the ruins of the door. They each dispatched one of the guards with ruthless efficiency and turned to face the Grand Master who was already looking at them as the stormed in.

'It's too late vampire,' the Grand Master said as he began to laugh a croaking laugh, 'your kind are swelling the city.'

Azerrad turned to Nestor and immediately Nestor understood. He turned and raced out of the chamber, grabbing Arjan's arm and dragging him with him as the pair raced down the stairs. They burst into the great hall in a ruckus to find a great crowd gathered already. Bemused they looked for familiar faces, but their interruption was interrupted by a watcher carrying the soaked and trembling form of one of the city's civilians with her.

'The city is swarmed, there are creatures all over,' the watcher said breathlessly as she and the civilian crashed to the floor.

'The old bastard has started his war, but it is not one we were meant to survive,' Nestor cried, 'get your weapons,' he directed to the gathered soldiers as he and Arjan burst out into the dismal night racing to the city's aid. In the hall, Gassis organised the crowd as soldiers raced to arm themselves, she separated the librarians into groups and made preparations for the city's inhabitants to seek refuge in the Citadel as its soldiers fought to take back the city.

Azerrad did not respond to the Grand Master's taunt and instead raised the pistol he had taken and cocked it. Gallion immediately recognised the pistol he had presented to Carstair and for a moment he looked genuinely saddened as he knew what the vampire holding the pistol represented.

'I trust he died well,' Galion said remorsefully.

'Stop this madness,' Azerrad fumed.

'Stop?' Gallion laughed once more, 'In all the time you guarded those books you never took the time to read them? There is no stopping what I have begun.'

'We were smarter than that,' he rebuked Gallion's jibe.

'I suppose you think you are here to kill me?' Gallion asked.

'I'm here to see you pay for your crimes,' Azerrad replied as he circled the Grand Master, his sword scraping on the polished wood of the chamber floor.

'Crime? What crime? All I have done is liberate my people from the doldrums.'

'You have liberated nothing,' Azerrad spat, 'you have condemned the city and its people to a fate worse than death.'

'You would know about that, wouldn't you vampire?' Gallion venomously retorted the smile never leaving his lips.

'There is no way out of here Gallion, you will come with me, or you will die.'

'What do you care anyway? These aren't your people, they aren't even your kind, your kind are ravaging the city or burned up in the tunnels beneath it,' Gallion's eyes flickered into life like wicked flames.

Azerrad's eyes reflected Gallion's as the old man spoke of his dearly departed. In a blind rage he pointed the gun at Gallion and pulled the trigger over and over, but the gun was silent and no bullets emerged from its barrel as the Grand Master began laughing again.

'That pistol is of no use here,' he advised Azerrad, 'the room is warded, it will not fire.'

'Then you shall taste the edge of my blade,' Azerrad cried leaping through the air towards the old man.

Azerrad leapt with preternatural speed, but Gallion

moved remarkably agilely for an old man and emerged unscathed, though his cloak bore the mark of the vampire's attack – a great slash running down it.

'Why waste your time? My men will be upon us in moments,' Gallion gloated at the seething vampire.

'Are you sure?' Azerrad fired back as he slashed with the curved edge of his blade once more.

More of Gallion's cloak paid the penalty as the necromantic Grand Master struggled to match the vampire's skill and speed and for the first time Azerrad saw the look of certainty flicker from his face.

'Quite,' Gallion replied, though he sounded far from certain as he spoke the word.

'See for yourself,' Azerrad said gesturing to the window with the blade as regained his composure.

Gallion did not want to leave himself open to attack but he could not abide the certainty with which the vampire spoke, and he whisked off to the open window, passing between the flowing drapes. He gazed out to the city below and from the ruined archway and mighty doors of the Citadel, he could see the soldiers of the Order swarming out like ants in different directions into the streets to fight Gallion's monstrous army.

He watched in horror as his plan seemed to be unravelling as soon as it had begun, his fist balling in rage and fury.

'Curse you and the weakness in my people,' he screamed angrily into the night.

'I am already cursed,' came the response, no more than a whisper but it felt as though it was delivered from right beside Gallion's ear. He spun cowering, his hands pushing at the air for there was nothing there.

In his chamber, he saw that while he had been looking out, the creature had extinguished all the lights.

'You, however, will be damned,' the voice spoke, louder this time as a shadow passed across the drapes in the blink of an eye causing them to swirl. Again, Gallion pawed pointlessly at them, his heart beating faster than it had in a long time, and for the first time in his life he felt afraid.

'Parlour tricks,' he cried into the darkness, not knowing where to direct his anguish.

Stepping into the room once more he saw the shadows dance like a macabre marionette show and whispered a short incantation before pointing towards one of the candles on his desk. It burst into flame at his behest and lit a small portion of the room allowing him to glimpse the form of Azerrad as he darted around. The Grand Master lit another candle, but as he did so the wispy shadow evaded the light and put out the first candle he had lit.

Becoming more irritated at the game occurring, he tried to conjure candles into life quicker and quicker, but he could never light the room enough to catch the form of the vampire. He tried to move himself across his chamber towards the door and his possible salvation, but every time he made a meaningful advance, he would feel the wind on the back of his neck and he would cower off in a direction he did not intend.

Azerrad revelled in the psychological torment he was inflicting on the devious Grand Master but knew that the game could not play out forever. He flitted and fluttered by until only one candle remained lit. The Grand Master began the incantation again, but Azerrad kicked the set of fire pokers over into the hearth and the resultant noise distracted Gallion long enough for Azerrad to destroy the remaining light, the last light the Grand Master ever saw.

Azerrad entered the Great Hall tired from the evening's events. He found Gassis and Agatha orchestrating the members of the Order that had not already departed and strode over to them. Seeing him appear, Gassis ran to him and threw her arms around him hugging her long lost friend.

'Nestor?' Azerrad asked not seeing time to waste.

'He left with the first of the soldiers to enter the city,' Gassis confirmed, 'Gallion?'

'Expired,' Azerrad said in a cold hard way before seeing a librarian walking by with a bowl of water.

He rushed over and soaked his face with the fresh water, the coldness invigorating him as pink water fell to the floor of the great hall. He thanked the disgruntled librarian who now had a bowl of partially bloodied water before returning to Gassis and Agatha.

'I will find him,' Azerrad promised to Gassis, and he turned to venture out.

'I'm coming too,' Gassis exclaimed grabbing Azerrad's arm to halt his escape.

'It looks like you have found your calling Gassis,' Azerrad replied fondly, 'make sure he has something to come back to.'

Azerrad exited the great hall through the gate, stepping out into the courtyard he could see the ruined gateway where the lightning had torn it down and beneath the crumbling archway refugees from the city poured in. As he pushed his way through the jostling crowd he was met with fear and anger as they saw his pale skin, blue eyes, and fangs, but he took no notice and entered the drenched city to find his friend and help with the cleansing of the city.

From the street he looked up at the citadel's tower and could see the Grand Master's window still open. The drapes billowing in the breeze, but all was dark inside. From inside, Gallion's chamber all was dark and the outside through the window looked like an abyss. The weather had begun to recede, however, and a final fork of lightning split the sky, the light of which briefly illuminated the Grand Master's chamber, revealing the old man skewered to his desk through the chest, his lifeless form limply hanging in the eerie dark, his eyes wide and lifeless.

Chapter 30

In the city, the fight to save its people raged on for hours. Nestor, Azerrad, and the entire garrison of the Citadel fought in the bloodied streets to eliminate the threat that the creatures Gallion had unleashed posed. The revenants that made up the bulk of the monsters assaulting the city were easier to dispatch than the vampires and werewolves as they possessed no natural lethality, but their weight of numbers posed their own problems.

As the creatures began to thin, some of the braver citizens made their way back into the streets with improvised weapons to aid the valiant soldiers in the unrelenting task. As streets were cleared more and more of the population tried to make it to the safety of their homes or the Citadel, often aided by the mysterious appearance of the Order's watchers who would materialise as if out of nowhere; the camouflaged angels guiding them out of harm's way.

Azerrad had found Nestor, Arjan, and a host of soldiers embroiled in a lethal fight with a pack of werewolves as several feral vampires skirted the edges of the fight like a pack of rabid hyenas baying for blood.

As the first rays of sunlight burst over the houses and

buildings of the city, Nestor finally threw down the last of the monsters, its head rolling across the blood slick cobbles. Nestor's chest heaved as he tried to breathe as hard as he could.

The night had taken a toll on all of them physically and mentally, they had been fighting for more hours than any wanted to count, and they had seen their friends fall and the people ravaged in one of the darkest moments of the city's history, but they had won. Azerrad put his hands on Nestor's shoulders as the young soldier rested doubled over.

'It is done,' Azerrad said confidently.

'There may be more, we cannot delay,' Nestor said trying to stand upright once more.

'The sun is rising, these monsters have no master anymore, they will flee to the shadows,' Azerrad assured the soldier.

'Then we will follow and cut them down,' Nestor spoke angrily.

'There will be time for that. They will return and you will be ready, but for now it is done,' Azerrad repeated.

At the Citadel, Gassis paced nervously as the warming rays of sunshine broke the terrible darkness of the night. She ushered civilians into the courtyard but was occupied with knowing her friends' fate. Finally, watcher after watcher emerged from different parts of the city all proclaiming the same news: the creatures were destroyed or were fleeing as the sunlight drove them off. The Order had won but at a great cost.

At the edges of the city, hidden enclaves of watchers took out the fleeing beasts where they could with long range rifles, but they could not eliminate them all.

It had taken from those first rays of light almost to the last of the day for the Order to clear the streets of the dead. Great pyres were set in each quarter of the city, piled high with the bodies of those slain in the night and the destroyed bodies of the monsters who had murdered them. The fallen soldiers of the Order had been returned home and placed upon a pyre of their own in front of the ruined gates of the Citadel.

The city had come together to help with the clean-up. The able-bodied helped take the fallen to the pyres and the older citizens threw bucket after bucket into the street to try to remove the taint of blood that had been left in their wake.

The civilians who had sought shelter at the Citadel were taken back to their homes by escorts of the Order and any whose properties had burned in the fires were found refuge in the homes of their friends and neighbours.

Inside the great hall, the Order was gathering. A great crowd amassed and was a mixture of confused faces and exhausted ones. With the Grand Master gone, who was going to lead them now? They looked to the senior soldiers and librarians that were gathering at the front of the crowd for answers. Whispers abounded guessing at who was going to take over, some assumed one of the two remaining senior officers would, others thought that one of the learned librarians would make a better choice. The whispers began gaining momentum before the senior soldiers quietened them down.

Sister Agatha stepped forward and prepared to speak.

'I know many of you are exhausted. This has been one of the most difficult nights since the Order's inception, but our job is not yet done,' she began, and the crowd looked on in agreement of her opening statement. 'Gallion had fallen into madness, but his evil has been wiped from this place with the blood, sweat, and tears of our people. We have sacrificed everything to keep the city safe and it is for now, but we must choose a new leader to lead us into the dawn.'

The crowd looked at each other and a gentle murmur spread across it as the speculation rose.

'I know who that leader is,' Agatha said with surety and the crowd anticipated her succession as Grand Master of the Order. 'In this trying time, one has shown the capacity and compassion to lead... Gassis come here.'

The crowd fell silent, Gassis looked on surprised and Agatha's usual icy demeanour thawed as she smiled and beckoned the librarian forward to join them at the front. Reluctantly, she made her way to the front and Agatha placed her hands on Gassis's shoulders, stoic as she presented her to the crowd.

'I have seen your courage to fight with your brothers and sisters and for what you believed to be right, I have seen your compassion to grant mercy to those who sought to take everything from you, and I have seen the wisdom and temperament to take charge in difficult times and I am certain you have what it takes to become the leader that this Order truly needs,' Agatha spoke her endorsement and the other older members of the Order began to clap as they agreed to Agatha's choice.

As the group began to clap, the hall erupted into noise as the crowd began to clap and cheer along with their senior peers. In an instant the leadership and rebuilding of the Order was thrust upon Gassis who didn't know whether to smile or weep. She did graciously accept the accolade that had been granted her and as a bloodied Nestor and Azerrad entered the hall to the raucous scene she broke from Agatha's grip and ran to embrace her friends.

'You stink,' she said, laughing at their return.

'What's going on here?' Nestor said ignoring the

playful insult.

'I think your hugging the new Grand Master,' Azerrad said, his perception as impeccable as ever.

Gassis smiled and nodded embracing the pair again.

'Come now,' Agatha bellowed over the excitable crowd, 'we all have things that need doing, there will be time to celebrate later, come on, come on,' she continued waving her hands and disbursing the crowd to return to the tasks they had been set.

'Grand Master, eh?' Nestor said, unsure whether to punch her in the arm or kneel before her.

'You drop to your knees, and I'll excommunicate you,' Gassis said sensing Nestor's thoughts. 'I'll need a new senior officer now; a vacancy has uh... arisen.'

'Any idea who you'll choose?' Nestor said missing the point altogether.

'I did have an idea, but he might be too dense now I think about it' she said smiling and shaking her head.

Nestor looked to Gassis then to Azerrad a little confused, before the penny dropped and he began to turn a colour that would rival a beetroot.

'It would be my honour,' he said embarrassed.

'Good,' Gassis said emphatically, 'now come on there is plenty to do here, someone made a real mess of my door I hear.'

'Not us,' Nestor said nudging Azerrad and smiling.

As night descended on the city of Uvrenmouth, many of its tired citizens arrived at the gates of the Citadel. Throughout the city, in the midst of the horrendous clean-up operation that had been undertaken, rumour had spread of an address that would be given by the mysterious and reclusive Order, the likes of which none of the citizens could ever remember happening in their lifetime.

In what remained of the ruined archway that had led into the courtyard in front of the Citadel, a stage had been erected. It was simple in its construction and was lit by two huge braziers that had been built at either side. The flames of the fires that burned within cut the night as it tried to draw in around the crowd and gave a small hint of warmth as the cold wind swept in with the oncoming gloom.

In front of the stage the citizens huddled together, still weary form the night before and chilled by the growing breeze. They fidgeted unsure as to what was going to happen or what else may be revealed. Groups whispered amongst themselves, with younger citizens speculating on the possible future that was being ushered in and the older ones talking of curses and bad omens that few remembered.

Behind the stage many of the Order were gathered in support. They had washed and changed to appear less repulsive to the crowd and on the stage several people stood. Two stood in a soldier like uniform with swords at their waists. They were slightly older men and looked tired and hungry, their eyes dark and their faces somewhat gaunt. Next to them stood two more people, a man and a woman, both were older and wore blue robes instead of uniforms and appeared unarmed. As impressive and dominant as the older woman appeared, the man was her opposite; he looked meek and fragile, though his face showed a wealth of wisdom in it.

Finally, some movement appeared at the doors of the Citadel and the crowd parted a little letting a dark-skinned woman emerge from the members of the Order and descend the steps towards the stage. She was dressed in a simple but clean and form fitting robe that gentle rustled as she moved. Her face was contrite, and her hair was pulled back giving her a serious and dominant aura.

Behind her followed another soldier in a full, clean uniform. A great sword hung from his waist that shifted as he moved. The soldier was younger than the others on the stage but up close his eyes revealed a wealth of experience that belied his young age. His face was soft and features neutral, but his stature made him an imposing escort.

To his side was the tall slender figure of the vampire Azerrad. He was in black skin-tight trousers and brown boots buckled up to the knee. He wore a loose-fitting shirt under a brown leather waistcoat, over which a black jacket lay. He moved effortlessly with so much grace that even Gassis's beauty could not draw the gaze of the crowd from the vampire's descent. Azerrad's long hair rippled in the breeze and as he glanced around the crowd his piercing blue eyes transfixed all that he caught the gaze of.

They made their way into the stage and the vampire, and the soldier flanked Gassis as she prepared to address the city.

'Citizens of Uvrenmouth,' She began in a stately voice, 'I am Gassis, the new Grand Master of the Order,' she was met with silence by the crowd as they waited to see what that meant to them. 'The events of last night have shaken the city to its core and I will not lie, it was one of our own that brought about those terrible horrors,' the crowd began to murmur their disapproval. 'But we have dealt with that rogue element, and we are united now in our goals for the future.'

She looked out across the crowd and saw their discomfort.

'You know now what stalks the night and that is something that we cannot change, but these monsters are nothing new for the city, you have been kept safe from the night by the ignorance we have allowed you to wallow in.'

The crowd began to look at each other some bearing expressions of confusion, others of fear.

'For a thousand years this city has been kept safe by

my people, by the Order, and we have kept you in the dark to protect you. But that is not possible anymore. The blood of the Order was spilt in the streets alongside the blood of its citizens and now we are bound,'

Gassis continued, her fiends marvelling at the assured nature of the address and her statesmanship.

'Our vow to you this day is that we will continue to keep this city safe by the sacrifice of the Order, your lives can continue, and tonight we will remember the fallen heroes of our city who gave their lives so that the rest of us may see the dawn,' as she spoke the words a librarian ran onto the stage with a torch and handed it to Gassis.

She accepted the torch and in silence she made her way from the stage passed the crowd and towards the pyre of the Orders fallen heroes. She held the torch over the lower echelons of the great funeral pyre and looked back to the crowd.

'To Uvrenmouth united,' she said in a loud and proud voice before dropping the torch onto the closest bodies, which set the whole pyre ablaze in a burst of flame as the gathered crowd and the members of the Order applauded and cheered, others cried in grief of their loss and the relief that they were protected.

As the funeral pyre burned high into the night it lit the surrounding area in a warm orange glow and throughout the city one by one, little orange glows could be seen as the other pyres were lit in conjunction with the first.

That night, the taverns were packed as soldiers, librarians, and civilians mixed and exchanged stories and drank together in the warm fires of the taverns' hearths.

Gassis stood in her new quarters and watched the pyres burn into the darkness as glowing beacons of hope for a unified future. She turned as she heard footsteps approaching to see the form of Azerrad enter the chamber. His eyes were looking around the room he had fought in not that long ago. The room was bare now, but it still bore the signs of his battle.

In the hearth the irons were still scattered amongst the ashes of the last fire that burned there. There were scratches and stains on the carpet and floor where blood had spilled, and swords had been drawn and the doorway still lacked an actual door.

'I want you to stay with us, to help me lead these people, to help me fight the creatures of the night,' Gassis said sensing that Azerrad was not intending to stay.

'What did you have done with the books?' he asked dodging the request.

'They are sealed into the crypts beneath the Citadel, no one will command that power again,' Gassis said firmly.

Azerrad nodded his consent.

'So will you stay?' she asked.

'I can't,' he replied regretfully, 'there are things I must see to, but one day I will return.'

Gassis looked sadly at him. She was still reeling from the loss of Edryd and Katerina, now she would lose Azerrad too.

'You are strong, you will make the right choices and you have your loyal friends,' Azerrad added as he turned to leave.

'Not all of them,' she replied mournfully. 'I asked Nestor to bring Edryd's body to the pyre, he said he had been moved?'

Azerrad turned and gave Gassis a knowing smile before departing the room through the open doorway and disappearing into the dark.

Gassis smiled back hopefully before returning to the window to watch the city, her city, for a while.

Epilogue

A new dawn rose on Uvrenmouth that morning. The suns warming rays banishing the coldness of the night. Throughout the city the pyres began to burn out and the people of the city awoke to the great task of rebuilding the city.

For the Order, some form of normality was found. The watchers went back to their post keeping their ever-vigilant eyes on the city's boundaries and Nestor and Gassis began the reconstruction of the Citadel's destroyed gates.

High over the city, the mountains looked over the bustling crowds as sunshine flooded the streets. From a secluded ledge towards one of their peaks, Azerrad watched the town burst into life as the sun penetrated its dark shroud. He leant against an ancient stone alter that had been lost to the annals of history, its crumbling form the last indication of the religious sect that had once dwelt in the mountains and kept watch over the city.

At his feet lay a battered and worn satchel heaving against its own seams as it struggled to contain its cargo. Azerrad smiled as he watched the city emerge from its cocoon and ran his hands across the altar's surface, brushing away the moss and debris that had gathered.

Around its edges small intricately carved runes were just visible, almost eroded away over the centuries, but he did not need them.

Carefully he reached into the satchel and began to remove the ancient books it held, laying them gently on the cold stone.

'She's not going to be happy when she finds those missing,' a familiar voice said from behind Azerrad.

'Then pray she doesn't notice they are dear friend,' Azerrad said with a wicked smile as he turned to see what Edryd was doing.

The now eternally young librarian was gathering the last of the herbs that he had been asked to find, still having to shield his eyes from the sun's rays, something he had not yet grown accustomed to.

'You'll get to used to that in time, Edryd,' Azerrad assured him.

Edryd smiled, revealing the pointed fangs he had acquired after his battle with Carstair. He shuffled over to the altar and placed the bouquets of herbs next to the open book as Azerrad was flicking through the pages.

'Are you sure you know what you're doing?' Edryd questioned as he watched his friend read to himself.

'Yes?' Azerrad replied in question form suggesting to Edryd he did not. 'Gallion was a fool, he cobbled together a few spells from bits and pieces of the books but he never unlocked their real power.'

'And you have?' Edryd once again questioned his friend worriedly.

'Mastered, no, but I know how to conduct this ritual,' Azerrad replied confidently. 'Now help with this.'

Edryd shrugged and turned with Azerrad to fetch the bundle that lay carefully on the grassy verge of the ledge, wrapped in an immaculate white cloth and bound with golden ties. The bundle seemed large and cumbersome but as the two gently lifted it from the grass, Edryd found his new strength made the task quite simple. Carefully they laid the parcel on the altar next to the books and herbs before Azerrad picked up the herbs and lit them so that they began to gently smoke.

The smell made Edryd feel nauseous but Azerrad showed no sign of discomfort as he circled the altar chanting from the books as he went. Impossibly the smoke from the herb bouquet gathered ethereally around the cloth-embalmed parcel, shrouding it almost from sight. Edryd watched in amazement as Azerrad performed the ritual until the herbs had burned out and a grey viscous cloud now hung over the Alter completely obscuring what it held. Azerrad dropped the husk of herbs to the floor as the cloud gently pulsated in place and drew a small, curved blade from his jacket.

Standing at the top of the alter he drew the blade across his palm and clenched his fist causing the blood to run smoothly from the wound dripping in a steady stream in the cloud below. Azerrad continued to chant and though they could not see through the cover, the blood fell onto the white covering and slowly absorbed into it, spreading in a great red circle and dropping onto the contents below.

Finally, when Azerrad was content he had spilled enough blood he withdrew the hand, quickly wrapping a strand of material from his shirt around the wound, before completing the chant and stepping back from the altar. The pair looked on anxiously as nothing seemed to be happening until eventually the cloud began to move.

From the eerie cloud the two vampires saw their quarry begin to stir atop the altar, a form rising in the mist, before it stepped down from where it had lain and broke from its ethereal cover, causing the cloud to dissipate entirely.

There in its absence stood the confused form of Katerina, her skin as beautiful and porcelain as it always had been, her chestnut hair flowing in alluring locks over her shoulders and her ruby lips stained with the blood of her lover. As her eyes regained their focus, the pair looked at her cautiously.

'I fell,' she whispered as her throat struggled to remember her voice, 'in darkness and blood,' she continued running her hands over her skin to find where there should have been a thousand cuts and bites.

'Calm my love,' Azerrad soothed, 'I could not walk this life alone.'

Turning around and seeing the altar for what it was, the books open, their pages flickering in the wind, 'What have you done?' Katerina looked up at her lover with dread in her eyes.

'Returned you to this world,' Azerrad said smiling and trying to comfort Katerina. She continued to stare for just another second before throwing her arms around Azerrad and kissing him deeply, longingly, like she hadn't in a lifetime. Edryd shuffled in discomfort, waiting for the pair to finish.

'Things have changed my love,' he said as she let him go from her tight grasp. He began to gather up the books and return them to the satchel he had taken them from earlier.

'I can see that,' she replied staring at the pale skin of Edryd.

Edryd felt almost embarrassed under her gaze and tried to shy away but reached out, her fingers invading his lips to reveal his fangs to her as she examined him like a doctor might a delusional patient. He swatted away her hands, unnerved by her protruding digits and helped Azerrad clear up the altar.

'Come my love,' Azerrad said throwing an arm around Katerina and hurling the satchel at Edryd with the other, 'I will tell you all about it.'